# Just One Kiss

## Whisper Lake #4

## BARBARA FREETHY

Fog City Publishing

# PRAISE FOR BARBARA FREETHY

"I love the Callaways! Heartwarming romance, intriguing suspense and sexy alpha heroes. What more could you want?" — *NYT Bestselling Author Bella Andre*

"I adore the Callaways, a family we'd all love to have. Each new book is a deft combination of emotion, suspense and family dynamics." — *Bestselling Author Barbara O'Neal*

"Once I start reading a Callaway novel, I can't put it down. Fast-paced action, a poignant love story and a tantalizing mystery in every book!" — *USA Today Bestselling Author Christie Ridgway*

"A fabulous, page-turning combination of romance and intrigue. Fans of Nora Roberts and Elizabeth Lowell will love this book." — *NYT Bestselling Author Kristin Hannah on Golden Lies*

"Powerful and absorbing...sheer hold-your-breath suspense." — *NYT Bestselling Author Karen Robards on Don't Say A Word*

"Freethy is at the top of her form. Fans of Nora Roberts will find a similar tone here, framed in Freethy's own spare, elegant style." — *Contra Costa Times on Summer Secrets*

"Freethy hits the ground running as she kicks off another winning romantic suspense series...Freethy is at her prime with a superb combo of engaging characters and gripping plot." — *Publishers' Weekly on Silent Run*

# PRAISE FOR BARBARA FREETHY

"PERILOUS TRUST is a non-stop thriller that seamlessly melds jaw-dropping suspense with sizzling romance, and I was riveted from the first page to the last...Readers will be breathless in anticipation as this fast-paced and enthralling love story evolves and goes in unforeseeable directions." — *USA Today HEA Blog*

"Barbara Freethy is a master storyteller with a gift for spinning tales about ordinary people in extraordinary situations and drawing readers into their lives." — *Romance Reviews Today*

"Freethy (Silent Fall) has a gift for creating complex, appealing characters and emotionally involving, often suspenseful, sometimes magical stories." — *Library Journal on Suddenly One Summer*

Freethy hits the ground running as she kicks off another winning romantic suspense series...Freethy is at her prime with a superb combo of engaging characters and gripping plot." — *Publishers' Weekly on Silent Run*

"If you love nail-biting suspense and heartbreaking emotion, Silent Run belongs on the top of your to-be-bought list. I could not turn the pages fast enough." — *NYT Bestselling Author Mariah Stewart*

"Hooked me from the start and kept me turning pages throughout all the twists and turns. Silent Run is powerful romantic intrigue at its best." — *NYT Bestselling Author JoAnn Ross*

**JUST ONE KISS**

# CHAPTER ONE

"IT'S JUST ONE LITTLE FAVOR."

Hannah Stark frowned as her mother's voice came across her phone speaker. *Had Katherine Stark been drinking? Were her mother's words slurred? Or was her hypervigilant scrutiny of her mom playing tricks on her?* There was no reason to think her mom had fallen off the wagon. On the other hand, her mom had rarely needed a reason. Although, there had been one good reason, but all the others...those had just been excuses.

"I really need your help," her mother continued.

"Mom—stop," she said, cutting off another plea. "I'm already on my way. You don't have to convince me."

"Oh, good. I'm sorry to give you more work, Hannah. I'm sure you've had a long day. But we're going to lose this rental if there's no hot water."

"It's fine. I'll take care of it." She turned right at the next light and headed away from her townhouse and the hot bath she'd been looking forward to for the past eight hours.

As an ER nurse, she spent a lot of time on her feet, and today had been a rough one. It was Friday night, five days before Christmas, and Whisper Lake was full of holiday visitors eager to experience the charm of a small-town Christmas and the beautiful white powder of the surrounding mountains. Some of those visitors had already ended up in her ER with torn muscles and broken bones. The slopes were exciting but sometimes unforgiving.

She smiled to herself, thinking that description probably fit her as well. She had a difficult time with forgiveness, especially with the people she loved the most. Her mother was at the top of that list. But despite their complicated relationship, she'd step in and help, because that's what she did. She kept the family together. She kept things on track. She'd been doing that since she was thirteen years old, and she didn't see that stopping any time soon.

Her phone rang again. This time it was her brother, Tyler, who at twenty-four was five years younger than her. She'd been Tyler's second mom for as long as they both could remember.

She answered the call. "Hi, Ty. What's up? I hope you're not calling to tell me you're not coming home for Christmas."

"Well…"

"No," she said quickly. "You promised you'd make it home. It can't be just me and Mom. We need you here."

"I'm trying to get home, but my flight for Sunday already got canceled because of the weather. The earliest flight I could rebook is Tuesday morning."

"That's Christmas Eve," she said in dismay.

"I know, but it's all I could get. It's not just Chicago weather that's the problem; there are storms in Colorado, too. If I miss that flight, I'll probably just have to come after Christmas. I'm planning to go to Aspen for New Year's. Maybe I'll just stop in Whisper Lake first."

"No way. You have to make it for Christmas." She felt an almost desperate need to convince him. "You haven't been home since August, and you know how difficult the holidays can be, especially for Mom."

"Which is why I will do my best to be there," he promised. "You sound particularly stressed. Is there something going on I don't know about? Has Mom fallen off the wagon?"

"I don't think so. But she's still being annoying. I'm on my way up to the cabin. Apparently, the tenant is having some issue with the hot water, and I'm the only one who can deal with this crisis."

"Isn't that Mark's job?" he asked, referring to the property manager.

"Mark left for Hawaii with his family, and his assistant left a message with Mom that she's in Denver for the day. Mom is too busy to go herself, so I'm off to save the day."

"You wear a superhero cape quite well."

"I wish I had one. Hopefully, the problem can be fixed if I relight the pilot. There's snow coming in tonight, and it is damn cold already. If I can't fix it, I'll have to find a place to move them to, which will not be easy at this time of year, and we'll lose the rental money."

"I have confidence you can fix the problem. You always do."

She appreciated his confidence in her, because she had worked damned hard to make sure her younger brother never had to live with the same fears and doubts that had plagued most of her life. "Thanks, Ty. I'll see you soon."

As she ended the call, she let out a breath. She felt a little guilty for pressuring Tyler to come home. She wanted him to have his life, and as a third-year law student at Northwestern, he had his hands full. However, she did want him to make it home for a few days. They might not have much of a family left, but what they still had, she wanted to keep together.

She turned on the high beams as the road wound through the mountains with the majestic peaks and thick groves of trees casting dark shadows all around her. While a drive around the lake could be beautiful and incredibly scenic, in the winter it felt dangerous and risky. The west shore highway ran high above the lake with some hairpin curves that, while familiar, still occasionally made her palms sweat. Thankfully, there was little traffic as most of the tourists were either at the ski runs or in town.

She took the turnoff for the part of the lake known as Wicker Bay, happy to see that it had been recently plowed. While the road crew was incredibly good at keeping the main highways clear, some of the side routes could be thick with snow.

The road to the cabin ran through more tall trees and down a fairly significant decline, eventually crossing over the Whisper River and ending at a picturesque cove where four family cabins had the bay completely to themselves. The cabin had been in her family for generations, having first been purchased by her grandfather, who had used the nearby dock to launch his fishing boat every summer morning. After her grandfather had passed, it had been used more as a vacation rental than a family getaway.

As the air grew colder, she turned up her heater, and then gasped as a loud bang gave her a jolt, and the car began to spin and slide down the road. She hung on to the wheel, trying to remember to turn in the direction of the skid, but the car kept slipping across the ice. Thankfully, she was able to bring it to a stop before she hit anything. She let out a breath, her heart beating way too fast.

When she got out of the car, she saw that her front tire was shredded. *Damn!* This was the last thing she needed right now. She could change the tire, because she'd long ago learned how to take care of herself, but she really didn't want to do it. It was freezing cold and about to snow. She reached back inside the car for her phone, but she couldn't find a signal. Reception had always been spotty between the road and the cabin. With no way to call for assistance, she was just postponing the inevitable. She would have to change the tire herself. Unless…

As headlights lit up the area around her, she whirled around. A black four-door Ford Ranger truck pulled over, and she instinctively stiffened. Whisper Lake was a pretty safe place, but they weren't immune to crime. Then she recognized the owner of the truck and she stiffened for another reason.

As Jake McKenna stepped out of the vehicle, a wave of anger ran through her. Jake had once been her best friend, then her first crush, followed by heartbreak and a teenage humiliation she should have gotten over by now but still couldn't quite seem to get past.

Everything between them had happened a long time ago, when they were both seventeen years old. In the twelve years since then, she'd left Whisper Lake for almost eight years to go to college and to nursing school, and Jake had also gone off on adventures that had taken him around the globe. But three years ago, she'd come back to Whisper Lake, and two years ago, Jake had made his return. She'd tried to avoid him ever since then, and most of the time she was successful. But not always.

Jake strode toward her, wearing jeans, boots, and a navy-blue parka. "What happened?" he asked.

Her stomach tightened, which made her jump to anger so she could deny the fact that she still found him to be one of the most attractive men she'd ever met. He had brown hair and eyes and a deliciously scruffy beard. He was muscled and lean from all the exercise he did. As the owner of Adventure Sports, he was often the one leading groups on the steepest climbs and the most daring ski runs. He also had a cocky smile that she'd once loved and now hated with the same amount of passion.

"What do you think happened?" she snapped. "I got a flat."

"What are you doing out here?"

"Our cabin has a hot water problem."

"Hannah to the rescue," he said with a slight smile. "Want some help with that tire?"

She really wanted help, but she hated taking anything from him. On the other hand, it was about to snow, and she wasn't stupid even if she was hanging on to a very old grudge. "Yes, I'd like help." She opened her trunk and the compartment where the spare tire should be, only to find herself staring at an empty spot. She suddenly remembered her mother telling her about the flat she'd gotten three months earlier when she'd borrowed her car. "Damn, my mom never put the spare back. I'll have to call for help."

"If you can get through. Do you have a signal?"

She checked her phone once more. "No."

"Why don't I give you a ride to the cabin? I'm headed that way anyway. I can drop you home after that and you can figure out how to get your tire fixed tomorrow."

"Why are you going to Wicker Bay?"

"One of my employees is staying in a cabin there, and I'm concerned about him. He's not answering his phone, and he's going through a bad breakup. Now, do you want a ride, or are you going to let your stubbornly persistent dislike of me make you say no?"

She hated that he could read her so well. "I'll take a ride." She grabbed her bag out of her car, locked the doors and then followed him over to his truck. She hopped into the front seat, happy with how warm it was inside. She rubbed her icy hands together, wishing she'd thought to put gloves on, but she'd only planned on driving the three miles between her house and the hospital today.

"How long were you standing outside?" Jake asked.

"Not long."

"It's a good thing I came along when I did, considering you didn't have a spare."

"We don't have to talk, you know," she said curtly.

"Oh, I know. You're not one to hide your feelings, Hannah Banana," he said with a teasing reference to her childhood nickname.

She crossed her arms in front of her chest and gave him an annoyed look. "Don't call me that. Or I'll have to refer to you as Jake the Snake."

"Who called me Jake the Snake?" he asked, as he drove down the road. "Wait, let me guess, it was you."

"Actually, I think Keira came up with it, but I thought it was more than appropriate after what you did." She blew out a breath, feeling like she became seventeen again every time she saw Jake. She needed to start acting like the adult she was. "Who's your employee, the one you're concerned about?" she asked, wanting to change the subject.

"Trevor Pelham. Do you know him?"

"I know the Pelhams own the cabin at the far end of the bay, but I don't know Trevor personally. He's a lot younger than me."

"Trevor has had a rough time the last year. His mom died of cancer, and the girl he's been living with broke up with him two weeks ago. He thought he was going to marry her. Now he's facing a Christmas alone, and he's been on a week-long bender. He missed a couple of days of work, and I'm worried about him. He said he was going to come up here to dry out. I decided to check on him."

"I'm sorry to hear that. I knew about his mom, of course. She was a nice lady." She paused. "It's nice of you to be concerned."

"I can be nice," he said dryly. "In fact, you used to think I was very nice."

"You were also a lot of other things."

"So were you."

She couldn't really argue with that, and she was relieved when he headed across the short bridge that crossed the river and led into Wicker Bay. They were only a half mile from the cabin now, and she was already eager to be out of his truck. She wasn't going to think about the long trip back to town that would soon be coming. Maybe if she could get a signal in the cabin, she'd just call for roadside assistance.

As he rounded the last curve, she could see the four cabins, spaced about a hundred yards apart, each surrounded by an isolating thicket of trees that provided a great deal of privacy. The other two cabins had changed hands many times over the years, and she had no idea who owned them now, only that they were also used for vacation rentals.

Her cabin was to the far right, and every window was blazing with light. There was no car in front, but it was probably parked in the garage. Jake had barely come to a stop when she jumped out of the truck. She thought he'd continue down the lane, but instead he parked and followed her up to the porch.

"Why don't you check on your friend?" she asked, as she rang the bell.

"How much experience do you have fixing water heaters?"

"I know how to relight the one in this cabin."

"And if it's not the light…"

"You think you'll know what to do?"

"Maybe."

Since the most important thing was getting the water heater fixed fast, she let him stay. She pushed the doorbell again and then knocked. She frowned when there was no answer. But she could hear noise inside the cabin. It sounded like the television was on.

She knocked again, then reached for the doorknob. To her surprise, it turned. She opened the door. "Hello?"

She stepped into the living room and stopped abruptly at the sight of a little boy sitting on the floor. He had blond hair and green eyes and appeared to be about four years old. He was holding two small stuffed puppies and watching a cartoon on the TV.

She gave him a friendly smile. "Hi there. Where's your mom or your dad?"

He stared back at her but didn't answer, his gaze traveling to Jake.

Jake immediately squatted down, and she did the same, seeing the fear on the kid's face.

"Hey, bud," Jake said. "I'm Jake. This is Hannah. What's your name?"

"Brett."

"Nice to meet you, Brett," Jake continued. "Where's your mom?"

"She left."

Uneasiness shot down Hannah's spine. "Who's watching you, Brett?"

"She said someone was coming to watch me. Is that you?" He held out one of his puppies. "Frisco is scared."

Her heart melted and she immediately wrapped her arms around both Brett and his puppy. "There's no reason to be scared," she assured him.

"I'm going to look around," Jake said, a thoughtful look in his eyes.

As he headed toward the bedroom, she sat down on the floor next to Brett. "Tell me about Frisco," she said as her gaze ran down his body. He looked healthy, and his jeans and sweater were clean. His hair was combed, and he smelled like soap and shampoo. She looked around the rest of the living room. It was neat and tidy. There was no indication anything had happened here, but she had a bad feeling churning in her gut. Something was wrong. This little boy was alone. *Why?*

"Mommy said Frisco will protect me," Brett told her.

"Did your mom say where she was going?"

"No."

"What about your dad?"

"I'm hungry."

"Well, let me see what's here to eat." She got to her feet and moved into the adjacent kitchen. There was a bowl of cereal on the table as well as a glass of milk and another glass of orange juice. They were untouched.

Brett ran into the kitchen. "Did you make me cereal?" he asked.

"It was already here, Brett. Your mom must have left it for you."

He scrambled into the chair. "Can you pour the milk into my cereal?"

"Sure." She poured some of the milk over the cereal and left the rest for him to drink.

As he started to eat, Jake came out of the bedroom and motioned to her.

She joined him in the living room. "What's going on?" she asked in a quiet voice, not wanting to alarm Brett.

"You need to see for yourself." He led her down a short hallway into the one and only bedroom. There was a small suitcase on the bed that was open but completely packed. On top of the neatly folded clothing was a note.

She picked it up and read aloud, "Please watch over my son. I'll be back as soon as I can. Don't call the police. He won't be safe if you do." She met Jake's gaze, her stomach churning. "What the hell is this?"

"Trouble," he said, meeting her gaze.

She thought so, too.

"And by the way," he added, "the hot water works just fine. It was just a ruse to get you out here."

"But this woman had no idea how long it would take for

someone to come up here. He's a small child, and she left him alone."

"What are you going to do?"

She looked at the note once more and frowned. "She says not to call the police, but I have to." She lifted her gaze to his. "Don't I?"

# CHAPTER TWO

HANNAH DIDN'T NEED Jake to answer that question, because she already knew. "Of course I have to call the police. I'll reach out to Adam or Brodie. They'll know how to handle this and keep Brett safe. I trust them."

"That's the right move," he agreed.

She took her phone out of the pocket of her jacket, relieved to see she had a signal. "Phone is working again."

"Good."

"Jake, I may need you to give both me and Brett a ride into town."

"Absolutely."

"What about your friend?"

"I'll check on him now. What do you think will happen to Brett?"

"Child welfare services will be called," she said slowly. She hated the thought of that sweet little boy spending Christmas in foster care.

"Maybe the mom will be back soon."

That was Jake, the eternal optimist. He always looked for the bright side, and while she'd really liked that about him, there had come a time when she'd also hated the fact that he couldn't seem to

understand that not everything would be all right. But this wasn't
the time to get into the past, so she simply followed him into the
living room. She wanted to check on Brett once more before she
called the police. Maybe he could tell her something about
his mom.

After Jake left, she sat down at the kitchen table across from
Brett and gave him a smile. He'd eaten every last bit of his cereal,
leaving behind a milk moustache. She picked up the napkin that
had been set next to the bowl and wiped his mouth.

As she did that, she couldn't help thinking about the little
details that had been carefully planned—the folded napkin, the fact
that the milk had not been poured into the bowl so the cereal
wouldn't get soggy, the warmth of the cabin, the bright lights, the
television, and, of course, the note. It all seemed to imply that
Brett's mother had spent some time planning her exit. She'd tried to
think of everything, but she'd left the biggest thing to chance, and
that was who might respond to her call about a broken water
heater.

"Can I have a cookie now?" Brett pointed to the bag of chocolate chip cookies on the counter. "I always get a cookie when I eat
my dinner."

She didn't think cereal and cookies were the best meal, but at
least he wasn't going hungry. At this moment, her first priority was
to keep him happy. She got him a cookie and brought it back to the
table.

His smile made her heart melt. He had a sweet, angelic face, a
trusting innocence that made her want to do everything she could
to make sure he was safe. In some ways, he reminded her of her
little brother Tyler. She'd been thirteen when her father had died,
when her mother had fallen apart, and Tyler had only been eight.
She'd fed him cereal and cookies, too. Or she'd made him jam
sandwiches because it was all she could find in the fridge. And
sometimes there had only been enough for one of them to eat. Not
because there hadn't been money for food—just no one to get it.

Her heart hardened at the memories, and she felt a rush of

anger toward the unknown woman who had left her son to the mercy of strangers.

*What if she hadn't been the one to come to the cabin? What if her mom had sent the handyman?* Old Blain wouldn't have known what to do with a small child. *And how could the unknown mother trust someone she didn't know with her child?*

Some people really shouldn't have children.

"When is my mommy coming back?" Brett asked, drawing her attention back to him.

"I'm not sure."

"Are you going to read me a story?"

"Maybe later. Do you know how old you are?"

He held up four fingers.

"Four. You're a big guy. Do you know where you live?"

"In a yellow house. It looks like the sun."

"That sounds nice. Is it here in the mountains?"

"No. It's far away."

"Do you live there with your mom and dad?"

"My mom lives there."

"Do you know her name?"

"Mommy."

She smiled at his pragmatic answer.

"What about your last name? Do you know that?"

He gave her a blank look, then said, "Can I play?"

"Sure."

As he slid off the chair and ran into the living room to play with his puppies, she got to her feet and took the cereal bowl to the sink. With Brett caught up in some imaginary game, she took out her phone and called her mother. She wanted to know more about the repair request before she contacted Adam.

"Did you get the water heater fixed?" her mom asked.

"The water is fine. I need to know who called you about the problem."

"I got a text on my phone from the tenant. Why?"

"What exactly did it say?"

"I don't remember exactly. Why are you asking me these questions, Hannah?"

She didn't want to get into it just yet. Her mom always complicated matters, and she needed to keep this situation as simple as she could. "Just tell me what the text said. Can you look on your phone?"

"I'm at Marty's house. Can't this wait?"

She didn't much care for Marty, who was a fifty-seven-year-old divorcee who had recently moved to Whisper Lake from Denver. He seemed like a party guy, and that was not the kind of man her mom should be with. "This can't wait," she said forcefully. "Just read me the text. It will take you two seconds. I drove all the way out here for you. It's the least you can do."

"Fine." Her mother paused, then read the text aloud. "Water heater is broken. Please send someone right away. We can't make it through the night without hot water. This is urgent."

"And what did you say?"

"After you told me you'd go, I texted her back that you were on the way."

"What's the name of the tenant?"

"I don't know. Mark did the booking."

"Did her name appear on the text?"

"Just a phone number."

"Can you forward it to me? There must have been a name on the rental agreement. Do you have that?"

"Mark has all that information. His assistant Debbie can get it for us, but I told you she's driving back from Denver."

"How would the tenant get your number? Why wouldn't she text Mark or Debbie?"

Her mother hesitated, then said, "I'm not sure. But I think my phone number is on the rental agreement as well as theirs."

"Okay, just text me what you have."

"I'm doing it right now. Can you tell me what's going on?"

"I'm not sure yet, but I'll get back to you."

"That sounds mysterious. Is everything all right? Wait a second, hold on."

She frowned as she heard her mother tell Marty to get her a sparkling water. It was good that her mom wasn't drinking alcohol, but Hannah couldn't help getting nervous when her mom put herself in situations where there was a lot of booze around.

"Okay, what were we saying?" her mom asked, coming back on the line.

"Never mind. I've got to go. I'll check in with you later."

After ending the call with her mother, she punched in the number her mother had forwarded to her. It went straight to voicemail. It was an automated message, with no indication of who the number belonged to.

She then called Debbie but got another voicemail. She left a message asking Debbie to call as soon as she got back to town. She'd no sooner finished that when Jake re-entered the cabin, concern on his face.

"Did you find your friend?" she asked when he came into the kitchen.

"No. He wasn't there, but the door was open, and the place was a pit, filled with fast-food garbage and two empty vodka bottles."

"That's not good."

His lips tightened. "No, it's not good. His car is not there. I really hope he didn't drive drunk."

She could see the strain in his eyes. While there were a lot of things she didn't like about Jake, she had to admit he'd always cared about his friends. "I'm sorry."

He gave her a nod. "Thanks. What's going on here? Did you talk to the police?"

"Not yet. I tried to get some information from Brett, but he just said they live far away and he's four years old. Thankfully, he's not scared anymore."

"The blessed ignorance of childhood."

"I also spoke to my mother. She gave me a phone number for the renter, but that person didn't answer. Our property manager and his assistant are currently unreachable."

"Did you tell your mother about Brett?"

"No. She's at a party, and she's not that helpful in a crisis. I'll call Adam now, but I'd like to do that from the bedroom. Can you watch Brett?"

"Whatever you need."

She kind of hated that Jake was being so supportive. She liked keeping a good strong wall of anger between them. It was much easier that way. But this was a situation she hadn't expected, and at the moment she needed him to distract Brett.

As Jake got down on the floor with Brett, she headed into the bedroom and took out her phone. There was a part of her that didn't want to make the call. The note had been so specific about the police putting Brett in danger, but she couldn't see how that could happen, at least not with Adam. However, as soon as she officially reported the mother's absence, Brett would probably end up in a foster home.

She'd spent two weeks in foster care a long time ago. It had been one of the worst experiences of her life. Luckily, she'd been able to go home, to be reunited with her little brother, thanks to the kindness of her aunt who had left her home on the other side of the world to come and take care of them until her mother got better. Hopefully, Brett had someone else in his life who could do that.

*But what if he didn't?*

She picked up the note and read it once more. Clearly, the mother was in trouble, maybe danger, since she implied Brett wouldn't be safe if the police were called. *What did that mean? Had she kidnapped the child? Was he even hers?*

Jake stuck his head through the doorway. "Did you call yet?"

"No. What's Brett doing?"

"Watching TV." He walked into the room, giving her a quizzical look. "Why are you stalling, Hannah?"

"I've been in Brett's shoes. It's hard to make the call knowing what will happen to him."

Jake's gaze suddenly filled with understanding. He was one of the few people in her life she'd told about that terrible time. "You're thinking about what happened to you when your mom disappeared for a while."

"Yes. I was ripped away from my family, made to stay with

people I didn't know, separated from my brother, my friends, anyone who knew me. It was awful. And I was lucky; it only lasted two weeks. What if Brett's mother can't be found for months? He's such a little boy. And he's so sweet. How can I do that to him?"

"What's the alternative? Are you going to take care of him? Can you legally even do that?"

She frowned at his questions. "Probably not. I just wish I had more information. Maybe his mom will be back really soon."

"We can wait, give her some time to return."

"Or I could wait. You don't need to stay."

"You have no working vehicle, there's a storm coming in, and phone signal is spotty. I'm not leaving you here alone."

"I can take care of myself."

"Well, then I'm staying for Brett, not you."

"I can take care of Brett, too," she said stubbornly. "I don't need you, Jake."

"You've made that abundantly clear," he said, meeting her gaze. "But I'm still staying. You can be stubborn; so can I."

"You are so annoying."

"Right back at you. Now, what do you want to do?"

She thought about her options. There was really only one choice. "I'll call Adam." Adam Cole was a detective and the brother of her friends, Lizzie and Chelsea. She had his personal number and could talk to him in a non-official capacity first. She punched in his number.

"Hello?" Adam said.

She could barely hear him with all the noise in the background.

"It's Hannah. Where are you?"

"Station Christmas party," he said. "Hold on a sec. I need to find a quieter place."

"Okay."

As Adam put her on hold, her gaze moved once more to the note, which she'd left on top of the packed clothes. As she picked it up again, she caught a glimpse of gold that she hadn't seen before. Moving aside a fuzzy sweater, she picked up the chain that had slid down between some clothes, her heart stopping at the sight of the small gold unicorn.

"Oh, my God," she murmured.

"Hannah? I'm back," Adam said. "What's up?"

She could hear Adam, but she couldn't find the words. That necklace was taking her back in time.

"Hannah?" Adam said again. "Are you there?"

"Sorry, Adam," she said quickly. "It's nothing. Never mind. I'll call you back."

"Are you sure?"

"Yes. Have fun at your party." She ended the call, her heart beating out of her chest.

"What's going on?" Jake asked in confusion, his sharp, questioning gaze seeking hers. "Why did you hang up on Adam?"

"Because I can't involve the police." She held up the unicorn. "I know who Brett's mother is, Jake. I know why she brought him here, why she left him for me."

"For you? I thought she texted the property manager."

"Actually, she texted my mother, whose phone number must have been on the agreement. But she must have figured I'd be the one to come."

"Who are you talking about, Hannah?"

She stared at him, a feeling of impossibility constricting her throat. It couldn't be, but it was. Now she knew why Brett reminded her of Tyler. "I'm talking about my sister."

"Kelly?" he asked in astonishment. "Have you been in touch with her?"

"Not in fifteen years, but this necklace belonged to her. In fact, I gave it to her on her fourteenth birthday, and she was kind enough not to tell me that it was way too young for her." It all suddenly made sense. "Brett is Kelly's son. That means I'm his aunt." She looked into Jake's confused eyes. "Where the hell is my sister?"

# CHAPTER THREE

IT WASN'T a question Jake could answer. In fact, he was still trying to follow the story Hannah had just pieced together. "Are you sure the necklace could only belong to your sister? It looks like something that could have been mass-produced."

"Even if there are thousands of these necklaces in existence, this one was in this suitcase, with this child, under these circumstances. There's no way it's a coincidence. Kelly brought Brett here. She sent the text claiming the hot water heater was broken, because she remembered how often we had to relight it. It was something she knew I could fix. She wanted me to find Brett."

"Why didn't she just say so in the note? Why didn't she address it to you?" he challenged. "Why leave a necklace and make you guess?"

Hannah didn't care for his questions, but he was used to that look of irritation in her eyes, so it didn't bother him.

"I don't know why she didn't do any of those things. But Kelly's actions haven't made sense to me in a long time. She left when I was fourteen and she was nineteen. I've never heard one word from her since then. I have no idea where she's been living, who she's been living with..." Her voice trailed away, then came back even stronger. "But I know she has a son. There must be a father somewhere. However, when I asked Brett about a dad, he didn't say anything and changed the subject."

Hannah sat down on the bed, her gaze thoughtful and worried as she stared at the necklace swinging between her fingers. She was determined to work the problem. She'd always been that way. When someone said she couldn't have something or do something, she became determined to prove them wrong.

He'd always liked that about her. She'd inspired him with her never-say-quit attitude more than she would know. But he also knew that she could get incredibly frustrated when she couldn't control the outcome of a situation, and this one was definitely not under her control.

As he watched her stare at the necklace, he thought it was probably the first time in twelve years that he'd had a chance to really look at her. Usually, when he showed up, she ran in the other direction. But not tonight. Tonight, a flat tire had thrown them together, had forced her to rely on him just a little, and he wasn't unhappy about that. He'd been wanting this kind of moment ever since he'd come back to Whisper Lake two years ago, but she'd been determined not to give it to him.

He understood her reasons; he just wanted her to see him now, to look past the boy he'd once been to the man he was today. But her gaze was on the necklace. Her thoughts were on the past—and not the past they had shared. The memories she was reliving were of her family, her sister, probably her mother and her brother, maybe even the father she'd lost.

He'd known a lot about her at one time in his life. She'd told him things she'd never told anyone else, and he wanted to be back in the warmth of that kind of incredible trust. But he definitely was not there. He wasn't giving up, though. As long as Hannah was still single, he wouldn't stop trying to break down her defenses. He just hoped that would happen before she fell for someone else. And he knew there were plenty of men who were interested in her.

She had a unique beauty, dark-red hair that was pulled back in a ponytail now but would flow over her shoulders and halfway down her back when she released it from the constricting tie. Her eyes were a dark-chocolate brown that could burn with the same fire as her hair when she was angry or excited or filled with desire. His body hardened as their most intimate memory filled his head. Hannah, with her hair down, her creamy skin flushed with heat, her bare shoulders revealing a delightful smattering of freckles. Her eyes had sparkled with desire when she'd looked at him, her mouth curving into a nervous smile.

He'd felt the same nerves, the same impatient, raw desire that had resulted in an experience he'd never forgotten. He wondered if she still remembered. He knew she didn't want to. She'd wanted to forget him after he'd broken their relationship beyond repair.

But she might remember. That might be the reason why she was so careful to avoid him, to never really look at him. Or maybe that was just wishful thinking.

He wanted her to want him again, the way he still wanted her. He just didn't know how to make that happen. Maybe it shouldn't happen. Perhaps, he should let the past stay where it was.

On the other hand, like Hannah, when someone put a mountain in front of him, he had to climb it, no matter the danger, no matter the risk.

But the risk wasn't his alone, and that's what gave him pause. He'd hurt her once; he didn't want to do it again.

Hannah finally lifted her gaze from the necklace. "Kelly is in trouble, and she needs my help with Brett. I'm not going to call Adam back, not yet anyway. I need to give Kelly some time to come back."

He nodded, as she brought his thoughts back to the present. "Okay."

"That's it?" she asked, as if surprised by his agreement.

"It's your family, your call. I am curious—have you heard from Kelly since she left?"

"No. She hasn't been in contact with any of us since the day she took a bus out of town. My mom looked for her in the beginning. I think she might have spoken to her once or twice, but then Kelly disappeared again. There was so much anger between them; they couldn't find a way to reconnect or maybe they just didn't want to."

"I know we talked about it in high school, but I can't remember all the details now. The relationship between Kelly and your mom took a turn for the worse after your dad died. Your mom blamed Kelly for the accident, right?"

"Yes. Kelly was a senior in high school. She had stayed out past curfew and my father went to find her. On the way home, on a very stormy night, he lost control of the car and died. Kelly was not injured. My mom told Kelly it was her fault. My dad never would have gone out that night if Kelly had come home on time."

He felt a little sorry for Kelly, even though he understood that the blame had come from a place of deep grief.

"I didn't blame Kelly," Hannah added. "I knew it was just an accident. But she and my mom could not get along. They were both in a lot of pain. Several months later, Kelly disappeared. I never thought she'd stay gone. I believed she'd return when she had a chance to calm down and grow up. But she never did. When Tyler and I were put into foster care, which happened about four months after Kelly left, the social worker said she looked for Kelly, but she couldn't find her. That's when I started to hate her. She hadn't just abandoned my mom—she'd abandoned all of us. It was selfish, but that's who Kelly was. Her drama, her problems, were always more important than anyone else's. Now, it's happening again. She has gotten herself into something, and I'm supposed to be there for her, even though she's never been there for me."

Hannah's voice was thick with emotion. She was angry and frustrated but also worried. Deep down, he knew she still loved her sister, because Hannah loved with her whole heart. He'd seen the way she'd taken care of her little brother, and even her mom, who often didn't deserve it. And for a while, she'd loved him like that, too. But when the love was gone, when she felt betrayed, there could be no end to her anger.

"Do you think I'm making a mistake?" Hannah asked. "Should I call Adam back?"

He was surprised she even cared what he thought, but if she wanted his opinion, he'd give it. "I think you should hold off on that call. Brett is safe. You're his aunt. See where this goes."

Relief filled her gaze. "I agree." She tilted her head. "I keep thinking about her note, about Brett not being safe if we go to the police. It makes me wonder if Brett's father is in the middle of this trouble. Was he hurting Brett? Did he have custody? Did Kelly take Brett and run to protect him?"

"Those are definitely all scenarios that make sense to me, including the idea that the father might be a cop."

"He could be, but he's not a Whisper Lake police officer. There's no way Kelly has been living in our small town. I just wish I knew where she was before she came here."

"That shouldn't be difficult to find out. There's a trail," he pointed out. "She had a vehicle. It had to be registered to someone. She booked the rental. I assume there was a deposit, a credit card involved. All those clues could lead to her whereabouts."

"And the police could probably find all that out in just a few minutes." She let out a breath of frustration. "I wish she'd left us more information in her note. It's so difficult to know the right move to make, and I still think she took a big risk that I'd be the one to respond to her call. What if I hadn't come right away? What if you hadn't driven up when you did? I could still be stuck on the side of the road. Did Kelly stick around to see if anyone would come, or did she just hope for the best?"

He started at her words. "When I walked over to Trevor's cabin, I saw a car leaving the area. Maybe it was Kelly. Maybe she waited until you arrived."

"That would make me feel better, unless the lights didn't belong to her car. Did you see anyone else?"

"No. There was a light on in the cabin next to Trevor's. Why don't I go knock on their door? Maybe someone saw something."

"That's a good idea." She got to her feet. "I also think we should take Brett to my house. With the storm coming in tonight, I'd rather be back in town."

He was relieved by that decision. "I would agree. I'll give you a ride whenever you're ready to go."

"Okay." She paused, an odd, tense look passing through her eyes.

"What?" he asked curiously. "Do you have something else to say?"

"Thank you," she said through tight lips.

He gave her a wry smile. "That sounded painful."

"I still said it," she retorted.

"Even though it made you want to throw up. You can't stand it when I'm nice to you."

"It's not like it happens all that often."

"It might if you didn't run out of the room every time you saw me."

"I don't do that."

"Yes, you do. Can't you be honest about that?"

"Do you really want to talk about honesty?" she challenged.

He had to admit he'd taken a wrong turn with that question.

Without waiting for his answer, she added, "I don't actually want to talk about anything that has to do with our past."

"You never do."

"And I still don't. There's no point. I need to deal with this situation."

"You always have an excuse."

"Do you really have anything new to say?" she challenged, as she put her hands on her hips. "What happened with us was a lifetime ago. I've moved on, and I'm sure you have, too."

"If you'd moved on, you wouldn't try to avoid me every chance you get."

She shook her head. "I can't do this right now." She turned and walked out of the bedroom.

He wasn't surprised by her quick exit; he was used to seeing her back. When he returned to the living room, Hannah was sitting on the couch next to where Brett was playing on the floor. Her entire demeanor changed when she looked at her nephew. Gone was the anger and the stress. There was nothing but warmth, kindness and love.

He really missed the days when she'd looked at him like that, but their very recent exchange reminded him that that would not be happening again any time soon.

As he watched Brett and Hannah together, he could see a family resemblance, even though Brett had green eyes and blond hair, no trace of Hannah's temperamental red. But there was something about Brett's expressions that reminded him of Hannah.

Hannah gave Brett a smile and said, "I was thinking you might want to come to my house and have a sleepover. What do you think?"

"Is Mommy going to be there?"

"I'm not sure when she'll be back. But I'll take really good care of you."

"Mommy said you would."

Hannah's jaw dropped at that comment. "She did? Did she mention my name? Did she say Hannah?"

"She said you'd be really nice to me and that we both like dogs. You had one named Tiger."

"I—I did," Hannah said, a tremor in her voice now. "What else did your mom say about me?"

"I don't know—stuff. Do you want to play?"

"Maybe for a minute. Then we need to get your things."

"You can be the vet. My puppy is sick," Brett said, handing her his small dog.

As Hannah and Brett began their imaginary game, Jake grabbed his coat and headed out the door. When he stepped onto the porch, he blew out a breath. Hannah got under his skin like no one else. She had so many sides to her personality. She was definitely a rough diamond, beautiful on the outside, but that beauty had been hardened through fire. She'd been through a lot in her life, and she'd come out stronger, but her toughness wasn't the whole story. She also had a tender, soft core and this situation with her sister was probably bringing her a great deal of pain.

Hannah had been trying to put her family back together since her father had died. He knew from their mutual friends that Hannah's mother's drinking had become a huge problem, much bigger than he'd seen in high school. He felt bad that he hadn't been there for her, although he knew she wouldn't have let him be there even if he'd wanted to. She was barely tolerating him now.

But she had let him into her life ever so slightly, and he would take advantage of that. He was going to help her with Brett and her sister. Whatever he could do to make this situation better, he would do. He owed her that much. Actually, he owed her a whole hell of a lot more, but at the moment, this was all he could do.

As an icy wind picked up, he lifted his gaze upward. The tall trees were swaying, the clouds overhead had turned black, and snow was beginning to fall. It would be a good idea to leave sooner rather than later. But first, he had to check with the neighbor.

He jogged down the road to the one cabin in the area that had lights on. He knocked on the door.

A man appeared on the threshold. He appeared to be in his fifties or sixties, his hair peppered with gray, his eyes guarded. "Who are you?" he asked bluntly.

"I'm Jake McKenna. My friend owns the cabin over there— Hannah Stark." He tipped his head toward Hannah's house.

"Okay. You got a problem?"

"A little boy was left on his own in the cabin. We're trying to figure out who left him. Did you happen to see anyone go into the house?"

The man's irritation turned to concern. "I saw a boy and his mom carry some groceries inside. That was a few hours ago. They seemed fine."

"Did you happen to see the woman leave?"

The man scratched his chin as he pondered that question. "I didn't see her leave, but I did see her talking to a guy at the cabin over there." He pointed to the cabin where Trevor had been staying, the one Jake had found littered with empty bottles and fast-food wrappers.

"Was that guy young with long brown hair and a beard?"

"That was him. What's going on?"

"I'm trying to figure that out. What kind of conversation were they having?"

"I couldn't hear what they were saying. They seemed friendly. It wasn't like anyone was scared or anything. That's all I saw."

"What about the woman's car? What was she driving?"

"I think it was a Prius." He shrugged. "I wasn't paying much attention. I came up here to get some rest, some quiet."

"I'll leave you to that. Thanks for your help."

"Sure thing."

As the man shut his door, Jake walked off the porch, taking another look at Trevor's cabin. *Was there any chance that Trevor and Kelly might know each other? Both families had owned cabins in the area for a long time. But Trevor was at least ten years younger than Kelly, and Kelly had been gone a long time. It seemed unlikely that they knew each other, but it was odd that they'd had any conversation at all.*

He was still pondering that thought when a gale force wind came roaring through the trees, sending snow straight into his face. It was snowing harder now. Visibility was diminishing quickly. He had a feeling they'd just lost their window to get back to town.

He jogged down the road, dodging a heavy branch as it fell to the ground. Another gust of wind almost knocked him off his feet. He opened the front door and had to forcefully close it behind him.

Hannah jumped to her feet as he shook the snow out of his hair.

"It's really windy out there," she said in alarm.

The windows in the house rattled at the end of her statement. "Yes. The storm is here, earlier than I expected."

"We should go now."

"I think we need to wait it out."

"We can't stay here."

"I don't like the wind," Brett said, getting up from the couch to wrap his arms around Hannah's waist. "It's scary."

Hannah patted Brett's head. "It's going to be fine, honey."

No sooner had she finished speaking when a branch hit the roof, sending Brett's arms tighter around Hannah, his face a picture of fear.

"I guess we'll stay put," Hannah said, meeting his gaze. "For a few hours anyway."

He thought it might be longer than a few hours, but he kept that to himself.

"Since we're staying," Hannah continued, "maybe I'll check the fridge and see if Kelly left us anything besides cereal and cookies."

"Kelly," Brett echoed. "That's my mom's name."

Hannah caught her breath. "Do you know where your mom went?"

"She said she'd be back soon, and I should be a really good boy because Santa is coming." Brett paused, concern in his eyes. "Am I being good?"

"Very good," Hannah replied.

"Sometimes I make people mad and they get angry," he said. "Mommy says I have to be quiet."

Jake didn't like what he was hearing, and he could see by the stress in Hannah's eyes that she didn't either. But she was trying not to show her emotions to Brett.

"Why don't you watch your show?" Hannah suggested with a forced smile. "Jake and I will see what other food there is."

"Okay." Brett got back on the couch, and Hannah covered him with a cozy blanket, then headed into the kitchen.

He took off his coat and followed her into the room.

As soon as they were out of sight from Brett, she turned around. "He's Kelly's son. He confirmed it."

"Yes, he is. But I'd like to know why he needs to be quiet and who he's making angry."

"Me, too. I need to find Kelly. I need to help her, to save her from whatever is going on, whatever she is running away from."

That was Hannah, always jumping into savior mode.

"I'll help you," he said, because that's the mode he usually jumped into as well.

"And after I save her, I'm going to kill her for leaving her son with no explanation," Hannah said with a fiery light in her eyes.

He couldn't argue with that. He completely understood why Hannah was furious with her sister. But he had to admit there was a part of him that wasn't that unhappy with the situation.

Hannah had been running away from him since they were seventeen years old, but tonight she wasn't going anywhere.

# CHAPTER FOUR

HANNAH KNEW Jake was not unhappy about getting stuck in the cabin together. He hadn't even tried to hide the gleam in his brown eyes, and that damn sexy smile of his had sent a shiver down her spine. She had a lot of reasons not to like Jake, and all those reasons made her angry, but what bothered her the most was that she was still attracted to him. She didn't understand how she could hate him and want him at the same time.

Turning away from him, she opened the refrigerator and was surprised to see more food than she'd expected. She'd thought the milk, juice, cereal, and cookies might have been the extent of the groceries, but there was a carton of eggs, a rotisserie chicken, a bag of salad, and cream cheese to go along with the bagels on the counter. She took out the chicken and salad.

"We won't starve," she said. "I'm surprised Kelly left this much food, but maybe she thought I'd stay here with Brett."

"Probably. The neighbor I spoke to said he saw her come in with a bag of groceries."

She'd completely forgotten about the neighbor. She'd gotten so distracted by the storm and the thought of having to spend more time with Jake. "What else did he say?"

"He saw her talking to my friend, Trevor. He didn't see

anything odd about their conversation. No one was angry or upset. They just seemed to be chatting. He said she was driving a Prius. That's all he knew."

"I wonder why she was talking to your friend."

"No idea. Since you don't know Trevor, I doubt Kelly would."

"She wouldn't. Trevor would be a lot younger than her. And Kelly has been gone so long. There's no way they know each other."

"I didn't think so, either, but it's odd that she would leave Brett and go talk to Trevor. If she needed something from a neighbor, she could have talked to the guy I spoke to, whose cabin is closer to this one."

She sighed. "Nothing Kelly has done so far makes sense to me." She grabbed plates out of the cabinet along with some silverware. "Do you want to cut up some chicken? I'll throw the salad in a bowl."

"Sure."

While he grabbed a knife, she put the salad together. It felt strange to be making dinner with Jake, something she never would have imagined them doing together.

He gave her a smile as he put slices of chicken on a plate. "I bet you didn't think tonight's trip would end up with us making dinner together."

Clearly, he was still good at reading her mind. "Definitely not. If I hadn't gotten a flat tire, our paths might not have crossed at all."

"Fate."

"Which usually doesn't work in my favor. I'd prefer if fate brought me a winning lottery ticket, but it never seems to go that way."

"I don't know about that. You could think of me as your winning lottery ticket. You're not stranded on the side of the road. You're not alone with Brett, because fate brought me to you."

"Fine, I'm not going to argue with you."

"That's a first," he said dryly.

"Keep being annoying, and that might change."

"I don't know how not to annoy you, Hannah. I take a breath and I make you mad."

His words made her feel like she was being childish, which she was. She hated that she couldn't seem to get over being pissed off at him. She should be more adult about it. They lived in the same town. They had some of the same friends. She wasn't a heartsick teenager anymore. She was an ER nurse. She handled life-and-death situations without missing a beat. *So, why did this man still throw her off her game?*

"Let's just eat," she said, taking the salad to the table. She moved back into the living room where Brett was watching a cartoon. "Do you want some chicken, Brett?"

"I'm not hungry," he replied, his gaze focused on the television.

"Are you sure you don't want a little more?"

He shook his head.

Since Brett had had cereal only a short time earlier, she decided to leave him be rather than force the issue. He was happy enough with the TV, so she'd let him keep watching. She could see him from one end of the kitchen table, so she took a seat there while Jake set a plate of chicken on the table and sat down across from her.

After the first bite, she realized just how hungry she was. She hadn't had much lunch and that had been hours ago.

"This isn't bad," Jake said with a pleased smile.

"Not bad at all," she agreed. "There are cookies for dessert, if you still have room."

"I always have room for dessert."

She couldn't help but smile. "I remember the night you ate an entire apple pie because Micky bet you that you couldn't." Jake had never been able to say no to a dare. If someone threw a challenge in front of him, he was determined to conquer it, no matter what it was.

"I won, but I felt bad afterward. I should have known better."

"You knew better; you did it anyway. You like having a mountain to climb, even if it's just eating a pie."

He tipped his head in agreement. "That's true. I like to push the envelope."

"Which I hear you do quite often. Some patients I've treated in recent weeks have talked about some harrowing rescues by you and Brodie and others on the search and rescue team."

"We've seen some bad crashes and some fairly stupid behavior. Not everyone conquers the mountain. Some people lose. Usually, because they didn't prepare."

"You believe in preparation? I thought you were more of a wing-it kind of guy."

"Not when it comes to battling nature. I respect the mountains and the weather."

"You weren't always that way."

"I grew up, Hannah. So did you. We're not the kids we once were."

"No, we're not. How's your business going?" she asked, wanting to immediately derail what might be another trip back into their past. She preferred to stay in the present.

"It's good. We've been very busy this season. I had to hire on some extra guides."

"How big is your team now?"

"Besides myself, we have six full-time guides and another four who work part-time, depending on the season. I have four other employees who handle the bookings and sell the limited amount of merchandise we carry in the store."

"Why limited?" she asked curiously.

"Because the focus of my business is the experience, the adventure. Gianna's parents already sell top-of-the-line equipment in their store, so I'd rather carve out my own niche. Plus, it's not that exciting for me to sell or rent skis. I'd rather show someone the thrill of coming down a virgin trail after the first snow."

His words took her back. "You showed me that."

He met her gaze, smiling as they shared that memory. "You loved it."

"I did. I had never been on that trail before. I didn't even know it existed. It felt like we were on our own private mountain, like no one had ever been there before us."

"And to think you were almost too afraid to go."

"But you talked me into it. You always pushed me to go further than I wanted to go."

"Wasn't it a good thing?"

"Most of the time," she admitted. "But it was different for you, wasn't it? I didn't push you; I held you back. I wanted to keep your feet on the ground, and you wanted to fly."

A frown drew his brows together. "It wasn't exactly like that, Hannah."

She shrugged. "Maybe we remember it differently. Anyway, it sounds like your business is going well." She picked up her plate and carried it to the counter. The window over the sink rattled from the force of the wind.

"I don't think we'll be able to go back to town tonight," Jake said, as he joined her at the counter.

She didn't want to spend all night in this small cabin with Jake and a four-year-old, who was going to go to bed soon, but she also didn't want to risk taking Brett into a fierce winter storm. "I think we have to stay here," she agreed. "I'm sorry that my flat tire got you into this."

"You know I'm not really sorry," he said, with a gleam in his eyes.

She didn't know what to say to that, so she said, "Can you handle the dishes? I want to spend time with Brett."

"I can do that."

She moved into the living room and sat down next to Brett. The little boy immediately snuggled up next to her. She put her arm around him, feeling a rush of tenderness for the small child who shared her blood. She would protect him and love him until his mother came back. She sent up a silent, pleading prayer that that would be soon.

After Jake cleaned up the kitchen, he came into the room, chomping on a cookie. He sat down in the armchair adjacent to the couch and they watched the cartoon together.

When it was over, Hannah couldn't help but notice that Brett was looking very sleepy. Glancing at her watch, she realized it was after eight.

"Bedtime," she said.

"Are you going to sleep in the bed with me?" Brett asked.

Since there was only one bedroom in the cabin and one bed, her choice was Brett or Jake. She was definitely going to pick Brett. Jake could take the couch.

"I'm sleeping with you," she told him.

"Okay," he said happily.

She took his hand as they got up and headed into the bedroom. She found his PJs, which were on top of the clothes in the suitcase. All of the items in the case seemed to belong to Brett, which made her wonder where Kelly's clothes were. She helped Brett change into his pajamas and brush his teeth, then tucked him into bed.

"Are you going to sleep now, too?" he asked her.

"I'll be in soon."

"Can you tell me a story?"

"A story, huh? What kind of story?"

"Do you know the one about the little girl in the balloon? She wanted to fly far away and have adventures."

Her heart flipped over at the mention of Kelly's favorite story, one which Kelly had shared with her many a night. Even as a child, Kelly had wanted to fly high and far away.

"I might remember part of—" She stopped abruptly, realizing Brett was already asleep. She blew out a breath of relief, because she didn't really want to relive that story.

She got up and turned off the light. She left the door ajar and then returned to the living room.

Jake was on the couch now. He had turned on the news, but he muted the sound when she appeared. "It's supposed to snow until midnight. If it clears after that, we should be able to get back to town in the morning."

"Good." She sat down on the couch, keeping some distance between them.

"You look a little more stressed than you did a few minutes ago. Why?" he asked curiously.

"It's silly. Brett asked me to tell him a story, and it was Kelly's favorite tale about a girl in a hot air balloon who flies away from all her problems."

"Sounds like your sister lived that story."

"She did fly away, but I have no idea where she's been living all this time. I have so many questions. What does she do for money? Who is Brett's father and where is he? And most importantly, why did she come back to Whisper Lake now? And why didn't she just ask me to help her?"

"Maybe she wasn't ready for you to see her, or she thought you might say no."

"I wouldn't have said no. But it does amaze me a little that even though she abandoned me and Tyler that she thought I would instantly step up for her."

He smiled. "It doesn't surprise me. Anyone who knows you, Hannah, would know that you would step up. That's who you are. You've always been that girl, even before Kelly left. And since then you've been taking care of everyone in the family."

It was nice to know that Jake could see the burden she'd been carrying, and she was a little touched by his description of her.

"Kelly knew you wouldn't turn your back on Brett," Jake added.

"But she was still afraid to ask or to explain. She should have done both."

"I don't disagree. But it is what it is. And no matter what you think about Kelly, you're already in love with Brett."

She smiled at his words. "I am. He's adorable."

Jake gave her a soft smile. "He is."

Under the warmth of his smile, she felt her anger toward him weaken, which scared her. Anger was what kept the wall up between them. *But did she really need that wall?* It wasn't like anything would happen between them ever again.

"What are you thinking?" he asked, giving her a speculative look.

"That I'm tired."

"You should go to bed."

"Not that kind of tired."

"Then what kind of tired are we talking about?"

"I'm tired of being angry at you," she confessed. The words had no sooner left her mouth than she wanted them back, but it was too late.

Relief filled his gaze. "Well, it's about damn time."

"I'm not saying I forgive you," she added quickly. "I just don't want to work so hard to avoid you. It's exhausting."

"Then stop, Hannah. What do you think will happen if you don't run out of every room I walk into?"

"I don't know, Jake. That's why I run. I don't like unpredictable situations. And you—you are the most unpredictable person I've ever known. You were my best friend. You were my first love, the first guy I had sex with, and three days later, you stood me up for the prom, cheated on me in a very public way, and humiliated me in front of the whole school."

With every word, the frown on his face deepened, as well as the regret in his eyes.

"I know I hurt you, Hannah. I was a seventeen-year-old kid, and I made a huge mistake. I've wished a million times that I could turn back time and do that night over again. But I can't."

"No, you can't," she agreed. "I thought we had something really special, but I was stupid."

"You weren't stupid. It was special until I messed it up. But I'm not that kid anymore, Hannah. You have to let me grow up. You have to see me for who I am now."

"Why? Why do I have to do anything?" she challenged. "Why can't we just not speak, not see each other, not relive some of the worst memories of my life?"

"Because we live in a small town. We hang out with the same people. And because we used to be friends, best friends. Don't you ever miss that?" he asked. "Because I do. I miss talking to you. I miss seeing your smile. I miss your wry humor and how funny and sarcastic you can be. But mostly I just miss being part of your life."

She felt the ice around her heart melt with his words. She did miss him, but she couldn't admit that. That would take this conversation in the wrong direction.

"You asked every single one of our friends to donate money for your booth for the winter carnival, but you didn't ask me," he added.

"I can't believe you're annoyed because I didn't ask you for money."

"Well, I can't believe you're annoyed every time I breathe, so there we are," he retorted.

"We shouldn't have started talking about the past," she said. "There's no point."

"Maybe there is a point."

"What could that possibly be?"

"You need to get your head out of the past, and I know how to make that happen."

"You don't—" she began, only to have her words cut short with a shocking kiss.

She didn't know what to do, how to react. Her brain was telling her to push him away, but as his arms came around her, as his mouth moved against hers, she couldn't think anymore; she could only feel. *This was Jake.* And the taste of his mouth took her back in time.

She suddenly remembered everything: the heated demand of his lips, the feeling of being swept off her feet and enveloped in a storm of desire and passion.

But this kiss was also different. Jake was a man now, and she was a woman who knew what she liked, what she wanted. Their tangled dance of tongues became a new adventure, a delicious melding of the past with the present. And she wanted more. She wanted to pull off his sweater and push down his jeans. She wanted to see him, touch him and taste him.

Her pulse pounded with the depth of her need. It was terrifying. This was why she'd avoided him for so long, because deep down she'd known the fire simmering between them could quickly get out of control. She had to stop. She had to push him away.

Finally, she found the strength to break the kiss, to slide down the couch, to put some much-needed space between them.

But it was still too hot. Her face was burning. And Jake's dark eyes were filled with a tempting promise of all the things she secretly wanted. "Why did you kiss me?"

"I wanted to get you out of the past," he said. "And you kissed me back."

"Only because you surprised me."

"That surprise lasted for several minutes."

"Well…" She found herself without any words.

"Well," he echoed. "It's not often you can't think of something to say."

"I'm going to bed." She got up and moved around the couch, then turned back to face him. "Don't do that again, Jake."

"I won't. Unless you ask me to."

Her stomach flipped over at that comment. "That will not happen."

"We'll see."

"You know one thing that hasn't changed, Jake? You're still cocky."

"And you still like it."

She really wished she could have had the last word, but escape was a bigger priority. She walked into the bedroom and closed the door, her heart still beating out of her chest.

He had surprised her, but she had kissed him back. Maybe they'd both wanted to see if the sparks were still there. Now they knew. The sparks were definitely there, and they were dangerous.

Jake had said he wouldn't kiss her again. It would be up to her. Which meant she was safe—at least from him. She wasn't so sure about herself.

But she needed to stop thinking about Jake and start thinking about the other male currently in her life—the little boy sleeping peacefully in front of her.

She took off her shoes and stretched out on the bed, pulling the heavy blanket over both of them. It was warm and toasty in the cabin despite the storm raging outside.

At her movement, Brett snuggled up against her and she put her arm around him. He immediately quieted, falling back to sleep. He trusted her. And she did not want to let him down.

She might be furious with her sister, but not with this little boy. He was an innocent angel, and she would do everything she could to keep him safe.

As the warmth of Brett's small body seeped into her soul, she closed her eyes, and the exhaustion of the day caught up to her. She didn't want to dream about anything, especially Jake, but there were other images sweeping through her mind.

Kelly with her long blonde braid and laughing smile around the living room using a hairbrush as a microphone, making up games as she watched over Hannah and Tyler. She'd been their babysitter a lot of times, not that she ever should have been. As soon as their parents would leave, Kelly would usually sneak a friend in, or take them on a walk to the corner store, which they were not supposed to do by themselves. And that was before Kelly got a driver's license.

Once Kelly had access to the car, she and Tyler had been Kelly's unwitting chaperones on cruising nights to boys' houses. But even when Kelly was breaking the rules, she was also fun. She made up games and helped them build forts out of pillows, blankets and chairs. She had an imagination that wouldn't quit.

Hannah felt an ache even in her dreamy state. She'd loved Kelly so much. When she'd gotten old enough to know better, she'd realized that sometimes Kelly made mistakes; sometimes her reckless attitude was too much. Sometimes the fights between her mom and Kelly had been so over the top, she couldn't believe what either of them were saying.

She'd tried to mediate between them. She'd loved both of them with all her heart, and Kelly had been her sister…until she wasn't.

It had been much more difficult to hold onto the love, especially as the years passed, as she had to raise Tyler and keep her mom sober. She'd thought how Kelly might come back a million times, but it had never been like this.

Brett moved in her arms. "Mommy?" he questioned.

She tightened her embrace. "Go to sleep. You're safe."

He was instantly reassured and why wouldn't he be? She'd just said the same thing to Brett that Kelly had said so many times to her when she'd gotten scared in the middle of the night, and she'd turned to her big sis for comfort.

Kelly had probably said the same thing to Brett.

He was safe. *But was Kelly safe?*

She had a terrible feeling that her sister was nowhere close to safe. But she hoped she was wrong.

## CHAPTER FIVE

JAKE COULDN'T SLEEP, and the hours of the night seemed impossibly long. The couch was short and narrow with a rock-hard lump in the middle. The wind was shaking the cabin with heavy branches and pinecones pummeling the roof. But it wasn't the couch or the weather that kept him too fired up to doze off. It was Hannah; it was her kiss, her taste, the scent of lavender that he'd always associated with her.

He'd traveled all over the world, and he'd thought he'd put Hannah and Whisper Lake far behind him. But whenever he caught a hint of lavender, it was like she was right next to him again. But it had always been an illusion, a bittersweet memory, until tonight…

Tonight, she'd kissed him back. It had been an impulsive, reckless, possibly foolish move to kiss her, but it had paid off. Taken by surprise, she'd responded exactly the way he'd wanted her to. Actually, she'd responded in a way that had been completely unexpected. She'd kissed him as if she wanted him, as if she were starving for him. It had reminded him of the past, but it had also shown him a different side to her.

She wasn't the somewhat shy and sweet teenage girl who had

been tentative and wary and a little unsure. He'd kissed a woman tonight, and he'd liked it even more.

They'd always had an unbelievable chemistry. And now they were as explosive as ever.

*So, what next?*

He wanted more, but she'd backed off when she'd come to her senses. She'd slammed the door shut between them. But she hadn't locked it. She would still try. He knew her well enough to know she didn't give up on a grudge that easily.

But something had changed. And that's what he'd needed to have happen. Since he'd come back to Whisper Lake two years earlier, he'd been trying to talk to her, to find a way to tear down her walls, to get back into her life. And she'd finally let him in. Well, the flat tire and no spare had done that, as well as Kelly's unexpected gift in little Brett. But now that he had a foot in the door, he wasn't taking it out.

He and Hannah had unfinished business, and he was determined to finish it. He couldn't continue living in a world where Hannah was a possibility. He needed to find out one way or the other if they could be together again.

As he rolled over once more, he opened his eyes and was relieved to see light coming through the curtains. It was morning, and the wind had died down. He decided to get up and make some breakfast with what was left over in the fridge. One thing he knew about Hannah was that she was always starving in the morning.

He smiled to himself, thinking about all the times he'd picked up a muffin or a donut on his way to school and surprised her in first period math. She'd always scarfed it down as if she hadn't eaten in a week.

His smile faded as a new thought occurred to him. Maybe Hannah had been hungry because she hadn't had breakfast. He'd never dug too deep into her life when they were young. She'd rarely spoken about her mom, and when she did, it was usually dark stuff, like her time in foster care. He didn't know how to handle those conversations. He'd tried to comfort her or offer helpful suggestions, but she'd usually just apologized for bringing it up and then changed the subject, and he'd let her.

Now, he wondered how much he'd missed, how much she'd suffered through that she hadn't told him about. It had probably been far worse than he'd ever imagined. And then he'd dumped even more heartbreak on her.

He felt physically sick every time he thought about what he'd done with her. He would have thought that the guilt would fade after twelve years, but while sometimes it lived in the back of his mind, it was never completely gone. He was the kind of person who hated to make mistakes. Failure was not his thing, and that had been a big fail.

There had been extenuating circumstances, things that Hannah knew nothing about, but none of that mattered. He'd hurt her, and then he'd left town to move on, to forget about her. But he hadn't forgotten. And even though he didn't deserve it, he wanted her to forgive him.

It was her forgiveness that had become his steepest mountain to climb. He hadn't gotten too far, but he might be one step higher than he'd been yesterday.

He swung his legs off the couch and then headed into the kitchen.

---

Hannah was relieved to wake up to sun peeking through the windows. It felt like it would be a better day already. And the squirming little boy next to her, who greeted her with a happy smile, made her heart squeeze with instant love. "Good morning," she said. "Did you sleep well?"

He nodded. "I'm hungry."

"I'll bet you are. I always wake up hungry, too. Shall we get some breakfast?"

He was already scrambling off the other side of the bed. She got up and followed him into the living room. She thought she might find Jake asleep on the couch as it was only a little past seven, but he was at the stove and he was cooking. She wanted to feel some anger for the kiss that shouldn't have happened, but it was hard to hang on to that when he looked so ridiculously handsome in his jeans and long-sleeve sweater. He must have snuck in a shower while they were asleep as his brown hair was still damp.

"Just in time," Jake said, giving her a cheerful grin. He'd definitely never been a moody guy. He was usually happy, positive, and looking forward to something. She'd always liked that about him. When Jake was around, it felt like her world was a little bit better. But she wasn't going to tell him that.

"You're making scrambled eggs," she murmured, her stomach rumbling in appreciation.

"Courtesy of your sister. Have a seat."

"I have to go to the potty," Brett said, running toward the bathroom in the hallway.

"I guess I should have asked him about that when he first got up," she said.

Jake grinned. "Seems like he's on it. Do you want eggs? Or do I even need to ask?"

"I'd love some." She avoided the knowing smile in his eyes by moving over to the coffeemaker, which was thankfully full. She poured herself a mug and took a sip, feeling instantly more alive. "How did you sleep?"

"Not very well. How about you?" he asked, as he scrambled the eggs with a spatula.

"Better than I thought I would. My mind was racing with questions, but eventually it got tired of trying to find answers that weren't there, and I was able to sleep."

"You were thinking about your sister?"

"Yes." She refused to admit he'd been part of her thoughts as well. "Snuggling with Brett, I couldn't help but remember the times when I was a little girl, and I'd sneak into Kelly's bed at night when I was scared. She always told me a story and made me feel better."

"So, there was a time when she was a good big sister?"

"Yes, but it was long ago." She took another sip of coffee. "I'm going to call Adam when we get back to town. I don't want it to be official business, but I need someone to tell me how to start looking for my sister."

"You don't think that will trigger a full-scale investigation?"

"I'm hoping not. But I don't think I have a choice. Do you?" She found herself wanting Jake's advice, because she was a little too close to the problem, and she didn't want to make a mistake.

"It's the right move. You're Brett's aunt, so I don't think anyone would take him away from you. By the way, I don't know if you noticed, but there's a car seat on the floor by the door."

Her gaze swung toward the front door. "I didn't see that before. Kelly must have left it in case I had to take Brett somewhere. This was planned, Jake. She thought of all the details. She put food in the house. She made sure it was warm, that there was something on the television so Brett wouldn't be scared when she left. And she even left the car seat. I just wish the plan had included a conversation with me."

"That would have been good."

Jake filled three plates with eggs. She took them to the table while he spread cream cheese on the bagels.

When Brett returned, she said, "Did you wash your hands?"

"I did," Brett said, holding them up.

Since they were still dripping wet, she knew he was telling the truth. She handed him a paper towel and they sat down at the table.

Jake's eggs were perfectly cooked, with a nice seasoning of salt and pepper. "Do you cook a lot for yourself?" she asked, as she took a bite.

"I'm good for breakfast. The other meals tend to be more of the eat-out or pick-up variety. I've had a lot of meals at Chloe's café, I will say that."

"Her chef is good."

"He is. How's Chloe doing these days? I heard she and Kevin have separated."

"Unfortunately, yes. He decided he wasn't done with being a soldier, and she decided she was done with him being a soldier. I know she has mixed feelings about it. She's taking the blame for breaking up the family, but it isn't all on her. Chloe had to give

birth alone while Kevin was missing in action. That was very trau-
matic for her, and she's been on her own for a long time. She runs
the café that was his family's business. I think Kevin should have
put his family first. He served over ten years. He has done his
duty."

"But it's not just duty to him. It's what he loves to do, what he's
always loved. Chloe knew what she was getting into."

"I think the idea of what she was getting into turned out to be
very different from the reality of being a military wife. I understand that Kevin should have a fulfilling job. I just also understand
how hard it's been for her. I like them both. I want them to be
happy. But maybe they can't be happy together."

"Or maybe they'll figure out a way."

"When Kevin is on the other side of the world? That's optimistic, but then you always were the optimistic one."

He shrugged. "What's wrong with being a positive person?"

"Not saying it's wrong. Just saying it's who you are."

"If you can dream it, you can make it happen. That requires
optimism." He paused. "I dreamt about you last night, Hannah."

That comment sent a tingle through her body. "I don't want to
hear about it. And whatever you dreamt will not happen."

"We'll see."

She didn't like that he was being optimistic about them. There
was no *them*. They were over. "Last night was a mistake, Jake."

"We'll see," he repeated.

"Oh, my God, you're so annoying."

"You said God. You're supposed to say gosh," Brett interrupted.

Now she was being reprimanded by a four-year-old. "You're
right. Are you done eating?"

He popped the last bite of eggs into his mouth and then said,
"Can I have a cookie?" with his mouth full.

"Finish what you're eating first."

He swallowed and smiled. "Now?"

"I suppose you can have one."

"I'll get it for you, buddy," Jake said, as he got to his feet. "I
want one, too. What about you, Hannah? Cookies for breakfast?"

"Why not? It seems like that kind of morning."

Jake brought the cookies to the table and then said, "We should leave as soon as we're done with breakfast. The guy I spoke to in the other cabin was plowing the road earlier. We should be able to get back to the highway."

"I'm fine with that. I still need to get someone to fix my tire."

"We'll figure that out once we get back to town."

"Can we play a game now?" Brett asked.

"Actually, we're going to take a ride," she told him. "Do you want to see my house?"

Brett suddenly looked uncertain. "What about Mommy? Isn't she coming back here?"

"Don't worry. She knows where to find you."

"Are you sure?"

"Yes. And at my house, I have some photos of me and your mom when she was a little girl. Would you like to see them?"

Brett gave a vigorous nod. She was happy he was too little to understand much, and he wasn't asking questions she couldn't answer.

"I'll get my puppies," he said, running out of the room.

As Brett left her alone with Jake, a new tension entered the air. "I don't want to talk about last night," she warned, making a preemptive strike.

"Did I ask you to?" he countered.

"I'm sure you were going to."

"I wasn't. Actions speak louder than words. What happened last night told me a lot."

"It didn't tell you anything. You took me by surprise, that's all."

"Whatever you say."

She frowned at his easy agreement. "Don't make it into something else, Jake. You and I are not going to be anything more than friends."

"So, we're going to be friends?" he asked with a sparkle in his eyes. "I like that. It's the first step."

He was deliberately baiting her, and she really shouldn't take that bait. But she couldn't seem to help herself. "It's not the first step or any step. It's nothing. We're nothing."

"Are you done?"

She gave him a long look. "You made a fool of me once; you're not going to do it again," she said. "Now I'm done."

# CHAPTER SIX

HANNAH HAD DRAWN her line in the sand, but Jake wasn't bothered by it, not with the memory of her mouth on his. There was something between them, whether she wanted to admit it or not. He didn't like being patient, but he could be when he had to, and earning Hannah's trust would take time. Her last stinging words had reminded him that he had a lot to make up for. But he wasn't leaving Whisper Lake any time soon, and neither was she.

Thirty minutes later, they were headed back to town, but it was a slow drive. The road was thick with snow but thanks to the neighbor's plow, they made it to the highway, which was in slightly better condition. He still drove carefully, very aware of the precious cargo he was carrying. Brett was in his car seat in the backseat, and Hannah was sitting next to him, her body tense, her gaze fixed out the window. They were physically close, but emotionally they were very far away.

Hannah's phone buzzed, and she quickly pulled it out of her purse to read a text.

"Is that from Kelly?" he asked.

"No, it's from Debbie, who works at our property management company. She said the cabin was booked to a Kimberly Slater, who used a credit card to pay for the rental. The address attached to the card was Miami, Florida." She looked over at him. "Kelly used a fake name."

"She could have changed her name a long time ago."

"But Brett said his mom's name is Kelly."

"True." He came up with more possibilities. "Kim Slater could be a friend of hers. Or it's possible Kelly stole the credit card from this woman."

Hannah frowned at that suggestion. "I would hope she didn't steal it."

"The good news is that you have a name and an address. That's a place to start."

"I'll pass it along to Adam. I texted him before we left. He'll meet me at the house in half an hour."

"Did you tell him what's going on?"

"No. I didn't want to get into it. I just said I had something important to talk to him about."

"It's the right play."

"I hope so."

As they neared Whisper Lake, he exited the highway and drove into town. "I know you live in Timber Heights, but I don't have your address."

"27 Chateau."

"Got it." A few minutes later, he turned down her street. Hannah lived in a townhouse in a relatively new development set in the hilly area above town. "Hard to believe this was nothing but open and inaccessible land when we were growing up," he commented. "Now, there are beautiful townhomes. Are you happy living up here?"

"Yes. I have a nice view of the lake from the deck off my bedroom. And everything is new, so I don't have to worry about something breaking, which is a great relief. My parents' house was a hundred years old and there was always something going wrong."

"Your mom sold the house a while back, right?"

"Five years ago. It needed a lot of repairs, and she was headed back to an expensive rehab facility in Denver, so she agreed to put it on the market. She got enough cash out of it that she could pay for rehab and get a small condo when she got out. She lives just off Main Street, and she enjoys being able to walk to work at Sonia's Flower Shop."

"Does she enjoy her job?"

"She seems to. She and Sonia have become good friends. In fact, Sonia introduced my mother to her latest boyfriend, who I'm unsure about."

"Who is he and why don't you like him?" he asked curiously.

"His name is Marty Guillory. He's a retired lawyer who bought a house by the lake, and now he dabbles in photography. I don't dislike him, but he has a party vibe to him, and I don't think that's good for my mother. But she doesn't much care for my opinion."

"Sorry."

She shrugged. "It's not like I don't want her to be happy. I just think she needs to be very careful, especially when it comes to men. She made a good decision when she got together with my dad, but everyone since his death has not been great. Most of them have encouraged her addictions. I was kind of hoping she might just stay single and work on herself, but when Marty moved to town a few months ago, she got all giddy and nervous. I told her to go slow, but she doesn't listen. She thinks I'm too hard on her, as if she didn't do anything to deserve my distrust."

He had a feeling that Hannah was hard on her mom. But he could also understand why. He certainly wasn't going to take her mother's side. He had his own battle to worry about.

He pulled into her driveway in front of the attached garage. As they got out of the car, Adam pulled up in a black SUV. He had dark hair and blue eyes and was not in uniform today, but rather in black jeans and a black leather jacket. Adam had moved to Whisper Lake a few years ago, shortly after his sister Lizzie had bought the Firefly Inn. He'd been working in Denver before that and was a top-notch police officer. Jake had every confidence that Adam would know what to do.

"Who's that?" Brett asked, as Jake helped him out of his car.

"That's Adam," he told him. "He's a friend."

Hannah gave him a questioning look. "Do you need to get to work right away? I know I'm asking a lot of favors, but could you possibly—"

"Yes," he said, cutting her off. "I'll hang out with Brett while you and Adam have a chat."

"Thanks," she said with relief.

He was more than happy to put her in his debt for another favor. He might need to use that sometime.

"Hi, Adam," Hannah said, as she put her arm around Brett. "This is Brett."

"Hi, Brett," Adam said with a cheerful grin. Then he nodded to Jake. "How's it going?"

"It's interesting," he replied.

Adam gave him a speculative look, which he suspected had more to do with the fact that he was with Hannah than with Brett. Everyone in their social circle knew that Hannah hated his guts.

"Jake rescued me from a flat tire," Hannah interjected, obviously feeling a need to explain. "On my way to the cabin last night. Why don't we go inside?"

She led the way into the house, dropping her keys and bag on the table in her entry.

He carried Brett's suitcase inside, impressed by the simple, clean beauty of her home. Off the entry, he could see a living room and dining room. There appeared to be a bedroom downstairs, with a staircase leading up to the second floor. The décor was clean and modern with light-gray hardwood floors and plenty of white and gray furniture with accents of blue and coral. The art on the wall was modern and impressionistic and there were flowers everywhere.

The scent of lavender swept through him. He wished it made him feel calm. But since it made him think of Hannah, the resulting action was the opposite of calm.

"Brett can sleep in the upstairs bedroom on the right," Hannah said. "Maybe you can show him where it is."

"I'm on it. Come on, Brett. Let's go check out your room."

As Brett followed him up the stairs, he saw Hannah take Adam into the living room. He wished he could be there to offer support, but what she needed most from him now was a babysitter, so that's what he'd be.

----

Hannah wished she could have sent Jake home, but having him keep Brett occupied was more important than getting him out of her house and out of her life. She waved Adam into a chair in the living room, while she took a seat on the couch.

"Okay, what's going on?" Adam asked, a questioning gleam in his eyes. "Your text was very vague."

"I know. Here's what happened: My mom got a message yesterday that the tenant in our vacation rental at Wicker Bay was out of hot water. I went up there to check it out. I found Brett all by himself. The hot water was just a ploy to get me up there. Brett's mother left a note asking me, or whoever came, to take care of her son. She didn't sign her name. She also said not to call the police as her son would not be safe if the police got involved."

"Okay," he said slowly, his sharp gaze assessing her story.

"But I need your help, Adam. I don't know if it's fair to ask, but could we start out unofficially?"

"Why?"

"Even though the mother didn't sign the note, I know who she is. She left her necklace behind, and that necklace belonged to my older sister, Kelly. She left home when she was nineteen. That was fifteen years ago. No one in the family has heard from her since."

He raised a brow as surprise flashed across his face. "I was not expecting you to say that."

"It was a shock to me as well. I checked with our property manager. The rental was booked by a woman named Kim Slater with a Florida address. But I know that the necklace was Kelly's, and Brett told me his mom's name was Kelly. I don't know if she used someone else's ID to book the cabin, but I'm sure she is Brett's mother."

"Why wouldn't your sister just call you and ask you to watch her kid or bring him here? Why leave him in a cabin in the woods?"

"I'm assuming she didn't want to see me or didn't want to give me a chance to say no. Since I'm Brett's aunt, and I'm perfectly capable of taking care of him, I'm hoping he can stay here." She gave him a pleading look, hoping she hadn't made a mistake in calling him. Adam did like to abide by the rules.

Indecision played through his blue eyes, but finally he gave a nod. "Let's see what we find in the next forty-eight hours. If we haven't tracked down your sister or gotten more information by Monday, then we'll have another conversation."

Relief ran through her. "Thank you. We need to find Kelly. She's clearly in trouble and Brett could be in danger."

"Not because you called me."

"I know I can trust you, Adam, and Brodie, too, but beyond that, I'm not sure. Kelly was very specific about not calling the police. Let me get you the note." She got up and retrieved the note from her bag, then handed it to him.

Adam gave it a good read. "What else can you tell me about your sister? Why did she leave home? Do you have any idea where she's been the last fifteen years?"

"After my father died, Kelly turned wild, and my mom became a raging alcoholic. They each blamed the other for my dad's death."

"Why?"

"It was a car accident, but the reason my father was out that night was to pick up Kelly, who had not come home by her curfew. It was storming, and it was an accident. But Kelly was the reason he went out at all."

"That's rough. I'm sorry."

"Thanks. Anyway, Kelly left home and I never saw her again. I think my mom looked for her at one time; I know others did as well, but to my knowledge, no one ever located her. I asked Brett a few questions, but he just said they live far away. He appears to be well taken care of. When I got to the cabin, Kelly had left food for Brett, and the heat was on. I'm pretty sure she stayed until I came.

Jake saw a car leave right after we got to the cabin." She paused. "But I don't want to defend her too much, because what she did was irresponsible and foolish."

"Or desperate," Adam suggested.

She was surprised that he was giving Kelly's disappearance a more positive spin. "Really? I thought you'd be ready to arrest her for abandoning her child."

"I might still do that. But first I want to find her, and if she needs help, I want to help her. She's your family."

"I want to help her, too, even though she probably doesn't deserve it."

He gave her an empathetic smile. "Family relationships can be complicated."

"Your family seems perfect. You and Lizzie and Chelsea are tight. I don't know about your other brothers."

"We're close, but we all have our moments. And we were fortunate enough not to suffer through the kind of tragedy that you experienced."

"You were lucky."

"Do you think Kelly kept in touch with anyone in this town?"

"No," she replied.

"What's your sister's full name?" he asked, pulling out his phone to take notes.

"Kelly Marie Stark. She was born on May 22$^{nd}$. She has blonde hair and green eyes. She graduated from Whisper Lake High School. I have no idea where she's been since she left town."

"All right. And your property manager?"

She gave him Debbie's information as well as the address of the cabin and an extra set of keys, because he wanted to drive up to the cabin and take a look around.

"What about your mother?" Adam asked. "Is she aware of the situation?"

"No, not yet."

"I'd like to talk to her about Kelly."

"She won't know any more than I do."

"It's possible she might," Adam countered.

She frowned. "I don't really want to involve her yet. She's not good in a crisis, and her sobriety can be tenuous. Can we leave her out for the time being?"

"You don't ask much, do you?" he said lightly, giving her a dry smile.

"I know I'm asking for a lot."

"It's fine. I'll dig into the information you've given me so far, and I'll let you know what I find out."

"Thank you so much, Adam," she said as she walked him to the door.

"No problem, Hannah. But talk to your mother, because I am going to need to have a conversation with her very soon."

As Adam left, Jake came down the stairs. "Brett is playing in the fort we built in your guest room with pillows and blankets," he said.

"You're a fun babysitter."

"I'm a fun everything," he said lightly.

She wasn't going to touch that comment.

"How did it go with Adam?" he asked.

"He's going to start looking for Kelly. He's happy to leave Brett with me until he gets more information."

"You must be relieved about that."

"I am. And I know that Adam is my best hope to find Kelly fast." She paused. "I do want to thank you, Jake. You've gone above and beyond."

"I'm happy to help. And I'd like to hear the update whenever it comes in. Why don't we exchange numbers?"

She hesitated as he took out his phone. The last number she wanted to have in her phone was his, but it seemed rude to refuse. She gave him her number, and he quickly sent her a text back.

"I need to take off now if you're good," he added. "One of my skiing guides just called in sick, and I have a group that wants to ski Skyhawk this afternoon."

"That's a little risky after such a big snow last night, isn't it?" Skyhawk was one of the most dangerous trails in the mountains above the lake, and there had been a couple of avalanches in the area.

"It should be fine. I know which trails to take."

Jake didn't seem at all bothered by the danger of that mountain, but it bothered her. "I hope the skiers know you can be over-confident."

He gave her a direct and pointed look. "I would never risk someone else's life, Hannah. I'm not reckless."

"I would hope not. But you do like to push the boundaries."

"So do these skiers. However, they're smart enough to know they need an expert guide to lead them down the mountain."

"It's still a risk."

"Life is all about risk."

"And sometimes that risk doesn't work out. I've patched up a lot of people who took a big risk and slid their way down the mountain and into a world of pain."

"And I've seen a lot of people face their fears and have the time of their life," he countered. "It's all about perspective."

She rolled her eyes. "Whatever."

"What are you going to do today?"

"I need to work the carnival later but before that I have to do something I really don't want to do."

"What's that?"

"Call my mother. Adam wants to talk to her, and I need to let her know what's going on. I just hope this doesn't send her off on a downward spiral. That would be the last thing I need."

"She's been good for a while, hasn't she?"

"It has been almost four years since her last relapse. But I don't want to see her sobriety tested."

"You can't control that, Hannah."

"You're right, and I hate it."

He smiled, taking a few steps closer to her. She shivered at his sudden nearness, her mind flashing back to his hot kiss from the night before.

"Don't worry," he said, a knowing light in his eyes. "I told you last night—the next time we kiss, you'll be the one who starts it."

"I wouldn't hold your breath."

He leaned in, and it was all she could do not to jerk away, or worse, kiss him.

He whispered, "We'll see." His warm breath brushed against her face, sending a wave of desire through her body. But then he was gone.

She told herself that was a good thing.

# CHAPTER SEVEN

Jake wished he hadn't promised Hannah he wouldn't kiss her again, because he really wanted to. On the other hand, he'd seen the desire in her eyes, and he liked that she was being forced to look at him in a new way. He'd wanted to shake up their antagonistic relationship for a long time, and that had definitely happened. Where they went from here, he had no idea.

After leaving Hannah's house, he drove across town to his home, which was a one-bedroom apartment over the commercial space that housed his company—Adventure Sports. His building was located next to Waverly Pier, which featured a half-dozen retail shops, as well as two larger warehouses: one for a local boatbuilder, and the other for a woodworking company.

Across from the pier was a park that was turned into a skating rink every winter, and today there were plenty of people out to enjoy the sunshine after the storm. A tented area had been set up with heaters and a snack bar, as well as skate rentals. Many of those skates had been purchased through his company, which had been a nice bonus for this quarter. But as he'd told Hannah, his main source of income, and the part of his business that was exploding was the adventure experience. There were plenty of opportunities to find excitement in the surrounding mountains in the winter and on the lake and rivers in the summer. While he'd spent a lot of time away from Whisper Lake, when he'd really thought about where he wanted to be, where he wanted to put down roots, he'd known it was time to come home.

There were still problems here. He didn't get along with his father, so family events could be complicated. And there was Hannah, who'd spent the past two years avoiding him. But there were also plenty of friends to spend time with. Adam Cole was one of those friends, and he had great respect for him. There was no doubt in his mind that Adam would find Kelly and hopefully reunite her with her son.

He parked behind the building and entered through the back door. The first floor housed the retail store and a large circular counter with monitors on the wall running looped videos of some of their adventure tours. Ashley, a twenty-two-year-old skier who was currently training for the World Cup circuit, was at the counter with Hank, a twenty-nine-year-old guide who specialized in rock climbing. In the retail section, Ruth, one of his mom's friends, was getting a child fitted for skis while Howie was helping a teenager with his snowboard selection.

As Ashley saw him, she motioned him over.

"Can you take the Skyhawk run this afternoon?" she asked worriedly. "Victor is fighting a fever, and I don't know what he was thinking by not calling in earlier. I promised my sister I would help her set up her booth for the carnival tonight, so I need to leave here by noon."

"No problem. I'll do it."

Relief filled her gaze. "Great. I don't want to let my sister down, even though, to be honest, I'd rather be on the slopes. But family is family. Speaking of which, your brother is in your office. He said he needed to use your computer. I guess the internet is down at your mom's house. I didn't think you'd care."

"I don't. Thanks for letting him in." He smiled as he headed for the office, happy to know that his favorite member of the family was back in town.

Paul was sitting at his desk when he entered the room. He immediately looked up and gave him a big smile. Paul was a thinner, shorter version of himself with sandy brown hair and brown eyes that had always been filled with curiosity and intelligence. They were four years apart in age, but light-years apart in every other area. But he loved his younger brother more than he loved anyone else in the world. Their bond had gotten tighter when Paul had gone through leukemia as a child. For three years, they'd been afraid every day that they'd lose him. Thankfully, he'd recovered. Now he was six months away from finishing medical school.

"You're back," he said as his brother got up to give him a hug. "How are you doing?"

"Great," Paul replied. "Hope you don't mind me using your computer, but the internet went out at the house and Mom is freaking out about all the cakes and cookies she has to finish baking by tonight. When I asked her where the router was, she gave me a look that said keep on walking."

He laughed at his brother's words, knowing that when his mother got focused on something, there was no interruption allowed. Since she was apparently responsible for filling at least one-quarter of a baked-goods booth with three of her friends, she was under a lot of pressure. "You were smart to come here and stay out of the line of fire, although Mom can never get mad at you."

"We've had our moments. What's going on with you? If I can be blunt, you look like shit."

He ran a hand through his hair. He'd gotten in a quick shower at the cabin, but that hadn't covered up the dark circles under his eyes.

"Did you sleep at all last night?" Paul queried.

"Not very much."

A grin spread across his brother's face. "What's her name?"

"You wouldn't believe me if I told you."

"Well, then tell me, because this sounds interesting." Paul sat down and leaned back in the desk chair.

He took the chair in front of the desk. "I was with Hannah."

Disbelief ran through Paul's eyes. "No way. Hannah Stark? The one who can't stand you and tries to avoid you whenever she can?"

"That's the one. It wasn't planned. It was the result of a random and somewhat bizarre set of circumstances."

"Now I'm even more interested. What happened?"

"It started with a flat tire. I gave her a ride because she didn't have a spare. She was heading to her family's cabin at Wicker Bay, and I was going to the same location to check on Trevor Pelham."

"What's wrong with Trevor?"

"He's going through a bad breakup, and after losing his mom earlier this year, he's been a drunken mess. He said he was going up to the cabin to dry out, but when I got there, he wasn't there. Anyway, that's not the most interesting part of the story. Hannah went to her cabin to check on a hot water problem for her tenant, but the only one at the cabin was a four-year-old boy. He came with a note from the mother asking for someone to watch out for her child and not to call the police because he wouldn't be safe."

Paul gave him a look of utter disbelief. "Seriously? That's crazy."

"It gets crazier. The child is actually Hannah's nephew, the son of her sister, Kelly, who ran away fifteen years ago. Of course, Hannah was shocked by the realization that her sister had a kid and that she'd left him alone in the cabin."

"That's quite a story."

"We ended up getting caught at the cabin, because the storm was fierce last night."

"I know. I was lucky to arrive just before it hit. So, you and Hannah spent the night together."

"With a four-year-old chaperone," he said dryly. "Not that we needed one."

"Hannah still hates you?"

He wished he had a different answer. "Yes, but I think we took a step out of the past, which is what I've been wanting to do for a long time."

"Did you kiss her?"

"There might have been a kiss."

Paul raised his brow in surprise. "I'm shocked. She let you kiss her?"

"She kissed me back. Until she remembered that she didn't like me."

"What happens now?"

"No idea. The ball is in her court. And Hannah is so damn stubborn. She sees everything in absolutes. There is no gray area. People are good or bad, right or wrong. In her mind, I'm bad, and I'm wrong."

"She wouldn't hate you so much if she didn't also like you. But this dance that's been going on between you and Hannah—it needs to end, Jake. It's gone on too long. Even when you're with other women, you're never really with them."

"That's not true," he said, frowning at his brother's analysis of his love life.

"Yes, it is. That's why no one lasts longer than a few months. No one is ever Hannah. If you want her, then go get her. Don't let the ball bounce around in her court. Take it, shoot it. That's what you do best. What you don't do best is wait."

"You have a point."

"You need to either get her back or let her go so you can move on with your life."

"Since when did you get to be so smart?"

"I've always been this smart. You just don't usually listen to me," Paul said dryly.

"Well, I hear what you're saying. It's good advice."

"Are you going to take it?"

"I think I will. But right now, I have to get ready to take a group down Skyhawk."

Paul grinned. "That sounds like fun."

"What are you doing this afternoon?"

"Helping Mom pack up her cakes and cookies for the carnival. Want to trade?"

"Not a chance," he said with a laugh. "But we should hit the slopes tomorrow or sometime this week."

"Maybe. I have some studying to do."

"It's Christmas."

"And I have six months left in medical school. I can't blow it now."

"You won't. I'm proud of you, Paul."

"Even though I'm following in Dad's footsteps?"

"You might become a doctor like him, but you are nothing like him," he said firmly.

"I wish you and Dad would find a way to get along," Paul said, his smile fading. "It would be nice to spend a Christmas with the four of us happy together, like the old days."

"We can't recreate the past."

"Isn't that what you're trying to do with Hannah?" his brother challenged.

"Actually, no. I don't want to go back to where she and I used to be. I want to discover where we can go now."

"You could do the same in your relationship with Dad."

He shook his head. "I don't think so."

"It's my fault, isn't it?" Paul asked, a serious gleam in his eyes.

He was shocked by his brother's question. "Of course it's not your fault. Why would you say that?"

"Because when I was sick, I took a lot of attention away from you. I know you got shafted."

"I did not get shafted. I wanted you to have everything you needed."

"And I did, but somewhere along the way, you and Dad lost your relationship, and I can't believe it had nothing to do with me."

"Well, it didn't." He didn't want to lie to his brother, but the situation between him and his father was much more complicated than Paul's illness.

"Then what was it?"

He let out a sigh. He was starting to realize that both his mother and his brother were losing patience with the situation between him and his father. They wanted him to fix whatever was wrong. He didn't know why it was on him to fix anything. "Let's not do this now. I don't have time, and it's Christmas."

"The perfect time to get the family back together," Paul said.

"It's not like you to just accept a bad situation and not try to change it. That's not who you are. You can't quit on Hannah. So maybe you should consider not quitting on your family."

He frowned, wishing Paul's words weren't echoing his own thoughts. He could see a connection between the way Hannah treated him and the way he treated his father, but the situations were completely different. "I'll think about it," he said. "In the meantime, I have to get ready to take on a mountain."

"Good luck, although I don't think you'll need it…unless the mountain's name is Hannah," Paul joked. "I still think that one might take you down."

---

Hannah paced around the living room, wondering if she'd made the right decision in calling her mother. Usually her mother's assistance created more problems than it solved. But Adam wanted to talk to her mom, and the news of Brett's appearance and her sister's disappearance would make the rounds of Whisper Lake no matter how quiet Adam kept the investigation.

Practically speaking, it would also be impossible to hide Brett's existence with so many holiday events happening over the next several days. She had to work Santa's house at tonight's Christmas Carnival, which meant she would have to bring Brett with her, and she would have to tell people he was her nephew. She would try to keep the problems with Kelly private, but even those would probably leak out. She'd accepted friendly, concerned gossip as an integral part of small-town life a long time ago.

As she waited for her mom's arrival, she went upstairs to check on Brett. She'd put him down for a nap earlier, and he was still fast asleep. She was grateful that he hadn't asked a lot of questions about where his mother was or when she was coming back, but she wondered if that just meant he was used to his mom disappearing. She hoped that wasn't the case. She hoped this was the first and only time that Kelly had abandoned her son.

The doorbell rang. She quickly closed the bedroom door, and

then went downstairs. She was greeted by her mother wearing an annoyed look on her face. It wasn't unusual to see that expression on Katherine Stark's face; Hannah got it a lot, usually because she was the one who forced her mom to deal with things she didn't want to deal with. Today was no exception.

"Come in," she said, waving her inside. Despite her mother's unhappy expression, she had to admit that her mom looked healthier and younger than her fifty-nine years. She wore dark jeans today with a soft-blue sweater under a white and gray striped coat. Stylish black boots completed the look. Her blonde hair was styled, her skin was clear, and her green-eyed gaze was sharp. She was slender but not as thin as she used to be when she had made booze the center of any meal. Looking at her now it wasn't easy to see the drunk she'd once been. Hopefully, she'd never see that woman again.

"What was so important that it couldn't wait, Hannah?" her mother asked. "I have so many things to do before the carnival tonight, and I would think you do, too. Isn't the hospital in charge of Santa's Workshop and the entire North Pole set?"

"Yes, and I will be heading down there later today, but I need to talk to you, Mom. It's about the tenant who called yesterday."

"Are we still on that? I don't have any additional information."

"I know, but I do. Let's go into the living room. You should sit down."

At her words, her mother gave her a wary look. "Really? I need to sit down?"

"Yes." She waved her mom into the living room.

"It's such a happy time of the year. Do I want to hear this?" her mom asked, as she took a seat on the couch. She'd always been one to prefer denial over awareness.

"You may not want to, but you need to. When I got to the cabin last night, I found a little boy. He's four years old and his name is Brett. He'd been left at the cabin by his mother, and the hot water complaint was just a ruse to get me or you up to the cabin."

"What are you talking about?" her mother asked, surprise and confusion flitting through her eyes.

"There was a note. It said Brett was in danger and needed someone to watch out for him. With the note was a necklace." She paused, waiting for her mother's gaze to meet hers. "It had a unicorn charm on the end of it. It was Kelly's necklace, Mom, the one I gave her for her birthday." She wished she still had the note and the necklace, but she'd given them both to Adam.

Her mother paled at her words. "No. That's impossible."

"Brett is Kelly's son. She's the one who rented the cabin. She's the one who left the text message. She's the one who wanted us to find her son and take care of him."

"Maybe you're wrong—"

She cut her mom off. "I'm not wrong. Kelly may have booked the reservation in a fake name, but she is Brett's mother. He confirmed his mom's name is Kelly. And he knew about our dog—Tiger. Plus, he looks just like Tyler did when he was small."

"Kelly has a son?" her mom murmured in bemusement. "But she left him alone? That doesn't make sense. But then, Kelly did a lot of things that didn't make sense. It sounds like she's still irresponsible and impulsive."

"I can't argue with that. I brought Brett home. He's taking a nap upstairs."

"He's here?" her mom asked in surprise.

"Yes. He's my nephew. He's your grandson. I couldn't let him go to anyone else. I did call Adam Cole. He's going to try to find Kelly. If we don't hear from her or he hasn't located her by Monday, then child welfare services may need to get involved. But I have no intention of giving Brett up. He's ours. He's family."

"Your sister left our family a long time ago."

"Brett didn't. He's an innocent child. He's very sweet—a little angel."

Her mother stared back at her with pain in her eyes. "Kelly was a sweet child, too. But then she got older, and she lost that angelic quality. She was sassy, always talking back and thinking she knew better. She was reckless, impulsive, and very self-centered. By the time she was a teenager, it was all about her, all the time. Never mind that I had two other kids to raise, Kelly seemed to need more and more and more. Whatever I gave her was never enough. And your father felt the same way."

"Really?" She couldn't help but interrupt her mother's rant. "I always thought Kelly was Dad's favorite. Even when she was getting into trouble, she could make him laugh. They'd be fighting and then suddenly they were smiling at each other, and he couldn't remember what she'd done wrong."

"She did have the ability to get her way with him." Her mom drew in a shaky breath. "He adored her; that's why he went out to find her that night."

"But it was an accident, Mom. It was raining hard. Visibility was low. I know you blame Kelly because he went to look for her, but the car crash wasn't her fault. I just don't understand why you had to pin it all on her."

"I know it was an accident, but she was the reason he was in that storm, and that's a fact," her mother argued. "If she'd come home on time, we wouldn't have lost him."

She gave her mom a long, pointed look. "You have to find a way to forgive her. Not just for her sake, but for yours. It's important for your recovery."

Pain filled her mother's eyes. "You're right."

"I am?"

"Yes. It's difficult for me to admit that I took my grief out on Kelly. But I didn't kick her out of the house. She left. I tried to find her, and I couldn't."

She was glad to see her mom taking some responsibility, but there was still a lot of defensiveness in her answer. "You didn't try that hard to find her. You couldn't, because you were drinking all the time. You fell apart after she left. You were wasted by four in the afternoon. I know you think you tried, but you didn't."

Hurt filled her mom's eyes. "You can be so harsh, Hannah."

The criticism stung. Maybe she was harsh when it came to her mom's alcoholism, but there was a part of her that hadn't yet been able to forgive her mother for everything that had happened to her. And she knew she had to follow her own advice and find a way, but today wasn't about them.

"Let's focus on what's happening now. Have you ever heard from Kelly? Has she ever sent a postcard, dropped you a text? Have any of her friends' mothers told you they know something about her life?"

"She has never reached out to me or my friends. I'm sure if she was going to contact someone in the family, it would be you or Tyler."

She'd tried calling her brother earlier, but she hadn't reached him yet. Hopefully, he'd call soon. "I've never heard from her. I don't think Tyler has, either."

"Well, there you go. Kelly doesn't give a damn about any of us until she needs something."

In this instance, it was difficult to argue with her mother, although she could tell her mom that the apple didn't fall far from the tree, because her mom tended to take a lot more than she gave.

"I have to go," her mom said, getting to her feet.

She stood up, surprised by her mom's words. "Go? Just like that? I need your help."

"To do what?"

"Don't you want to meet your grandson?"

Indecision played through her mom's eyes. "You said he's asleep."

"You could peek in."

"I—I don't think I can." Her mother shook her head. "Kelly really hurt me, Hannah."

"Kelly did, but Brett didn't."

Her mom swallowed hard. "I'm just afraid, Hannah. I don't want to go back into the past. I've finally gotten to a good place in my life. You know how hard I've battled to get here."

"Which means you're strong enough to deal with this now," she said, wishing desperately that for once her mom would step up and be the strong one. Maybe she just didn't have it in her.

"Well, perhaps I could do it later today or tomorrow. I need a little time. I have to meet Marty now. We have things to do before the carnival."

"So do I."

"I'm sure your coworkers will cover for you," her mom said, dismissing her comment with an airy wave, as she practically ran toward the door. "I'll see you later."

Her mom was out of the house before she could get another word out.

Shaking her head, she walked quietly up the stairs to check on Brett. He was still asleep in her guest room, a small figure protected by pillows on either side of him as he lay in the middle of the queen-sized bed. His cheeks were rosy red, and he was the picture of innocence. He had no idea what was going on in his life and how bad it might get.

An overwhelming feeling of protectiveness swept through her. Brett might not have his mother or his grandmother, but he had his aunt, and she would take care of him. She would give him everything he needed and more. He deserved nothing less.

But she still felt a little alone in her resolve. She wished her mother had stayed. She wished her brother would call her back. She even missed Jake, which was the craziest feeling of all, and one she could not allow to seep into her soul.

She'd had such a hard time getting over him when she was seventeen. She'd probably cried for a year straight. Every time she'd thought about him, she'd been filled with a deep pain that came from her soul. It shouldn't have hurt so much. It should have just been her first teenage heartbreak, but the feelings had lasted long beyond her teen years. And now, when she'd finally gotten to a good place, those emotions were coming back.

*Why did Jake have to come home?*

It wasn't as if this town had ever been enough for him. She'd certainly never been enough for him, which was why his sudden desire to have her forgive him, to welcome him back into her life, seemed ridiculous.

*Was she just a challenge that he had to prove himself against? Did he just want her back to prove he could get her?*

As the questions swirled around in her head, she told herself to stop thinking about him. She had enough problems without worrying about him. If she just kept enough space between them, he'd give up. He'd probably even leave town eventually. He wanted everything in his life to be extreme, to be exciting and thrilling, and he'd run out of that excitement in Whisper Lake.

*Wouldn't he?*

## CHAPTER EIGHT

THE MOUNTAIN almost kicked Jake's ass, not just because it was a tough run, but because the three college buddies who had booked the trip were nowhere near as good as they thought they were. Jake managed to coach them through some of the toughest and steepest parts of the trail, and while one of the guys had taken a hard fall, he'd only ended up with a broken finger and a big story to tell his friends who had stayed back on the less challenging slopes.

When he got back to his apartment, he took a long, hot shower and thought about the night ahead. While he was physically tired from both the skiing and the near-sleepless night, he also felt amped to see Hannah again. He'd been thinking about her all day and wondering if there was any news about Kelly. He hoped she would text him or call him with an update, but even though she'd taken his number, he wasn't sure she'd actually use it.

But it wouldn't be difficult to find her tonight. She'd go to the carnival. Everyone in town would be there. The hospital always hosted Santa's Workshop, which involved an elaborate set featuring Santa's house, his toy shop, a barn with a live reindeer and a grand throne upon which Santa, played by his father, would grant small children their most heartfelt wishes.

His mother's bakeshop, which was hosted by the hospital's

volunteer group would be next to the North Pole, providing baked treats, hot chocolate and cider as well as some very Irish coffee. While he'd avoided that particular part of the carnival last year, this year he was willing to risk running into his father if it gave him a chance to see Hannah again.

After hopping out of the shower, he dressed in jeans, a sweater, and a heavy coat. While it wasn't snowing, it was damn cold. He walked into town. The carnival was set up only about a mile from his apartment, and he enjoyed walking the streets of Whisper Lake. The town had grown a great deal since his childhood years. There was more of everything: business, retail, restaurants, homes, and, most of all, people. The resort community had tripled in population in the years he'd been gone.

His father now ran a state-of-the-art hospital. The police and fire department had also expanded. His volunteer search-and-rescue team had doubled in size in the past six months. And his business had taken off. He was booked solid through February.

Despite the growth, Whisper Lake had still retained its charm. Some of the buildings dated back a hundred years and the more modern structures had been designed with a taste of the old and the feel of the mountains and the landscape that surrounded them. Nothing was more than three or four stories high, and there were plenty of wood structures with large bay windows offering views of the lake and the mountains.

He sidestepped a group of pedestrians who were trying to get into the Fudge Shoppe. The stores were busy tonight with holiday shopping, the retailers taking advantage of the tourist traffic and the winter carnival that would officially kick off at five, which was in about fifteen minutes.

Finally, he made it to the main square that was situated in front of city hall. The area had been turned into a winter wonderland with Christmas lights, tall, decorated trees, and an array of festive booths. While the carnival started in the square, it extended into the park with booths hosted by local businesses—everything from holiday gifts, to baked goods, clothing boutiques, photographs, antiques, glass-blown collectibles, cozy quilts, and jewelry. There were also booths featuring paintings, books, Christmas center-pieces, and home décor. In the park, the carnival became more about the kids starting with Santa's Workshop and moving into game booths offering participants a chance to win stuffed animals and other trinkets.

The park was already packed with young families, probably eager to partake before it was time to get the younger children into bed. As he scanned the faces of the little ones nearby, he found himself looking for Brett and for Hannah.

His brother had told him it was time to either go get her or let her go. He'd thought he had let her go, but once he'd come back to town, he'd wanted to get her back. And the more she didn't want to talk to him, the more he wanted to talk to her.

*Did he just want her because he couldn't have her? Was it the challenge that intrigued him? Or was it more?*

He believed it was more. Hannah had been the first girl he'd ever loved. He'd first become aware of her in middle school, but there had been a lot going on with her then. Her father had died, and her mother was falling apart. He'd been too scared of all that loss and grief to know how to talk to her, so he'd pretty much stayed away. But once they got to high school, they'd become much better friends.

By their senior year, things had changed a lot for Hannah. Her mom was sober, and Hannah was showing up at parties with her fiery red hair, shimmering brown eyes, and blossoming curves. He'd fallen hard, and so had she. They'd always been able to talk to each other, but now there was a smoking-hot attraction going on, too. And they were both in a place in their young lives where they were looking for a good time.

He'd lived through years of his brother's illness, and she'd lived through her mom's alcohol addiction, but for those six months that they were falling in love, everyone else was okay, or at least okay enough that they didn't have to worry about them. They could just have fun, and that's what they did. They'd gone on hikes and boat trips. They'd spent hours swimming in the lake. He'd taught her how to snowboard and helped her take her skiing to a new level.

He'd pushed her out of her comfort zone, and in some ways, she'd done the same for him.

While he excelled in physical activities, Hannah brought a whole new dimension of intelligence and curiosity to his world. She read endless books and talked about science and wanted to learn everything that she could. When she'd passed books onto him, he'd thought he'd pretend to read them, but once he started, he couldn't stop. It was ironic that the books she lent him had actually inspired him to leave Whisper Lake, to see the world, to have his own adventures.

He knew she'd had some adventures, too. She'd left the lake and moved to Denver to go to college and nursing school. She'd built a life for herself outside of this small town, and while he didn't know much about that life, except what he'd heard from their friends, he wanted to know more. But mostly he just wanted to know her again.

Being with her last night—actually talking to her, eating a meal with her, helping her—had reminded him of how good they'd once been. He'd messed it all up, and his actions that night were the biggest regret of his life. But he didn't want to keep going back there. He wanted to move forward.

He'd put the ball in her court, but that didn't mean he wouldn't make a few plays of his own...starting now.

As he walked under a vine-covered archway leading into the North Pole, he saw Hannah and Brett coming in through the opposite arch. His body tightened as his gaze ran down her body, and the very sexy red and green elf costume she had on that consisted of a fur-lined short dress, white tights, and furry boots.

When she saw him, she froze, her hesitation obvious. He did not want to go back to the place where she ran out of the room as soon as he entered, and it looked like that might be happening. But then Brett saw him and sparkled with joy. He let go of Hannah's hand and ran straight to him.

He caught the little boy and lifted him high into his arms, as they exchanged a happy smile.

"I'm going to see Santa tonight," Brett told him.

"That's cool. What are you going to ask him for?"

"I can't tell you. It's a secret."

"Got it."

"But I've been really good, so I'm pretty sure I'm going to get my present."

Jake looked over at Hannah, seeing a mix of emotions in her eyes. He was actually glad to see more than anger there. It felt like progress.

"I didn't expect to see you here," Hannah said. "You usually avoid the North Pole."

"It's not the North Pole I avoid. It's Santa."

"I know."

"Why don't you want to see Santa?" Brett asked curiously, reminding Jake that this kid picked up on everything.

"It's not important." He turned back to Hannah. "Did you get your car back?"

"Yes. Thanks for calling Juan. He delivered it to me with a new tire. I owe you for that."

"It's not important."

"But I will pay," she said firmly.

"Sure. Whatever you want. What's your job tonight?"

"I'm in the toy booth." She tipped her head toward the booth where Keira Blake was setting up goodie bags. "We're giving out small toys to all the kids who visit with Santa and get their picture taken. No one goes home empty-handed."

"That's nice."

As he finished speaking, Keira came over to join them. She was an attractive brunette with dark hair and eyes, and she was wearing a similar costume to the one Hannah had on.

"Santa has beautiful elves," he said.

Keira gave him a curious smile. "Thanks, Jake. Who's this little guy?"

"This is Brett," he said, turning his gaze to Hannah to fill in the blanks.

"Brett is my nephew," she told Keira.

Keira's eyes widened. "Your nephew?"

"He's Kelly's son," Hannah explained. "He's staying with me for a few days."

"Well, that's...interesting," Keira said. "Even more interesting to see you and Jake having a cordial conversation—actually, any kind of conversation at all."

"Tis the season for conversations," he said lightly.

Hannah shrugged at Keira's enquiring gaze. "What he said."

"Okay. I'm going to need more details later," Keira said.

"Is that a reindeer?" Brett asked, pointing to the barn.

"It is," Keira said. "Would you like to meet Rudolph?"

"It's Rudolph?" Brett asked with surprise.

"Well, it might be one of his brothers," Keira amended. "Can I take Brett to meet the reindeer, Hannah?"

"Uh, sure, thanks," Hannah said.

He set Brett down on his feet, and the little boy slipped his hand into Keira's. He was certainly a trusting soul.

"No problem," Keira said. "Actually, there is a problem. Santa has been delayed by a surgery. And the line is getting long. You might want to think of a Plan B. You can do that while I show Brett the reindeer."

"I think I'd rather do the reindeer," Hannah said, but she was too late. Keira was already leading Brett away.

"Damn," Hannah muttered, taking out her phone to read a text. "Your father won't be here for thirty minutes."

"The kids will survive."

"Will their parents?" she asked, tipping her head toward the line where the children were growing increasingly restless and their parents were looking more than a little frustrated.

"What other option do you have?"

She tilted her head, giving him a considering look. "Santa's suit is in the house. I could get a sub for just a short time."

He did not like the way she was looking at him. "No way. I'm not playing Santa. That is my dad's role."

"Does it really matter whose role it is? Think of the kids. They're dying to tell Santa their secret wishes. All you have to do is listen."

"I can't believe you're asking me to be Santa. Haven't I done enough for you this weekend?"

"But this isn't just for me; it's for the kids."

He hated her pleading smile, because he didn't want to play Santa, but he also didn't want to say no to her. If he did help her out, he needed to get more than a thank-you. "On one condition," he said.

"What's that?" she asked warily.

"I want a date."

"A date?" she echoed in astonishment. "With me?"

"Of course with you."

"Why?"

"Because we started down a new path last night, and I think we should keep going."

"I don't want to keep going."

"Well, I don't want to play Santa Claus. So that's where we are. You can make me dinner, or you can take me out, but I want a date that includes a meal and at least one hour of your delightful conversation."

He loved seeing the dilemma in her eyes. She only had one choice and they both knew it.

"Do you really want to have dinner with someone who doesn't want to have dinner with you?" she challenged.

"I want to have dinner with you. What's your decision?"

"I have to take care of Brett," she said, with one last desperate attempt to get out of it.

"I didn't say when it had to happen, just that it happens. If it's tomorrow or a week from now, I'm good."

She let out a breath of resignation. "Fine. I'll have dinner with you sometime. I can't guarantee delightful conversation, but I will talk."

"Then I'll be Santa. Deal." He extended his hand.

She reluctantly slid her fingers into his, and the touch came with a wave of intense heat. She immediately jerked her hand away, her face flushing. "Let's get you into your costume."

He followed her into Santa's house, having to duck his head to enter the fake log wood cabin. He was surprised to find it decorated on the inside with two armchairs and a cooler of drinks. Apparently, this was where Santa took his breaks.

"Here you go," she said, handing him a pair of extremely large red velvet pants and a big pillow. "You're going to look awesome."

"I think I forgot what Santa looks like," he grumbled.

"It gets better," she said, picking up a white wig with a long beard. "And when you're talking to the kids, try not to make any specific promises. That gets Santa in trouble with the parents."

"I should have bargained for more than dinner."

She gave him a happy smile. "You probably should have. I'll see you outside. Don't take too long. The kids are waiting."

He shook his head as he got into his costume. He'd never had to work this hard for a date. But just taking her hand had caused a crazy explosion of heat between them.

It was time to take that fire higher or burn it out completely.

---

Hannah watched Jake take Santa's throne with a feeling of wonder and amusement. He looked ridiculous, but he didn't seem to care, as he patted his knee and the first child sat down. The five-year-old girl had a head full of golden curls and was completely adorable as she whispered in Jake's ear. Hannah didn't know what he told the child, but the little girl looked ecstatic. Hopefully, he'd remembered her advice to not make really big promises.

It was ironic that he'd stepped into his father's shoes. He'd been at odds with his dad since high school, and their relationship had only gotten more estranged with time. She had no idea what was really between them, and while she was curious, she knew better than anyone that some family problems were too personal to share.

She forced herself to stop watching Jake. She had a job to do, too. Now that the kids were going through the line, they'd be stopping at the toy booth. She walked around the counter as Keira brought Brett back. Keira had picked up another one of their friends along the way, Gianna Campbell Barrington. Gianna was with Hailey, her eight-year-old stepdaughter, and Hailey and Brett already seemed to be fast friends. But then, Brett seemed able to make friends with anyone within ten seconds. He was very much his mother's son in that regard. Kelly had been one of the most popular kids in school.

"Can I see Santa now?" Brett asked eagerly.

"I have to work the booth, honey, but we can go on my break," she told him.

"Actually, if you don't mind," Gianna said, "he can wait in line with Hailey and me. We've already bonded."

"Are you sure?"

"Absolutely. Keira tells me Brett is your nephew. It must be fun to have him here at Christmas."

"It is," she said, seeing the questions in Gianna's eyes, but thankfully her friend didn't ask any of them.

"We'll talk later," Gianna said.

"Of course. Brett, do you want to go with Hailey and Gianna?"

Brett nodded as Hailey took his hand.

"I'll be here in the booth when you're done," she assured him, not that he seemed concerned. "Make sure you stay with Gianna and Hailey."

"I will," Brett promised.

As they walked away, Keira moved next to her. They handed out a couple of goodie bags and then Keira said, "We need to talk, Hannah."

"I can't explain right now about Brett," she said, giving Keira an apologetic look. "It's a long story, and there are too many people around."

"Fair enough. Let's talk about Jake then."

She groaned. "Do we have to?"

"Yes. You've barely been able to tolerate thirty seconds in the man's company and now you're hanging out with him and looking very friendly. What is going on?"

"Jake helped me out yesterday with Brett. I had a flat tire, and he was there. It wasn't planned." She paused to smile at the next child and hand the little boy his goodie bag. "Now Jake seems to think we should be friends again."

"Just friends?"

She felt her cheeks warm at the question, and it didn't help to see Keira giving her a knowing smile. "I really don't want to talk about it," she said.

"Tough, Hannah. I was in high school when Jake cheated on you. I was there to pick up the pieces of that heartbreak, and I have watched you snub the man every chance you've gotten since you both moved back here. But it's happening again, isn't it? You're starting to like him."

"Well, you like him," she said defensively. "You and Gianna and Chloe have always been after me to make peace with him, so that it's not awkward when we're together. You should be happy."

"I am happy—if you're happy."

"I don't know what I am, honestly. And I have bigger problems than Jake at the moment. I don't know where my sister is, Keira. I don't know when she's coming back or if she's coming back."

Keira frowned. "I'm sorry. I didn't know that."

"I haven't heard from Kelly in fifteen years. Now, she leaves her child for me to watch, a boy I didn't know existed."

"He's very sweet."

"I know. I love him already, which makes it even harder. I need Kelly to come back, but she's clearly in some sort of trouble."

"Have you talked to Brodie or Adam?"

"I spoke to Adam. He's looking for her."

"Then you don't have to worry. Adam will find her. He'll help you figure this out. In the meantime, we'll all be here for you. And I'm thinking I might be able to include Jake in that promise since he's already playing Santa Claus for you."

"He's doing it for the kids."

Keira laughed and rolled her eyes. "Not a chance. He's doing it for you." She paused. "What's he going to get in return?"

"A date. That's right, I had to agree to a date to get him to play Santa Claus."

"Well, that should be fun."

"Will it be fun? Or will I be opening a door that should stay locked?"

"It doesn't have to be that dramatic."

"It doesn't have to be," she agreed. "But somehow I think it will be. Because that man...he gets under my skin, Keira. I should hate him. And I do hate him. But I also kind of like him. Oh," she groaned. "Why does he have to be nice now? Why does he have to be so damn good-looking? Why couldn't he have gained a hundred pounds or lost his hair or broken his gorgeous face?"

Keira laughed. "Because then it would be too easy. Frankly, I think it's good you have to deal with him. Ever since he came back, you've barely dated anyone. Everyone is so boring to you. Jake is not boring, and maybe you have unfinished business."

"I'm not sure I want to finish it."

"Well, one way or another, I think you're going to have to."

# CHAPTER NINE

JAKE HAD MORE fun than he would have thought playing Santa Claus, and he had to admit he was happy to see the annoyance on his dad's face when he finally showed up and realized who had taken over his role. He took a break to remove the costume while his dad went to talk to Hannah. When he was back in his street clothes, he left Santa's house and the costume inside and walked over to the toy booth. His father, who had been hovering nearby, gave him a brief nod, which he returned, and then his dad went to change.

Brett was playing in the back of the booth with a sleepy golden retriever, who belonged to one of the other elves, while Hannah and Keira were spreading holiday cheer with their goodie bags.

"Can I help?" he asked.

"You've done enough," Hannah told him quickly. "Thank you for playing Santa."

"It wasn't bad. I made some mental notes on some of the Christmas wishes. I jotted them down on a piece of paper that I left in Santa's house. Some of the kids were vague, but there were a few who were very specific. I'm not sure what you can do with them."

"We'll share the wishes with the parents."

"Nice job," Keira put in, a twinkle in her eyes. "I never thought I'd see you stepping into your dad's shoes."

"I prefer to think of them as Santa's shoes."

"Either way," Keira said with a laugh, as she moved away to talk to some friends and their kids.

"It was nice to have you step in for your dad," Hannah said. "I think Davis was a little stunned that you'd agreed."

He shrugged. "I don't really care what he thinks."

She frowned. "I wish you two could get along."

"What does it matter to you?"

"Well, maybe it doesn't matter to me, but I'm sure it bothers your mom and your brother. I do remember a time when you and your father had a good relationship."

"That was so long ago I can barely remember." He knew Hannah didn't understand, because he'd never told her why he and his dad no longer got along, and he couldn't tell her now. "Let's talk about our date," he said, changing the subject. "Where do you want to go?"

"The date is not going to happen any time soon."

"But you're not getting out of it. We have a deal."

"I never renege on a deal, but I need to deal with Brett and Kelly first." She stopped abruptly, her gaze filling with worry. He turned and saw who had created so much stress in her eyes. It was Adam. And he was walking purposefully toward them.

Hannah licked her lips and put a steadying hand on the counter.

"It's going to be okay," he said quietly.

"You don't know that."

She had a point. "You're right, but it's always best to stay positive."

"Hello, Hannah, Jake," Adam said. "Do you have a minute to talk?"

Hannah looked over her shoulder at Keira, who clearly sensed something serious was going on.

"Go," Keira said. "I'll take care of Brett."

Hannah gave Keira a grateful look and then they followed Adam into a shadowy part of the park away from the carnival. She probably would have preferred to do this without him, but since she hadn't told him to go, he was going to stay close.

"Have you found my sister?" she asked.

"Not yet," Adam replied. "But I do know more about her life since she left Whisper Lake fifteen years ago, and I want to fill you in."

"Okay. What do you know?"

"Kelly got married five years ago to Travis Hill, an army lieutenant who was killed in action three months after the birth of their son, Brett."

"Oh, no," she whispered, putting a hand to her mouth. Brett's father was dead. That was terribly sad.

At her emotional reaction, Jake couldn't help himself. He moved closer, taking her free hand into his, and she let him.

"Kelly and Brett were living in South Carolina at Fort Jackson when Travis died," Adam continued. "After that, they moved to Florida for a while and then to Colorado Springs eighteen months ago."

"I can't believe Kelly came back to Colorado," Hannah said. "She always wanted to live by the ocean. I figured she'd ended up at a beach somewhere."

"She did for a while. When she got to Colorado Springs, she got a job as a checker at a grocery store. I spoke to her boss, Tracy Vaughn. Ms. Vaughn said Kelly was a good worker, and she had no problems with her until about two months ago when she abruptly quit, saying the hours weren't good for her because she was a single mother. She had gotten some work she could do from home and no one at the market saw her again after that. She gave me Kelly's last known address, and I had an officer from the Colorado Springs Police Department check it out. Her landlord said she saw Kelly three weeks ago putting suitcases into her car. She said she was taking a vacation and was headed to New Mexico. The landlord did not see her after that and Kelly missed her rent payment, which was five days later. She has not shown up or returned the landlord's texts, emails or calls. The police officer went into Kelly's apartment with the landlord, and it looked like she'd left in a hurry. There were clothes and toys and food that was rotting in the refrigerator and the cabinets."

Hannah's fingers tightened around his. Like him, she didn't care for where this story was going.

"What else?" she asked tightly.

"The landlord said Kelly had a boyfriend—Russ Miller. He worked as the night manager at the Bentley Hotel. I called the hotel to speak to him, but he disappeared three weeks ago, and no one has seen or heard from him since."

"The same time as Kelly," he muttered, as Adam's gaze swung to his.

"Yes," Adam confirmed. "Kelly withdrew $300 from an ATM two days after she was last seen at her apartment. Russ Miller did the same one day later. Neither one has used a credit card since then or accessed their bank accounts. Mr. Miller has not been in contact with his employer."

"What about the credit card in the name of Kim Slater?" Hannah asked. "The one she used to book our cabin."

"I contacted Kim Slater. She is one of Kelly's friends from her time in Florida," Adam replied. "She hasn't seen Kelly in over a year. She said Kelly might have been able to access her credit card number from the computer she gave her, but she has the actual card in her purse, and she hasn't paid much attention to it because she just had a baby a few months ago. She did say that Kelly had called a few months ago and mentioned that she was having trouble with a guy."

"What kind of trouble?" Hannah asked.

"She said there was a man who was harassing her, but she was handling it. When Kim tried to press her, she just told her to forget she'd said anything."

"If the boyfriend was harassing Kelly, maybe he's the reason she's on the run," Jake interjected.

"And why she left Brett with me," Hannah said, turning her head to meet his gaze. "She wanted to put her son somewhere safe. But I still don't know why she didn't go to the police or warned me against doing so." She looked back at Adam. "This

Russ Miller doesn't have any ties to the police department, does he?"

"No. It's still early in the investigation, but from the surface read I did on Mr. Miller, I don't see any link between him and the police. He also has no history of domestic violence or legal problems. I haven't been able to talk to his coworkers yet, but I will be following up with them as well as his neighbors."

"Maybe Kelly's boyfriend has a relative or a friend that's a cop, someone that he's using to hold over Kelly's head," Hannah suggested.

Adam shrugged. "Possibly."

"If Kelly left Colorado Springs three weeks ago," Hannah continued, "and she showed up at our family cabin yesterday, where has she been in between?"

"She was in Denver two days ago," Adam said. "That's where she rented the car—with Kim Slater's credit card. We've sent out an alert on the license plate."

"That's good. Do you think Brett is in danger?" Hannah's gaze moved back toward the carnival.

"I don't know," Adam said. "But my gut tells me that your sister is the one in trouble, and we need to find her as soon as possible."

Jake's stomach twisted at the somber tone in Adam's voice. And he could feel Hannah's tension as her fingers curled around his once more. She probably didn't even realize she was holding his hand. But he liked the fact that her instinct was to rely on him, to trust him to be there for her.

"What can I do?" Hannah asked.

"What you're doing," Adam said. "You're taking care of Brett."

"I will do that, but I also want to do more."

"Everything that needs to be done is being done," Adam assured her. "And I'm sorry, Hannah, but this investigation is now on the books. I need the resources of the department and the manpower. I've read Brodie in, and he'll be my right-hand guy on this. There's nothing we want to do more than bring your sister home for Christmas."

"I would really like that, too," she said, her voice thick with emotion. "Thanks for getting on this so fast, Adam, and working on the weekend."

"No problem. I'll let you know as soon as I hear anything else. And if you hear from Kelly…"

"I will get in touch with you immediately," she promised.

Adam smiled and tipped his head. "Exactly the answer I was looking for. Take it easy."

As Adam walked away, Hannah let out a breath and then suddenly started. She let go of his hand with an awkward look, as if she'd just realized she'd been holding hands with him.

Clearing her throat, she said, "What do you think, Jake? I don't know what to make of everything Adam just told me. My head is spinning. My sister's life sounds complicated and sad and worrisome. She lost Brett's father. She's moved a couple of times. Now she's apparently on the run, maybe from her boyfriend. And she stole someone's credit card number. What kind of person is Kelly? Who has she turned into?"

"She sounds desperate to me, Hannah. And if she stole the credit card to get out of a bad situation and protect her kid…"

"I know I shouldn't judge her without knowing all the facts, but what I know so far is disturbing. It's also frustrating to have to just wait."

"I completely understand. But you are doing everything you can to help your sister."

Hannah frowned, doubt in her eyes. "I feel like I should be looking for her."

"The police can do that far better than you. And you're doing the most important thing for Kelly. You're taking care of her son."

"He cannot lose his mother, not after having lost his father. That little boy needs at least one of his parents."

"Kelly will make it back to him." He tried to infuse as much confidence as he could into his words. "And you can tell me again that I don't actually know that, but I'm still going to keep the faith that that will happen."

"I want to believe it, too. But sometimes bad things happen, and I need to prepare myself for that."

She'd been through far worse things in her life than he had, but he also knew there was nothing she could do to prepare. "You can't control the future, Hannah, or even the present. But you can focus on the positive, what Kelly has done right so far. She was smart enough to get Brett to safety. She left him food. She was on top of all that. She's working some plan in her head. Maybe it's a good one, maybe it's not, but she's trying to handle her problem the best way she knows how."

"That's true," she said slowly. "It's hard to trust in someone I haven't seen in fifteen years. And in my experience, Kelly didn't always make the best decisions. But I will try to think positive, because I have to. Now, I should get back to Brett."

He fell into step with her as they walked back to the booth. Brett was now not only playing with the dog, but also Chloe's toddler son, Leo, and Gianna's stepdaughter, Hailey. Chloe, Keira, and Gianna were in a very quiet conversation when they approached, and he had a feeling that they were talking about Hannah and him, or maybe just Hannah. They'd all gone to high school together, and there had been a time when all four women had hated his guts, but Chloe, Keira and Gianna had found a way to at least tolerate him and accept that he'd changed for the better.

"Is everything all right?" Keira asked, her gaze full of concern.

"Adam is trying to make everything all right," Hannah said, choosing her words carefully.

Jake didn't think she had to worry about Brett picking up on too much. He was very caught up in the dog and the other kids.

"Keira has told us a little," Chloe said.

"Because I only know a little," Keira added.

"If we can help…" Gianna put in.

"I will let you all know, and I will fill you in at some point, hopefully when there's more news and it's all good," Hannah replied.

"We're going to play some games in the arcade," Gianna said. "Can we take Brett with us?"

"Actually, I'll go, too," Hannah put in. "I could use a break, unless you need me, Keira?"

"Not at all. I'll be fine. Lizzie and Chelsea are coming in ten minutes to take an hour shift. Go have a little fun."

As Hannah, Chloe, Gianna and the kids left, he was about to go his own way when Keira said, "Not so fast, Jake."

"What?" he asked warily.

"I want to know what's going on."

"Hannah said she'd fill you in."

"Not with Kelly. With you and Hannah. When did the cold war end?"

He grinned. "Last night, thanks to a flat tire."

"It's quite a fast turnaround."

"But a long time coming."

"So you're friends now?"

"That might be stretching it a bit, but I'm hoping to keep going down this path."

"There's nothing I would like more than to not have to watch the two of you shoot daggers at each other."

"That's Hannah, not me. I'm on the receiving end of those daggers."

"True. But you earned every one of them, Jake. And I don't want you to hurt her again. Whatever you have in mind, you better think long and hard about it," Keira warned. "Or you'll have me to deal with, and I won't be throwing imaginary daggers."

"I get it. And you can believe me when I say the last thing I want to do is hurt Hannah."

She gave him an assessing look. "Okay. But you do know there's a good chance she could hurt you, right? Our Hannah doesn't forgive or forget—not easily anyway."

"Well, I don't like it when things are too easy. I'll see you around." Despite his cocky words, Keira's words rang through his head as he left the booth.

*Was he chasing an impossible dream?* Well, it wouldn't be the first time.

# CHAPTER TEN

HANNAH HAD JUST FINISHED MAKING Brett breakfast Sunday morning when her doorbell rang. She was surprised and tense when she walked out of the kitchen and down the hallway. If it was Adam, it could be bad or good news. But it wasn't Adam; it was Jake, and while she was still surprised, the tension was much, much different.

"Good morning," he said with a smile that immediately sent butterflies through her stomach.

"What are you doing here?"

"I'm picking you and Brett up." He waved his hand toward his truck.

"To do what?"

"Go sledding. We're all meeting at Northstar for sledding, tubing, snowman building... Gianna set it up last week. Don't you remember?"

She frowned. She'd completely forgotten that Gianna had set up a group outing for today. "I don't think I can go."

"Why not?"

"I have Brett."

"Hailey and Leo will be there. It's a family-friendly day. You were planning to go, weren't you? Or were you waiting to see if I'd be showing up?" he challenged.

"You really don't factor into my decisions, Jake." She was beginning to realize how petty she'd been when it came to Jake. She was a little disappointed in herself. But that didn't mean she wanted to spend the day with him. While he might not be her mortal enemy anymore, she didn't really know what else she wanted him to be. Even now, she was feeling far too many tingles just standing a few feet away from him. And she still had to get through that date she promised him, which she planned on putting off as long as possible.

"Prove it," he said. "Come to the snow park with me."

"I don't have to prove anything to you."

He sighed, as if she were the most trying person in the world. "Everything is such a battle with you, Hannah. It will be fun. What else are you going to do? Sit around and worry about Kelly?"

He had a point. She didn't know what else she was going to do, but she would drive herself crazy and probably Brett, too, if she stuck around the house all day. "Fine, I'll go," she said slowly. "In fact, this could be our date."

Jake immediately shook his head. "No way. That's the two of us alone for a meal and at least one hour of conversation. Where's Brett?"

"He's having some oatmeal."

"Is that why it smells like cinnamon?"

"Maybe. But don't get too excited. It's out of a box."

"Any extra?"

"You seriously want oatmeal?"

"I seriously do," he said with a laugh, as he walked into the house and headed for the kitchen.

As soon as Brett saw Jake, he jumped out of his chair to give Jake a hug, reminding her of how good Jake had been with the kids waiting to see Santa. He'd always loved working with children— something she'd forgotten about him. Back when they were teenagers, he'd volunteered to coach youth leagues in football, soccer, and basketball, and he'd always been great with his little brother. If Paul had ever needed anything, Jake had been right there, even if it was just to tell him a silly joke or make him smile.

In fact, they'd often bonded over the fact that they both had younger siblings to look out for. Tyler and Paul had only been a year apart in age, and there had been more than a few times when they'd taken them out for pizza. Unfortunately, Paul had been sick for several years so more active sports like snowboarding or sledding had been out of the question. But Jake hadn't cared. He'd willingly give up a more extreme adventure if Paul could join for something less strenuous. That caring trait had been one of the reasons she'd fallen for him in the first place. That, and the fact that he was really good-looking, funny and charming.

She frowned, telling herself not to get carried away. He'd had a few bad traits, too—one, in particular. He couldn't be trusted.

But once again she was going back into the past, and it was time to stop doing that. She moved over to the stove and spooned some oatmeal into a bowl, added some fresh blueberries, and set it down on the table in front of Jake.

He put his heavy coat around the back of his chair and took a seat, giving her a really sexy smile, his gaze filled with a promise of pleasure that he'd never failed to deliver on. But that pleasure was not happening now...or ever, she told herself firmly.

"You're not eating?" he asked, as she sat down at the table and sipped her coffee.

"I already ate." She turned to Brett. "Do you want anything else?"

"No. When is Mommy coming to get me?"

"I'm not sure, but we're going to have fun today." She put a bright smile on her face. "We're going to play in the snow and ride a sled. Would you like that?"

Brett gave a vigorous nod of his head. "When are we going?"

"Very soon. Why don't you see if you can use the bathroom before we leave?"

Brett slid off his chair and ran out of the room.

"Has he been asking about his mother a lot?" Jake enquired.

"A couple of times this morning. But he had fun at the carnival last night, and I'm sure the snow park will distract him today."

"It will. I'm surprised you forgot about it."

"I've had a lot on my mind."

"I know. I'm sure you've been thinking about Kelly nonstop."

"I have. I tried to ask Brett a few questions, but he was no help. I asked him if his mom had a friend. And he told me her friend was a purple unicorn, who flew into the sky."

Jake smiled. "Sounds like a fun friend."

"He also told me that he's going to ride an alligator in the summer, his mom is getting him a horse, and his teacher, Miss Lane, has red hair like mine."

"It's like two truths and a lie," Jake said. "You have to decide which two are true and which one is a lie."

"Or it could be three lies."

"I don't know. Maybe Kelly is getting him a horse."

"The only one I believe is that his teacher might have red hair."

He scooped another spoonful of oatmeal into his mouth. "Let's play. Give me two truths and a lie about yourself."

"I don't have time for games."

"There is always time for games," he told her, reminding her of how many times he had stolen her away from her books to play a silly game or go somewhere fun.

Jake had definitely expanded her world. He had pushed her to try things she never would have tried. But look where pushing those boundaries had gotten her—a world of pain.

"Come on," he said, bringing her focus back to the present. "Let's play."

"You already know way too much about me."

"We'll see if I still do."

She hesitated. It was kind of silly, but on the other hand, it was probably better than talking about their pasts. "Okay. Let's see." She thought for a moment about the life she'd lived away from Jake's view. "I ran naked through the quad at the University of Colorado in Denver."

"Interesting." He gave her a thoughtful look. "What else?"

"I won a contest and got to sing on stage with the Jonas Brothers."

"That's two."

"While I was training to be a nurse, I had to go to the morgue one day, and when I pulled the sheet off a corpse, he moved his foot. I screamed and went running out of the room." She smiled. "That's three. What do you think? Which ones are true, and which one is a lie?"

"I believe the morgue story," he said slowly. "The lie is either singing on stage with the Jonas Brothers or the naked dash through the college quad. I've seen you do karaoke, so it's possible you got on the stage. I've never seen you run naked anywhere, and the time we went skinny-dipping in high school, you kept on your underwear."

She flushed at that memory. "I forgot about that."

"I've never been able to. Even in underwear, you were spectacular."

"I was too skinny."

"And too critical of yourself."

"We're getting off track," she told him, not wanting to think about the fact that while she'd kept on her panties and bra, Jake had stripped all the way down, and his body had been more than a little impressive. "Which one is the lie?"

"The naked run."

She was happy he didn't know everything. "You're wrong. I did that on a dare and a couple of shots of tequila."

"I'm impressed."

"By that? I don't think your bar is very high for being impressed."

"I'm impressed you let loose and ran free."

"Things were definitely loose," she said with a laugh, as he grinned back at her. "And don't imagine it."

"Too late. I can't help myself."

"Your turn," she said, wanting to get his gaze off her body, as her nerves were tingling in all the right places. "Two truths and a lie." She was actually curious as to what he would say. She might get to learn something about him without having to show any interest. And that was another truth—she was interested to know more about the man he was now, even though she'd spent the past several years trying to keep his name and face out of her head.

"All right," he said, a sparkling gleam in his brown eyes. "I got to take batting practice with the Colorado Rockies, and on the first pitch, I hit a home run."

She nodded, thinking that actually sounded feasible, although it reminded her of one of his teenage dreams. He'd been the star shortstop in high school. Of course, he'd also been the football quarterback, and the high-shooting forward in basketball. Jake was the guy who did everything well. "Next," she said.

"I climbed Mount Kilimanjaro. And in college, I played Romeo in *Romeo and Juliet*," he finished.

"You're making this too easy. I can see you hitting with the Rockies. I can see you climbing Mount Kilimanjaro. Romeo has to be the lie."

"You're…right," he said.

"So, I win. What's my prize?"

"We didn't agree on a prize."

"How about you let me out of the date?"

"Nope. You should have negotiated before we played. And I should have come up with a better lie."

"You should have," she agreed, as she sipped her coffee. "When did you climb Mount Kilimanjaro?"

"The summer after college graduation."

"What was it like?"

"It was grueling. It's a six-day trip—four days to get up, two to come down. I thought I'd trained. I thought I was prepared, but I have to admit the altitude got to me. I had to battle headaches and nausea on day three, and the last day was a nine-hour trek that tested my will and my body."

"But you made it."

"I did," he said, meeting her gaze. "And it was an incredible view from Uhuru Peak. We spent fifteen minutes on what they call the roof of Africa, and it was a stunning experience. Definitely worth the pain and the effort."

"That's incredible. It also sounds very difficult."

"Most incredible things are."

She nodded, thinking that was the philosophy Jake lived his life by. She'd been much more content to read about others' adventures, while Jake had wanted to experience them first-hand.

"After that climb," Jake continued, "I knew I wasn't ready for a nine-to-five job, so I turned a summer of traveling into two years of exploring the world. I spent two months in Africa and then I went to India, China, Vietnam, Thailand, and Singapore."

"How did you support yourself? Or did your parents float you a loan?"

"My parents were definitely not involved. My father was furious that I wasn't looking for a real job after paying for my college education. My mom occasionally sent me some spending money, but I worked along the way, picking up whatever jobs I could find. After the Asian swing, I moved on to Europe. I settled in Switzerland for almost two years, working at a ski resort where I taught skiing, snowboarding, rock climbing, whatever needed to be done. My experience in the Alps was what inspired me to create my own business."

"And you didn't want to run that business there?"

"No. It was time to come back to Colorado. We have some fairly spectacular mountains here, not to mention a beautiful lake."

"I know your parents were thrilled when you made that decision."

He shrugged. "It is nice to be closer to my mother again. And I'm fairly sure Paul will be headed here after medical school."

"Your dad can't wait for your brother to join the staff at the hospital."

"I'm sure," he said dryly. "He loves the idea of Paul following in his footsteps. I personally think Paul should work somewhere else for a while. Whisper Lake isn't going anywhere, but there's a whole world out there for him to see first."

"I agree with you."

"You do? I'm shocked."

She made a small face at him. "I was grateful for the experiences I had in two different city hospitals before I came back. I think they made me a better nurse. I hope Paul will consider all his options."

"My dad will pressure him to come here. And Paul won't fight him."

"I'm not sure your father will pressure him," she countered. "He knows that there's valuable experience to be had elsewhere. He'll want the best for Paul. Just as he wants the best for you, Jake. I know you two don't get along and God forbid I should mention either of your names to the other, but in some ways you're more alike than you realize."

"I am nothing like him," he said flatly. "Please don't compare us, Hannah. You can say anything else you want about me, but don't say that."

She was taken aback by the strength of his negative response. "I—I'm sorry. But your father is a great doctor and a good man. I don't see how a comparison is so bad."

"Because you don't know him the way I do."

"Want to enlighten me?"

"No. I don't want to talk about my father at all. And you should know better than anyone that parents are not always who they appear to be to the outside world."

She couldn't disagree, since her mother had clearly shown a different side at home than she had out in the community. But she was curious as to what Davis had done to turn his eldest son against him. "I wish—"

Jake cut her off. "Let's change the subject. Let's talk about you. I know you went to school in Denver. What was that like?"

She didn't really want to change the subject, but she could see the determination in his eyes to move the conversation along. "It wasn't the typical college experience," she said.

"Why not?"

"You don't know?"

He gave her a speculative look. "Know what?"

"I took Tyler with me to college. My mom had a relapse the summer after I graduated from high school. I postponed going to the university for two years so I could stay at home and take care of Tyler. I did my general courses at Lansing Community College. But when I was done there, I knew I needed to get us both out of Whisper Lake. I transferred to the University of Colorado, and I got us an off-campus apartment in Denver. Tyler was fifteen then and a sophomore in high school."

"I'm surprised he wanted to leave his friends."

"He didn't really have a choice, and he needed a break from Mom. She was in and out of the house, embarrassing herself and both of us. It was easier for him to go to a school where no one knew he had a crazy, alcoholic mother. We actually had a good time together."

"It must have been hard on you to manage college and take care of your brother."

"In some ways, but it wasn't bad, and it was the best situation for Tyler. We made it work. When he graduated and went off to college at Northwestern, I felt pretty proud of myself for helping to make that happen. Now, he's finishing up law school."

Jake smiled. "Your little brother is going to be a lawyer, and mine is going to be a doctor."

She smiled back. "They're showing us up."

"And we're both proud."

"We are," she agreed. "Remember when we used to play Monopoly with them? Tyler was cutthroat at buying up properties. Paul analyzed every purchase with careful deliberation."

"Whereas you and I were mostly winging it," he said with a laugh. "We always lost to them when we played in teams."

"Because you got distracted."

"By you," he said, meeting her gaze. "Do you know that wherever I go in the world, I smell lavender and I think of you?"

Her cheeks warmed at his words. "I guess I overdid it a little with the lavender; I just love the scent."

"You also loved those vanilla candles."

"I can't believe you remember that."

"I remember a lot of things, Hannah. We were good together."

"For a while," she conceded. "But all good things end."

"That's not true."

"From my experience, it is." She cleared her throat, realizing how personal they were getting. "Anyway...what were we talking about?"

"What did you do after Tyler went to Northwestern."

"I went to nursing school and worked in Denver for several years. I ran into your dad at a medical conference there, and he told me they would be opening a new medical center in Whisper Lake, and he'd love to see me come back. My mom had just finished a stint in rehab and was living a sober life, so I decided to come home. That was three years ago."

"And you're happy?"

"Yes. I love Whisper Lake and it's different now. I'm an adult. I live in a home that is all mine and has no bad memories. I have my friends. I can keep an eye on my mom if needed, although, thankfully, she hasn't needed me. She's been sober for almost four years. I pray that it continues, but who knows what might trigger a relapse? I want to stop feeling like the other shoe is about to drop, but I can't quite get there."

"I can't imagine being in your shoes, but I think you're an amazing woman for taking care of your brother the way you have. You've always put him first. I hope he appreciates you."

"I think he does, but I didn't do it for his appreciation. I took care of him because I loved him, and I'll always be there for him, no matter what."

"I wish I'd known how hard everything got for you after high school," he said, regret in his eyes. "What about the rest of your family? Your aunt? Your grandmother? How did you support your brother? How did you pay for Northwestern?"

"My aunt paid for Tyler's college, and my grandmother left me and Tyler two condos in Aspen that we could rent out and use the rental income to pay our own rent. To be completely honest, I also learned how to withdraw money from my mom's bank account early on. When she went off the rails, I took a chunk of her savings and put it in my account. I only used it for emergencies; I kept most of it. I actually gave it back to her a few months ago. She was shocked. But it was her money."

"Money she should have used to support her kids."

"True. She did have to sell our old house to cover her rehab stints. She managed to hang on to the cabin, though. She actually lived there for a while until she got her act together. Now she has a condo here in town. It's very modest, but she's happy there."

"Are you close now?"

"Not really. However, I feel a duty to take care of her. I just wish...never mind."

"What were you going to say?"

She shrugged. "It will make me sound terrible."

"You feel duty but not love," he guessed.

"I want to love her. She's my mother. But there's all this stuff between us." She drew in a breath. "I don't know why I just told you all that."

"Because I was interested."

As Jake finished speaking, Brett returned. "Who's going to play with me?"

"We're both going to play with you," Jake said with a grin. "Have you ever gone sledding?"

Brett shook his head. "Is it scary?"

"No, it's super fun," Jake replied. "Do you want to ride with me?"

"Can Hannah come, too?"

"Absolutely," Jake said, giving her a smile.

A shiver of desire ran down her spine at the look in his eyes. She felt like every second she spent with him was playing with fire but couldn't seem to say no to whatever invitation he offered. She told herself she was doing it for Brett. Everything she'd done with Jake so far had been to make Brett's life safer and more comfortable. But that wasn't the whole story. She knew it, and she had a feeling Jake knew it, too.

As Jake drove Hannah and Brett to the snow park, he couldn't help but think about the sad story she'd told him. Her life had gotten really hard after high school, and he wished he'd been there to help her. She probably wouldn't have let him, but maybe he could have done something.

He also couldn't help but think how differently both their lives would have been if he hadn't cheated on her, if he hadn't broken her heart and his at the same time.

But that chapter was part of the bigger story of their lives, and he wanted to write another one, one that didn't have an unhappy ending.

"Are we almost there?" Brett asked from the backseat.

"Almost," he said, flinging Hannah a smile. "When's the last time you went sledding?"

"I can't remember."

"What about skiing or snowboarding?"

"I went skiing twice last year but not this year yet. I have to admit I've lost a little enthusiasm for the mountains after patching up patient after patient with blown knees, broken bones, and head injuries."

"That would be a downer," he agreed. "But think of all the people who don't end up in your ER after a successful run."

"I wouldn't know. We're very busy during the winter. The summer is never as crazy, although we've seen some bad injuries from rock climbers and hikers who did not have enough skill to be doing what they were doing."

"That can be a problem, which is why my guided tours provide a lot of instruction as well as hands-on attention."

"No one ever gets hurt?"

"We've had a couple of broken fingers," he admitted. "And one teenager sprained his ankle because he was texting instead of paying attention while we were hiking by Embers Lake."

Embers Lake was a small lake that fed into Whisper Lake and had been named for the beautiful orange sunset that made its water look like simmering embers. "I love Ember Lake. I haven't been there in a long time, either."

"What do you do for fun if you avoid the mountains?"

"I sing karaoke with the girls at Micky's," she said.

"You've always had a good voice."

"I can carry a tune, and I'm loud, but I'm no Chelsea," she said wryly, referring to her friend, who was a very successful and well-known country music singer.

"Few people are. What else do you do? Do you still bike?" They'd spent a lot of days biking around the lake when they were younger.

"Yes. Tim Hodges at the bike shop hooked me up with a sweet deal on an off-road bike that can get me down any rough road."

"I think old Tim Hodges might be sweet on you."

"He's seventy."

"And he's still a flirt. However, I'm sure you can do better than a seventy-year-old."

"Well, thanks," she said dryly.

"Do you have someone that you're dating?" He tried to make the question sound as casual and as disinterested as he could. He'd seen her around town a few times with different guys but not one guy on a consistent basis.

"Lots of someones."

"Haven't found Mr. Right?"

"I'm not even looking for him. But Mr. Fun For a While wouldn't be bad."

"You don't want a relationship?"

"They're a lot of work and, frankly, no one has made me want to do the work in a long time."

"When was the last time you were in a relationship?"

"Why do you care?"

"I'm just curious. Is it a secret?" he challenged.

"No. It was three years ago. It ended right before I moved back here."

"What happened?"

"Nothing dramatic. We met at a book signing. We both loved the mystery author, J.R. Welks, and we bonded while standing in line. Unfortunately, our mutual love of mystery thrillers didn't extend to much else in our lives."

"How long did you go out?"

"About a year." She shifted in her seat, giving him a thoughtful look. "What about you? Are you dating anyone?"

"Not at the moment."

"And before this moment?"

"I've had a few girlfriends," he conceded.

"Probably more than a few. You were always very popular," she said, a tighter, tense note entering her voice. "When was your last serious relationship?"

"Serious? I'm not sure I've ever had a serious relationship."

"Why not?"

"I've traveled a lot, which makes long-term anything difficult."

"I don't think that's the reason. And you've been back here for what—two years?"

"About that. I haven't been in a hurry to settle into anything. Anyone looking for Mr. Right would have to settle for Mr. Fun Right Now. That guy I can be." He gave her a grin. "Sounds like you and I might be on the same page."

"We had our run. I don't want another one."

"Are you sure? That kiss on Friday night..."

She frowned and shook her head. "We're not talking about that. You took me by surprise. Whatever you might think about my response, it was only because I didn't know it was coming."

"You're very defensive about your reaction."

"I'm not defensive. I'm being honest."

"No, you're not. You liked kissing me as much as I liked kissing you."

Conflict played through her eyes, and then she said, "Fine. We still have chemistry, but I'm not going to do anything about it. We had a bad ending, and I can't put myself in a position to have another one. I can't trust you, Jake. You want honest—that's me being honest. You hurt me, and you embarrassed me, and I don't let anyone do that to me twice."

"I wouldn't do it to you again."

"That's what you say. But I didn't think you'd do it the first time. My instincts about you were wrong. So, that's it."

"That's nowhere close to being it," he argued.

She sighed. "I don't know what you're trying to prove."

"I'm not trying to prove anything. I just want a second chance."

"You haven't earned it."

"Okay," he said. "Then I'll earn it."

"I didn't mean to make that a challenge."

"Too late. I've already accepted."

"Jake, give it up already. We can coexist more peacefully than we have. We can be friends, but that's it. We are not going to be what we were before."

"I have no intention of being what we were before. I want you to know me now, and I want to know you. I'm going to show you that I'm someone you can count on."

"Are we here yet?" Brett piped up from the backseat where he'd been watching a show on Hannah's tablet.

He'd almost forgotten Brett was there. Thank goodness he had been wearing headphones the past several minutes, not that he would have understood what they were talking about.

"We are just about there," he said, spotting the turnoff for Northstar.

"Is our sled going to go really fast?" Brett asked.

"As fast as you want it to go," Hannah put in, turning to look at Brett.

"I want to go fast. Mommy said she'd take me sledding but not until after."

"After what?" he asked, curious about Brett's comment. *Was there a much-needed clue about to come their way?*

"After my little sister comes," Brett replied, dropping not just a clue but a bombshell.

# CHAPTER ELEVEN

HANNAH COULDN'T BELIEVE what Brett had just said. *Was he telling the truth? Was Kelly pregnant? Or was this just another fantasy like the one about the unicorn?*

"When is your little sister coming?" she asked.

"Valentine's Day. We're going to make her a heart and name her Violet."

"That's a pretty name." She calculated the dates. If Kelly was having a baby in mid- February, then she had to be seven and a half or eight months pregnant. But Adam hadn't mentioned the pregnancy after speaking to Kelly's boss. *Wouldn't that person have said that Kelly was pregnant? And who was the father of Kelly's baby? Was it the boyfriend who had disappeared at the same time as her? The one who might have been harassing her?*

She was still trying to come up with answers when Jake turned into the busy parking lot at the snow park. As he searched for a spot, she took out her phone and texted Adam the information she'd just received. She didn't know if he was working on Sunday, but hopefully he'd get back to her. She felt like the stakes were even higher now that she knew Kelly might be pregnant. But maybe Violet was just a story in Brett's head. That was as plausible as anything else.

She didn't want to upset Brett by asking more questions, so she let the subject go as they got out of the truck and entered the park. They met up with the rest of the group in the great room of an enormous lodge that had once been the home of a wealthy landowner. It was spectacularly decorated for the season with an enormous Christmas tree and plenty of colorful wreaths. It also smelled like pine and cinnamon. Gianna, Zach and Hailey were there as well as Chloe and her son Leo, Lizzie Cole and her fiancé Justin Blackwood, and rounding out the group was Keira, who was flying solo today.

Lately, she and Keira had been the ones to do most of the solo flying as members of their group had started coupling up, but today Hannah had Jake by her side, and she knew their arrival together would raise a lot more questions. To her surprise, everyone acted as if it was completely normal to see her and Jake together. They must have made some sort of pact not to say anything, which was fine with her.

Eight-year-old Hailey immediately took Brett's hand and asked him if he wanted to go on the sled with her. Brett was thrilled to have the little girl's attention and immediately attached himself to Hailey as they headed out of the lodge.

The guys led the way, with Zach keeping a close eye on his daughter Hailey and her new best friend, Brett. Jake put Leo on his shoulders as he walked alongside Justin, and the women fell into step with her. The interrogation was on.

"What do you want to know?" she asked with resignation.

"First, any news on Kelly?" Keira asked.

"Nothing yet."

"Well, no news is probably good news," Chloe said. "And, by the way, we filled Lizzie in."

"I figured. Your brother is looking for my sister."

"Adam is the right man for the job," Lizzie replied, giving her a sympathetic smile. "I hope everything works out."

"So do I."

"Now, let's talk about you and Jake," Gianna said pointedly.

"You were with him at the carnival. You're with him now. What's going on? Are you back together?"

"No. He happened to be with me when I discovered Brett, and ever since then he's been helping me."

"But you hate him," Gianna reminded her.

"She doesn't hate him anymore," Keira put in with a mischievous smile. "Come on, Hannah, be honest. I saw the way you were looking at Jake last night, and it reminded me a lot of high school."

"I may not hate him as much as I used to, but we're not getting back together. He's being a friend, and I'm letting him. The only thing I'm concerned about right now is making sure my nephew has a great day."

"We can help you with that," Chloe assured her. "And I'm glad you and Jake are able to at least stay in the same space together."

"I agree," Lizzie said. "Let's concentrate on having a great day. We'll sled, we'll build snowmen, we'll get those spicy hot chocolates with marshmallows. It's going to be a great day."

"That's quite a positive declaration," Keira put in with a dry smile. "Since when did you become so calm and Zen, Lizzie? You're usually running around like a madwoman, especially during the holidays. Isn't the inn packed this weekend?"

Lizzie laughed. "We are sold out, but I'm trying to enjoy my guests instead of worrying about every little thing. Justin has had a surprisingly calming influence on me. Last summer, I was trying to keep my head above water, but now things at the inn are going really well. I just needed to reassess my priorities. Plus, I have a great man who believes in me, and has been willing to change his whole life for me. I feel really lucky."

"Have you set a wedding date yet?" she asked, happy to be talking about someone else's love life.

"Probably next summer. We're not in a rush."

"Well, I still hope you have a ceremony and don't elope like this one," Keira said, giving Gianna a wink.

"Hey, after all my disastrous non-weddings, I was just ready to be married," Gianna said. "But I think you should do it up big and grand, Lizzie, like you do everything else."

"It probably will be over the top," Lizzie admitted. "And you'll make my dress, Keira. It has to be even better than the one you made for my sister. But don't tell Chelsea I said that."

"Your secret is safe with me."

"How's the boutique going?" she asked Keira. "Will this upcoming year be the one where you ditch the real-estate and go full force into your fashion design business?"

"I hope so. We'll see."

"If I can help in any way..."

"I'll let you know. And by the way, we won't talk about your sister while we're with Brett, but just so you know, we have your back."

"Whatever you need," Gianna added, with Lizzie and Chloe smiling their support.

She appreciated each and every one of them. She might have lost her real sister a long time ago, but she had these women. Three of them had been her friends for most of her life, and Lizzie was becoming one of her best friends now.

For the next hour, they played on the bunny slope, taking turns riding down the hill of soft white powder with the kids, who were all in absolute heaven. She loved seeing Brett so happy. He hadn't known any of these people three days ago, but now he was one of them. He was Hailey's adored little friend and Leo's big brother figure. Most importantly, he was her nephew, and more and more, she saw not only bits and pieces of Kelly in his expressions and in his personality, but she also saw her dad. Her father had missed so much, and his passing had left a huge hole, but there was a new generation now. Brett had a lot of her dad's easy friendliness. His legacy lived on.

As Jake swept Brett up into his arms for another run down the slope, her smile broadened. Jake was like a big kid himself, and in this instance, all the children were benefiting from his zest for adventure. They were willing to follow him anywhere. She could relate to that feeling. He had a powerful charisma that had always made it difficult for her to look away. That's why she'd stopped looking at him. She could feel the pull even when their eyes didn't meet, but when they did...

Her heart flipped over as he caught her gaze now, his smile spreading across his lips, as something passed between them, something she didn't want to define.

"Nothing like watching a man with a child," Gianna said.

"What?" She forced herself to break the connection with Jake to turn to Gianna.

"Jake looks good with Brett," Gianna said. "When I first saw Zach and Hailey together, I was overwhelmed by the tenderness and love between them. They don't even share blood. He was her stepfather, but he loved her so much, and it touched me deeply. I was already falling for him again, but that was the real kicker."

"Zach is amazing with Hailey. I forget that he's not her biological father." She paused. "I also sometimes forget that you and Zach had a teenage history, too."

"It wasn't as long or as complicated as yours and Jake's, but summer camp was certainly memorable that year. Our story was also different, because I'm the one who hurt Zach, whereas Jake was the one who hurt you. I wasn't sure Zach could forgive me, but I'm lucky that he did, because it allowed us to get to this incredible place."

"You think I should forgive Jake?" she asked curiously, feeling like Gianna would understand her conflict better than anyone else.

Gianna frowned. "I don't know. I feel like you think we're belittling the pain you went through because we've accepted Jake back into the group. But we haven't forgotten, Hannah. We've just seen a different side of Jake, one that you haven't allowed yourself to see —until maybe now."

"I have to admit it has bothered me," she said honestly. "Everyone was so willing to welcome Jake home."

"Not at first," Gianna protested. "It took a while, but he and Brodie became friends through the search-and-rescue team, and Jake started working with Lizzie giving tours to her guests. Then he made Zach's day by taking him skiing down Skyhawk Trail.

The friendships started with the outsiders and then spread to us. Keira resisted the longest."

"She's under his spell now," she said dryly, seeing Keira laughing hilariously at something Jake had said.

Gianna smiled. "You kind of seem like you're warming up to him."

"I don't know how it has happened, but he does bring the heat," she muttered.

"That sounds interesting."

"Or dangerous. I don't want to make another mistake. I loved him so much, Gianna."

"I know. I was there."

"I thought we had the greatest love story of all time. I guess everyone thinks that at seventeen. I thought he believed that, too. But he didn't. He threw us away with that stupid, slutty Vicki Thompson." She took a hard breath. "I know he was drunk. I know he was sorry. But what I don't know is why. And he's never been able to tell me. He wanders all around the subject: everything from getting cold feet about how serious we were becoming to his friend Eddie plying him with alcohol, to some mysterious incident that he can't talk about. He clearly can't tell me the truth."

"Maybe he doesn't know the truth. Maybe he can't remember."

"You might be right, but I'm tired of alcohol abuse being the get-out-of-jail-free card for every bad thing you do in your life," she said sharply. "And I know that's mostly because of my mom, but in some ways, it feels the same. Everyone wants to apologize and to be forgiven for doing shitty things because they were drunk. Maybe just don't get drunk and do shitty things. Start there." She paused. "And I know I sound very harsh when I say that, so I don't usually say it. I usually accept the apology and agree to move on. I've certainly said that to my mom."

"But you can't say it to Jake."

"In some ways, I want to, but…I'm not there yet."

"I get it. You have to do what's right for you. Like you said, it's not on you to absolve everyone else of their sins."

"Right?" She felt a little better that Gianna got it. "I will say this, though. I can see that Jake is a better man now. He has built a good business, and he puts his life on the line to rescue people he doesn't know. He's certainly been very supportive since my sister left Brett with me, so I'm trying to let go of the past and see him as he is now. Beyond that, I don't know."

"Well, you don't have to know yet. See how things go. And maybe...just let yourself have some fun. The other thing I remember about you and Jake before the big breakup was how much fun you had together."

"That is true," she admitted.

A shrill clanging bell interrupted their conversation and the rest of the group came back as the announcement for the beginning of the snowman competition played across a speaker.

"I think we should split into teams," Keira said. "Make a friendly wager on who gets the highest score."

"That works for me," Justin said, putting his arm around Lizzie. "We'll take anyone on."

"We're in," Zach said, speaking for Gianna and Hailey.

"I'll team up with Chloe and Leo," Keira said.

Hannah sighed as Jake looked at her. "I guess you can do it with me and Brett."

"But I want to build the snowman with Hailey," Brett announced, clinging to Hailey's hand. "Can I? Can I?"

While she would have preferred to have Brett as a chaperone, she could hardly deny the request. "Of course you can," she said.

As they headed toward the meadow where the snowman-building competition would be taking place, Jake walked alongside her.

"You didn't do any sledding," he said. "Why is that?"

"I had fun watching all of you and taking photos."

"But you can't come to a snow park and not sled." He suddenly stopped walking and put a hand on her arm. "Why don't we concede on the snowman competition and take the lift up to Griz-zly's Peak?" He tipped his head toward the advanced run that was not for kids.

"I should stay with Brett," she protested.

Jake smiled. "I hate to break it to you, Hannah, but Brett has a big crush on Hailey. And he's very happy to be hanging out with her. I'm sure Zach and Gianna will watch him."

"I suppose," she muttered, torn between what she wanted to do and what she should do.

"I'll take that as a yes."

"It wasn't a—" Her words were cut off as Jake yelled to the rest of the group that they were going to pass on building a snowman and hit Grizzly's Peak.

Her traitorous friends just grinned and told them to have a good time. And then Jake's hand was on hers, spinning her around so fast she felt dizzy. Although, she suspected that the dizzy feeling was more from Jake than anything else.

His inviting smile was too sexy to refuse, and she didn't even pull her hand away as they walked toward the lift. They'd ride a chair up to the top of Grizzly's Peak about 200 yards, then grab a sled and come down the steep and icy slope. She felt both nervous and excited, which was pretty much how Jake always made her feel.

As they got in line, she saw a couple come flying down the mountain, crashing in a somewhat spectacular fashion at the bottom. But they picked themselves up with a laugh, brushing the snow off their clothes.

"Let's not do that," she told Jake.

"Amateurs," he said with a roll of his eyes. "Trust me. Our ride will not end like that."

"It already did," she couldn't help saying.

He frowned. "This ride will be different."

"I hope so." They stepped into place and then sat back in the chair as the lift swept them upward. As they rose up over the trees, they had a beautiful view of the park and the surrounding mountains. It was a gorgeous day, no trace of the storm that had kept them in the cabin all night together or the one that was forecast for later in the week. It was a perfect moment in time, and she was just going to enjoy it.

"You look happy," Jake commented.

She turned her head to meet his gaze. "Is it crazy to say that I love riding a lift up a mountain more than I like skiing or sledding down?"

"That is crazy," he agreed with a smile. "I like both."

"There's a peacefulness up here, swinging our legs above the treetops."

"The calm before the storm. But the race down the mountain brings the energy, the excitement, and the challenge. You can't beat that feeling of exuberance at the end of a good run."

His words made her feel like she was already on that run. This had probably been a really bad idea, but it was too late now. There was no other way down than sledding with Jake, and the excitement was already bubbling up inside of her. "Have you done this run before?"

"Nope. This place wasn't here when we were kids. And sledding isn't really my thing. I'd rather be snowboarding, skiing or freestyling."

"Then why the push to sled now?"

"Because I get to put my arms around you," he said with an honest and open grin.

She couldn't help but smile back. Thankfully, she didn't have to come up with a response as the lift had reached the top. They hopped off and grabbed one of the two-person sleds before making their way to one of the three runs that went down the mountain. When it was their turn, she had to admit to a little trepidation.

"It's very high," she murmured. "It didn't look this steep from the bottom."

"It will be fun. You will love it, Hannah."

"How do you know that?" She got onto the front of the sled, and he slid in behind her, wrapping his arms around her, and pulling her back against his very solid chest. And just like that, her fears slipped away.

"How do I know that?" he echoed. "Because deep down, you love to fly, Hannah."

She had no time to argue or even to think about that, because they were racing down the mountain. As their speed picked up, as the wind beat against her face, she screamed with both fear and excitement, appreciating the strong arms around her. It seemed like it would be impossible to stop, but there was just enough of an upward rise to slow them down and bring them to a stop in a spray of beautiful white powder.

Her heart was pounding against her chest as she rolled off the sled and jumped to her feet. Jake looked at her with sparkling brown eyes as he got to his feet. "Well?"

"That was amazing."

"Seems like the perfect time for a kiss. But it's your call," he said.

She must have lost her mind somewhere on the slope, because she found herself grabbing his arms and leaning in for the kiss she wanted as much as he did.

She closed her eyes as his mouth settled on hers with spine-tingling heat. There was cold surrounding them, but there was nothing but delicious warmth in their kiss. She'd always loved kissing Jake, and now the past was mixing with the present in the best possible way.

Until a flurry of snow hit her on the side of her cheek. She broke away from Jake as a sled came perilously close to running them down but managed to land a few feet away.

"Sorry," a woman said with an apologetic wave.

Jake grabbed their sled and they dragged it over to the lift area, sliding it onto a flat piece of metal that would take it back to the top.

"Want to do that again?" he asked.

"The sledding or the kiss?" she asked mischievously.

"How about both?" he returned, his hands sliding around her waist.

She immediately regretted her challenging question. She slipped away from him. "I think we're done."

"For today," he added. "The ball is now back in my court."

"We're not playing a game."

"Oh, it's not a game," he said purposefully.

"Jake…" Her voice trailed away as she really didn't know what to say.

"Let's go build a snowman," he said.

As he turned away, she said, "I don't have to do everything you say." She impulsively picked up a handful of snow, molded it into a ball, and threw it at the back of his head.

He jumped and turned around in surprise. "What the hell was that?"

"Oops," she said, giving him a look of mock apology.

"You want to play it like that?" he dared.

"I'll play any way I want," she shot back. She dodged his snow-ball and jogged across the meadow. He caught up with her within ten seconds. He grabbed her by the arm and spun her around.

She thought he was going to go in for another kiss, but to her shock he smashed a pile of snow right into her face. She sputtered. By the time she'd wiped the icy mess off her mouth, he was out of her range.

He flung her a quick grin, backpedaling as he did. "Ball is still in my court," he said.

"You just had a chance to kiss me. Why didn't you take it?"

"It wasn't the right time."

"There's not going to be a better time. We may never be this close again."

"Oh, we will be," he said, his promising gaze sending a shiver down her spine that had nothing to do with the snow still lingering on her face. "You'll see."

"Or I won't," she said, determined not to let him think he was getting his way.

"You will. Because you want it to happen as much as I do."

She wanted to argue that he was wrong, but her slight hesitation was all it took for him to spin back around and jog ahead, once again getting the last word.

She hated when he got the last word, but she had to admit that what she hadn't hated was his kiss. *But then, why would she hate it?*

They'd always had a crazy chemistry. It was everything else

that had gone to hell. That's the part she didn't ever want to live through again. So, maybe she needed to end this game before it went any further. Not that she was playing.

*Oh, who was she kidding?*

She'd kissed him. She was definitely playing. But not for long, she told herself firmly. They'd had some fun. That was enough.

*She really wanted it to be enough...*

# CHAPTER TWELVE

HANNAH HAD SURPRISED HIM, not just with the kiss, but with the snowball fight, with the smile that had stayed on her lips, the happy light in her brown eyes. He'd wanted to see her like this for a long time, and, finally, she'd shown him a side of herself that wasn't brimming with anger and resentment. He just wasn't sure he could make the mood last, but he was certainly going to try.

He'd always thought he needed a huge challenge to face and conquer in order to get to a happy place, to escape the darkness that resided deep in his soul, in a place that no one else ever saw. That's why he hiked the tallest mountains, climbed the most dangerous rock formations, challenged himself on the white waters of the wildest rivers, tested his confidence with parachute skiing and cave diving—anything that would put his life on the line, his skills to the ultimate stress point. But today, sledding and snowman building, and a hot kiss from Hannah, had put a grin on his face that he couldn't seem to get rid of.

Everyone else seemed to be having a good time, too. Lizzie and Justin managed to snag first place with their snowman, an elaborate creation that only the imaginative Lizzie could create, while the rest of the group had had to settle for ribbons for basically showing up. After the competition, they'd gone to the dining room at the lodge and ordered up burgers, wings, fries, and plenty of hot chocolate with whipped cream. Conversation had flowed fast and furious, although he'd been content to watch and listen for most of the time.

After their meal, Lizzie and Justin took off while Hannah, Zach, Gianna, and Chloe decided to take the kids into the arcade. He'd thought about going with them, but Keira had slid down the bench next to him, and it was clear she wanted to speak to him.

"So..." she began. "What's going on, Jake?"

"Just enjoying the last of my hot chocolate," he said, taking a sip.

"I mean with Hannah."

"I know what you mean, but I can't tell you."

"Why not?"

"Because I have no idea," he said candidly. "I was in the right place at the right time to help Hannah on Friday night. Since then, she's been a little friendlier. I think, or I hope, that she's starting to see me as who I am now."

"That would be nice. It has been awkward for the group with you two at such odds. But—"

"I figured there was a *but*... Let me have it."

She gave him an assessing look. "I don't want to see Hannah hurt again, and I'm not sure what to make of this sudden turn-around in your relationship. Two days ago, she hated your guts. Today, I felt like I was watching the Hannah and Jake show of our high school years, the sneaky little intimate looks and the ridiculously happy smiles."

"I don't think we've gotten back to that place yet."

"Still...I'm a little shocked that everything has changed so fast. I don't know what to make of it."

He shrugged. "I'm just happy she doesn't look like she wants to put a knife in my back as soon as I turn around. Beyond that, I have no idea where we're going, if we're going anywhere. She has a lot happening in her life right now."

"True. I've only heard pieces of the story, but I know Kelly is in some sort of trouble, which doesn't surprise me, since trouble was her middle name. But now she has a kid who needs his mother, so I hope she comes through whatever she's involved in."

"So do I." Despite Hannah's estrangement from her sister, anything bad happening to Kelly would shatter Hannah. "I don't want to see Hannah have to deal with another tragic loss."

"I don't either. She has had such a rough time with her mom all these years. You know she practically raised Tyler. She had him with her when she went to college because her mom couldn't take care of him. Can you imagine being a junior in college and having to deal with your sixteen-year-old brother making his way through a new high school?"

"She told me about that. I had no idea she'd had to do that."

"She rose to the challenge. That's what Hannah does; it's what she's doing now." Keira paused, her gaze moving toward the archway that led into the arcade. The group was headed back to the table. "Looks like they've run out of tokens." She turned to give him another pointed look. "Just remember this, Jake. You hurt Hannah again, and you will have to answer to not just me, but all of us. You know that, right?"

"What if she hurts me?"

Keira frowned. "Good question. I guess we're friends, too."

"I'd like to think so."

"Maybe you two should go back to keeping your distance. As annoying as it sometimes was to be around the two of you together, I never had to worry that things were going to blow up again. Now, I do."

"Relax, Keira. We're not rushing into anything. We've barely gotten past the enemy stage."

She gave him a thoughtful look. "Somehow I doubt that. And I know you, Jake. When you want something or someone, you go after that goal with everything you've got." She paused. "Hannah is the same way. So, I guess we'll find out what happens if one or both of you decides you want the other."

"It will be fireworks," he said with a grin.

She smiled back. "I hope neither of you gets burned."

Jake thought about Keira's words as he drove Hannah and Brett home a little after two. Brett was already drooping in his seat. He had a feeling the kid would be asleep before they reached the highway. Which meant he and Hannah would have plenty of time to chat, not that she'd had much to say since she'd gotten in the truck. Her mood had definitely changed from where it had been after the sled run. She wasn't being cold, but she wasn't being warm, either. She was thinking—probably about all the reasons why they shouldn't be friends again. That needed to stop.

"What do you have going on the rest of the day?" he asked, hoping to distract her from her thoughts.

"I have to bake cookies. The hospital Christmas party is tomorrow afternoon, and I've been tasked with bringing three dozen cookies. I guess Brett will have to help me make them."

"I'm sure he'll enjoy that. I think my mom is making cookies, too, or maybe that was for the carnival."

"She was on the carnival baking committee. The ER nurses are in charge of tomorrow's sweets. I was also thinking that I should get a tree." She took a quick look back at Brett. "He's already asleep."

"He had a lot of exercise today."

"I want to make this Christmas magical for him," she continued, as she turned her gaze back to his. "I don't usually decorate for the holiday, but I feel like this one should be everything it's supposed to be. It won't make up for his mom not being around, but maybe it will help."

"And maybe she'll be back by Christmas."

"I hope so."

His phone buzzed with an incoming text, and he pulled it out of his pocket. He handed it to Hannah, not wanting to be distracted while driving through the mountains. "Could you read that for me?"

"It's from Trevor. He's at the Motor Inn off Highway 7 in room ten."

He was relieved that Trevor had finally gotten back to him, but not that he'd ended up in a motel.

"Is that good news?" Hannah asked.

"I'm not sure. I don't know why he left the cabin, but I'm glad he finally got back to me. I've been texting him since Friday night."

"He sounds relatively coherent."

"I'll go by the motel after I drop you and Brett off."

"I'm sorry you have to take us all the way back."

"It's not a problem."

"When you talk to Trevor, maybe you can find out what he spoke to Kelly about."

"I will definitely ask him."

"He might have been the last person to talk to my sister. He could have information that no one else has."

"That's one reason I've been relentlessly texting him."

Hannah tapped her fingers nervously against her thighs. "I wish we could both go see Trevor, but I can't expose Brett to whatever is going on at that motel."

"No, you can't. I'll handle it, and I'll make sure to get any information he has. You can count on that, Hannah."

"Thanks."

Fifteen minutes later, they arrived at her house. He got Brett out of his car seat and carried him into the house and up the stairs to Hannah's guest room. After one very sleepy trip to use the bathroom, Hannah tucked Brett into the middle of the bed, surrounding him with pillows, so he couldn't possibly roll off the edge, and then they went downstairs.

The whole routine of putting a child down to sleep felt surreal, as if they were parents, as if Brett was their child. It was not an experience he'd ever had before, but he found himself liking it more than he would have expected.

They were almost to the door when the doorbell rang. A somber-looking Adam stood on the porch. He looked like he'd come from work, wearing a heavy wool coat over dark slacks and a button-down shirt.

"Is it bad news?" Hannah asked.

"It's news," Adam said quietly. "Can I come in?"

"Yes. Let's go in the kitchen. Brett is asleep, but I don't want to take a chance he'll overhear anything."

He followed Adam and Hannah into the kitchen. As eager as he was to talk to Trevor, he wanted to know what Adam had found out.

"We've been tracking Kelly's boyfriend, Russ Miller," Adam said, as they sat down at the table.

"The hotel manager?" Hannah asked.

"Yes."

"Did you find him? Does he know where Kelly is? Was she with him?" The questions poured out of Hannah's mouth,

"We found him," Adam replied, his lips drawing into a tight line. "At a campground outside of Denver. He was dead."

Jake couldn't believe what he was hearing. "He's dead?"

"Yes. Russ Miller was stabbed twice. His body was found near a river that ran through the campground. It was about a mile from the cabin where he was staying with your sister."

"Oh, God." Hannah put a hand to her mouth. "Is Kelly..."

"We didn't find her," Adam said quickly. "But she was with him at the campground. The attendant said that Russ checked in last Monday with a woman and a child. She identified the woman as your sister. Mr. Miller's body was discovered Saturday morning, and it appeared that he had been dead for over forty-eight hours. It's believed that the stabbing occurred sometime on Wednesday evening."

"Did anyone see anything?" he asked.

"No. It's winter, and the campground was mostly empty. Only a few cabins had been rented. The attendant said that Russ, Kelly and Brett showed up on Monday night and paid in cash for a week."

"What do you think happened?" Hannah asked.

"Mr. Miller was stabbed in the back and then in the neck. The neck wound was fatal. My guess is he was taken by surprise, disabled by the first attack and unable to fight off the second."

Hannah paled at Adam's gruesome statement, and Jake couldn't help but put a comforting hand on her shoulder.

She gave him a despairing look and then moved her gaze back to Adam. "Who do you think killed him?"

"I don't know."

Jake didn't know either, but he had a bad feeling, and he could see that Hannah was struggling with the same theory.

"If Russ was hurting Kelly, then maybe she…" As Hannah struggled to finish that sentence, he jumped in.

"It could have been self-defense," he said. "Kelly didn't want to be with Russ. She found a moment to take him by surprise. She stabbed him, and she took Brett and ran."

Adam met his gaze. "It could have gone down that way. If she was involved, self-defense or not, it would also explain why she didn't want anyone to go to the police."

"She could have been afraid she'd be arrested for her boyfriend's death," he added.

Hannah turned to him, grabbing onto his theory. "And Kelly didn't think anyone would believe it was self-defense." She looked back at Adam. "What happens now?"

"The investigation is continuing on multiple fronts. I'm working with the police in Colorado Springs and in Rocky Point where the campground is located. The rangers are also involved in collecting evidence in the park. We're, of course, still looking for your sister and following up with as many coworkers and friends of Kelly and Russ Miller as we can find."

"You got my message about Kelly being pregnant?"

"Yes. I have to tell you that no one mentioned it to me. The only photo we have of Kelly is from the ATM she used in Colorado Springs before she left town. In that grainy image, she doesn't look pregnant, but she was wearing a big coat over what looked like leggings and boots, so it was hard to tell. However, I will follow up and see what I can find out about that. I don't know that it changes anything, although it might play into some kind of motive."

"Should I feel relieved that Kelly isn't in danger from this man?" Hannah asked slowly.

"He definitely can't hurt her," Adam said, giving her a compassionate look. "How's her kid doing?"

"He's doing well. We went to the snow park with everyone today. I'm trying to distract him, but he keeps asking about his mother. I don't know what to tell him."

"As little as possible is probably good."

"I just wish I knew where Kelly is now," Hannah said, fear in her voice. "There's more snow coming in tomorrow. I hate to think of her out alone in the mountains somewhere."

"Your sister has been very resourceful so far," he interjected. "She's doing everything she can do to survive."

"I know, but she must be so scared."

Adam got to his feet. "Hopefully, we'll have more news soon, but I wanted to give you an update. I'll see myself out."

As Adam left the kitchen, Hannah let out a troubled, frustrated sigh. "I was not expecting to hear any of that."

"Nor was I," he admitted. "What do you think?"

"If Kelly killed a man, it had to be in self-defense. But I also wonder if she's ever coming back. Maybe she left Brett for me to raise. I know she'd never want to go to prison. She was incredibly claustrophobic. She once had a panic attack in a line at an amusement park when the space got small and dark. On the other hand, would she really run away and leave her son? And what about the baby she's carrying?"

"I think we're going to have to wait and see how this plays out."

"You need to go see Trevor. He could at least tell us if she is pregnant. He saw her and spoke to her. Did we ever tell Adam about Trevor?"

He frowned, as he got to his feet. "I don't think so. Let me see what he has to say, and then I'll fill Adam in."

"Okay."

As they walked out of the kitchen, the doorbell rang once more.

"Maybe Adam has already found out something else," Hannah said.

But it wasn't Adam on the porch this time; it was Hannah's mother, Katherine Stark.

He inwardly groaned. He hadn't had one conversation with Katherine since he'd returned to town, although he'd seen her in the distance a few times, but they'd both been happy to avoid each other.

"You," she said, her voice filled with anger. "What are you doing here?"

"I don't think that's any of your business," he said shortly.

Her lips parted in surprise, as if she couldn't believe he'd just said that.

"Jake is helping me with Brett," Hannah put in.

"Why?" Katherine asked.

"Because he is, Mom," Hannah snapped.

Katherine turned back to him, scorn in her gaze. "I told you to leave my daughter alone a long time ago."

"When did you tell him that?" Hannah cut in.

"Back when you were in high school. He came by to beg for your forgiveness, and I told him you would never ever forgive him, and he didn't deserve it."

Hannah appeared shocked at that piece of information. "You never told me that."

"I'm sure I did." Katherine gave him another searing look. "You still don't deserve forgiveness. You hurt my daughter."

He wanted to say she'd hurt her daughter far more than he had, but he thought it was better to just walk away. "I'm going to go," he told Hannah. "I'll be in touch."

She gave him a troubled look. "Let me know what Trevor says."

"I will," he said, then headed down the path.

He was almost to the truck when he heard Katherine say, "Seriously, Hannah, what are you doing with Jake?"

Unfortunately, he couldn't hear Hannah's answer. Maybe that was just as well.

# CHAPTER THIRTEEN

"I ASKED YOU A QUESTION," her mom said, as they stepped into the house.

Hannah gave her a warning look. "Don't speak so loudly. Brett is asleep."

"I just don't understand why you would be with a man you hate," her mom continued, as they moved into the living room and sat down.

"It's complicated, Mom. Jake has been helping me with Brett."

"Why aren't your friends helping you?"

"My friends?" she echoed. "A better question might be why isn't my mother helping me? You're Brett's grandmother, and you wouldn't even see him yesterday."

Guilt moved through her mother's eyes. "Well, I was busy yesterday, but I'm here now." She paused. "I'd like to meet him."

"I told you, he's sleeping."

"He certainly takes a lot of naps."

"He's four. Do you want to come back later?"

"Maybe I should just wait."

"You want to wait?" she asked in surprise. "It could be a while. I'm sure you have other things to do. Why don't you go home, and I'll call you when he wakes up?"

"I'd rather stay."

"Well, I can't entertain you. I have to make three dozen cookies before tomorrow."

Her mom's green eyes lit up. "I can help with that. I'm great at baking."

She actually wouldn't mind her mom's help. "All right. But we're not going to talk about Jake."

"I can't make that promise. When I see something wrong, I have to say something."

"Since when?"

"It's part of being honest and staying well. If I keep things inside, they only get worse. You can't keep secrets and stay sober."

Her mom's words came straight out of her Alcoholics Anonymous meetings, and while she wanted to say her mom had never really been that honest about anything, there was no point. Katherine Stark had a blind spot when it came to her own deficiencies. But she was trying, and she was sober. That was the most important thing.

"If we're going to be completely honest," she said. "Then you need to explain why you never told me Jake came by to see me after our horrible breakup."

Her mom's shrug was unapologetic. "I was protecting you. I saw how hurt you were, Hannah, and when he came by to apologize, I was afraid you'd take him back. Is that what you're doing now? Are you giving him a second chance?"

"I don't know," she said. "I haven't decided yet."

Her mother bit down on her bottom lip as if she was forcing herself not to say anything, which was fine with her.

"Okay," her mom continued. "We won't talk about Jake. What's happening with Kelly?"

She wanted to talk about Kelly even less. "The police are looking for her, but they haven't found her yet. That's really all I know." She didn't want to get into the boyfriend or what had happened at the campground. It would only upset her mom, and she didn't need her mother to fall apart on top of everything else. "Let's go into the kitchen. I need to get started on the cookies."

"I can't believe they put you in charge of cookies. You were always so impatient with baking," her mom said, as she followed her into the kitchen. "You never wanted to wait for the cookies to bake. Every time I turned around, you were sneaking raw cookie dough."

She smiled at the memory. "That is true. It was so good."

"And so bad for you with the raw eggs."

"Well, I survived," she said lightly, knowing she'd survived things far worse than raw egg cookie dough. "But tomorrow the cookies definitely need to be baked."

"Then it's a good thing I came by."

She didn't know yet if it was a good thing or not, but she was going to find out soon.

---

Jake drove across town fighting off waves of anger. The contempt in Katherine Stark's voice still grated on his nerves.

After the life she'd led, the terrible mother she'd been—how dare she judge him for one bad mistake? If she hadn't been such a complete and total burden on Hannah for the last decade, maybe he could admire her sticking up for her daughter. But it just felt hypocritical.

Unfortunately, her attitude toward him had also been another reminder of what a stupid ass he'd been. He didn't care what she thought of him now, but he didn't want her messing up the tentative truce between Hannah and him. But there was nothing he could do about it.

He needed to forget about Katherine and focus on Trevor and what information he might be able to provide that would help them find Kelly. Although finding Kelly might bring a whole new set of problems. It was difficult to know what to believe with the limited information that they had, but he thought there was a good chance that Kelly had killed Russ Miller and had run for her life.

It might be difficult to prove self-defense, but Kelly couldn't stay on the run forever. Or maybe she could.

*But what would that do to Brett?* She'd be sacrificing her son for her freedom. *On the other hand, what good would Kelly be to her son if she was in jail? And how hard would that be on Hannah?*

Hannah would take it on herself to raise Brett, just as she'd raised her younger brother when her mom was too drunk to do so. It would be a lot for her to handle. Raising a four-year-old child would consume her life, but she would do it. It just didn't seem fair. She'd spent a lot of time taking care of other people. At some point, it needed to be her turn. And he found himself wanting to be the man who took care of her, who eased her burden. She might not want him to help her, but he would do just that.

The Motor Inn was five miles out of town on a remote highway that led toward the town of Great Falls, fifteen miles south. There wasn't much else on the highway beyond gas stations, fast-food restaurants, and cheap lodging. When he pulled into the parking lot, there was no sign of Trevor's old Chevy Impala.

He turned off the engine and got out of the car, making his way up the exterior stairs to the second floor. He rapped sharply on room ten.

A moment later, Trevor opened the door. He looked like shit. His long, dark hair was greasy. His T-shirt and jeans were filthy, and his body odor made Jake wince. He also didn't like Trevor's bloodshot eyes and pale skin. But there was a clarity to his gaze that he hadn't seen in a while.

"How are you doing?" he asked, as he stepped into the room. His gaze swept the furnishings. There was nothing much there beyond a bed, a dresser and a small table. While there were food wrappers on the table, there was no sign of alcohol or drugs. It was a much different scene than the one at the cabin.

"I'm surviving—barely," Trevor said, sinking down onto one of two hard chairs.

He perched on the edge of the other chair. "Why did you leave the cabin? Why come here?"

"The cabin reminded me of Michelle. We used to go there when we were happy. Being there without her made me really unhappy. I hit up the nearby liquor store after ten minutes. When I finally sobered up on Friday night, I decided to leave, and I came here. I figured this shithole wouldn't remind me of anything happy, and I was right."

"I'm glad you're okay. I've been texting you since Friday night. You had me worried, Trev."

"I know. I'm sorry, Jake. I was detoxing, and it was all I could do to breathe my way through it. But I made it. It's been almost forty-eight hours since I took a drink."

He hoped this was the new start Trevor needed. "That's good. But you don't have to do this alone. I told you I'd help you pay for rehab."

"I appreciate that, but I have to do this my way. I have to be able to manage my addictions in the real world. I went to rehab once before, and it didn't stick. As soon as I got out, I went right back to it. I don't know if this will work, either, but I had to try something different. I'm a mess, Jake."

"Actually, for the first time in a while, I feel like you're on the right path. And when you're ready to come back to work, you have a job. That job lasts as long as your sobriety does."

"I get it. I know I screwed up a few times the past couple of weeks."

"You did. Now you have to do better." He paused. "How did you get here? I didn't see your car in the lot. I'm hoping you didn't drive."

"I got a ride from a woman who was staying at one of the cabins near mine. She came by to ask if she could borrow my car. I told her I had to leave, so if she wanted to drive me, she could take the car after that."

He was surprised by Trevor's words. "A stranger asked to borrow your car and you said yes?"

"Well, I wasn't exactly sober at the time," Trevor admitted. "I needed to get out of the cabin, and I knew I couldn't drive."

"At least you knew that much. Where was her car?"

Trevor gave him a blank look. "Uh, I don't know. She said her car broke down. Her kid needed something for Christmas. I told her if she dropped me off here, she could take the car and then bring it back when she got her vehicle fixed."

"But she hasn't brought it back yet. And it's Sunday afternoon. Do you seriously think she will?"

"Maybe not. Why are you asking me so many questions?" Trevor asked, running a hand through his hair.

"Because the woman who gave you a ride disappeared and left her kid behind."

"What? No." Trevor shook his head in confusion. "She said she left her kid with her sister. He would be fine until she got back. She kept saying that, over and over."

"What else did she say?"

"I don't remember. It's all a blur."

"Try. It's important."

Trevor stared at him for a long minute. "She said she was a good person. People might not believe that, but she was. She seemed agitated and stressed out."

"Was she hurt? Did she have any physical injuries? Bruises, broken bones?"

"I don't think so, but she was pregnant." A light came on in his eyes. "I just remembered that. She kept touching her belly. She was mostly talking to herself, or maybe to the baby. She said it was going to be all right. She would keep her safe. She would do what she had to do to keep her kids safe."

"Did she say where she was going?"

"I don't think so."

It wasn't much, but it was something. At least they now knew what car Kelly was driving. "I don't suppose you know your license plate number?"

"Dude, I can barely remember my name right now."

"Okay. It's fine. I'm sure the police can figure it out. Why don't you come to my place for the night? I've got a couch and food in the refrigerator."

"No. I have to stay here another night."

"What about food? You don't have a car."

"There's a pizza place across the road. They deliver."

"You can't survive on just pizza. I'll go to the store and get you some groceries."

"Why do you care so much?" Trevor asked, a questioning note in his voice.

"You're one of my employees, and we're friends."

"You should have fired me weeks ago, and I don't think I'm much of a friend."

"You're going through a hard time. You just need to turn your life around."

"What if I can't?"

"You're already doing it," he said, meeting Trevor's uncertain gaze. "You've made mistakes. You just need to recover and do better."

"I'm going to try, but—"

"No buts. By getting sober, you're giving yourself a second chance, and I'm giving you one, too. Don't let me down."

Trevor nodded. "Okay."

He got to his feet. "I'll be back in thirty minutes."

"Thanks."

He headed out the door and jogged to his car. On the way to the store, he punched in Adam's number. If Adam could track Trevor's car, maybe they could find Kelly. It was the best lead they'd gotten so far, and it felt good to be doing something proactive. Hopefully, the information would pan out and Hannah would get some good news.

---

They'd just started pulling ingredients together for the cookies when Hannah heard the pitter-patter of little feet coming down the stairs. Apparently, Brett's nap today was not going to be a long one. She moved toward the kitchen door as Brett came running down the hall. He launched himself into her arms, and she gave him a hug.

"Did you have a good sleep?" she asked him.

He nodded, his gaze moving toward her mother, who was

standing frozen in the middle of the kitchen, a look of shock on her face.

"Who's that?" he asked.

"That's my mom. And she's also your mom's mom, which makes her your grandmother."

"Hi," he said, with his usual friendly smile. "I'm Brett."

Surprise flashed across her mother's face at his warm greeting. "Uh, hello." She paused, giving Hannah an awkward look. "I'm not sure what he should call me."

"How about Grandma?" She looked at Brett. "What do you think about that?"

"I never had a grandma before. My friend Albie has two."

She couldn't help wondering about his father's parents, but, apparently, they didn't exist—at least, not in Brett's world.

"Are you going to bake cookies with us, Grandma?" Brett asked.

Her mother sucked in a quick breath at the title Brett had so quickly accepted. "I am," she said.

"We're going to make sugar cookies," she told Brett.

"I was thinking about that," her mom said. "Why don't we be a bit more creative? Remember when we used to make sweater weather sugar cookies?"

Her mom's words took her way back in time. "Yes. The cookies all looked like Christmas sweaters."

"I want to make sweater cookies," Brett announced.

"We could also do white chocolate cherry shortbread cookies," her mother added. "Those were your favorites."

"I don't think I have the sweater mold or the ingredients for the other ones."

"We could do peanut butter, too," her mom said. She was either completely caught up in the cookies or trying to avoid thinking about the little boy who was calling her grandmother.

Hannah suspected it was partly the latter.

"I love peanut butter," Brett said, getting more excited by the minute.

"And bittersweet chocolate crackle cookies," her mom continued. "Those were Kelly's favorites."

"Kelly is my mom," Brett said.

Her mother looked pained at that reminder. "I know." Her gaze moved to Hannah's. "He looks like Tyler more than Kelly, but she's there in his eyes. I don't know if I can do this, Hannah."

"Of course you can. Because all we're going to do is make cookies. However, I think one of us needs to go to the store."

"I can do that."

"Okay. But, Mom, you need to come back." She was slightly terrified that her mom would go to the store, walk down the liquor aisle, and use alcohol to stop thinking about Kelly and Brett. "I can't make all those cookies without you. And Brett wants to do them with you, too."

Her mother slowly nodded. "I'll come back, Hannah."

She wanted to make her mother promise to return, but what was the point? There were too many broken promises between them already.

As her mother left the kitchen, she set Brett on his feet. "How about a snack while we wait for Grandma to come back?"

"Can I have a banana?"

"Absolutely." As she walked over to the kitchen island that was already littered with ingredients, she really hoped the baking bonanza would work out, for a lot of different reasons. Not only would she have the cookies she needed for the party, but her mom would get a chance to bond with Brett. Plus, it would be the first time she and her mom would attempt to recreate one of their favorite shared experiences. While she had always been impatient with the cooking portion of baking, she had loved hanging out with her mom while she baked. It would be fun to do it again, but she had a feeling that it wouldn't just be the chocolate that was bittersweet.

An hour later, Hannah's kitchen looked like a bakery with flour, sugar, vanilla, and eggs cluttering up her counter. The heat from the first batch of cookies made the room not only warm and cozy but also filled with the scent of chocolate and cinnamon. Hannah felt a wave of nostalgia. Watching her mom patiently help Brett cut out sweater cookies, she saw herself in the same scene a very long time ago. She could also see a young Kelly pouring sugar into a bowl and Tyler toddling around in a diaper with chocolate smeared across his mouth.

Her heart ached as the image now included her dad coming in to steal a spoonful of raw cookie dough. Like her, he'd been too impatient for the cookies to bake. Her mom would tell him it wasn't good for him. But he never listened, and their playful argument often ended with a kiss.

She didn't know much about their relationship beyond what she'd witnessed, but she'd always thought it was strong. Her dad had been the solid anchor to her mom's neurotic and impulsive tendencies. They'd balanced each other out. And in the years when they were a whole family, there had been a lot of fun, a lot of good times.

More stress had entered the family when Kelly had gotten into her middle teens. She had inherited more of her mom's reckless impulsiveness than her dad's steady, plodding personality. But even with the fighting between Kelly and their parents, there was always a strong undercurrent of love. Her dad had had a patience with Kelly that made the two of them very close but had put a distance between Kelly and her mom. And then he'd died, and the family had shattered.

Watching her mom with her grandson now made her feel like some of the old family love was coming back. Or maybe it would be a new love, a new start.

They could never be what they were, but scenes like this gave her hope for the future. She just wished Tyler and Kelly were here, too. Tyler would be home Tuesday. But Kelly...

*Would she ever come back? Or would she keep running for her life?*

She wished Kelly would reach out. Then she could find a way to help her. Although, if Kelly had killed a man, regardless of her motivation, helping her might not be possible. But she could still help Brett. She could still try to make this Christmas special for him.

"When is Tyler getting in?" her mom asked, interrupting her thoughts.

"Tuesday morning." She paused, suddenly realizing that the guestroom she had reserved for her brother was now being used by Brett. "I'll have to put a blow-up bed in my office."

"That should work."

"I think we should make a big deal out of Christmas morning," she added. "We need to make it special."

Her mom met her gaze. "That makes sense."

"But I'm going to need some decorations." She paused and spelled out the rest. "A t-r-e-e and some g-i-f-t-s."

"Oh, that's right. Maybe you should run out now and take care of some of that."

"I don't want to leave in the middle of all this."

"I have things under control. Let's be honest, I'm much better at baking than you are."

"I know, but Brett is here."

Her mom let out a sigh. "You don't think I can watch a four-year-old? I raised three kids."

That was her mom, the queen of denial and make-believe. "You're glossing over some not-so-great years," she couldn't help saying. "Like the Christmas you almost burned the house down."

"You burned the house down, Grandma?" Brett echoed.

Her mother sent her a pointed frown and then looked back at Brett. "I did not. Hannah is exaggerating."

"What does exaggerating mean?" Brett asked her mother, always curious about everything.

"Never mind. Just keep stirring. I'll be right back." Her mother marched out of the room, motioning for Hannah to follow her. "I can watch Brett," her mom said, a note of decisiveness in her voice that Hannah didn't hear that often.

"I just don't want to put any stress on you, Mom."

"Do you think I'm suddenly going to drink because you leave me alone with a four-year-old for an hour?"

"I don't know. You've been triggered by very small things in the past. Yesterday, you didn't even want to see Brett. You were afraid."

"I was," her mother admitted. "I was afraid that my heart would break when I saw him, that he would remind me so much of Kelly that I wouldn't be able to handle it," her mom admitted. "But I didn't drink last night. And I came back today because I knew I had to see my grandchild, and I had to try to help you." She drew in a breath and let it out. "I've been sober for almost four years, Hannah. Four years! When are you going to believe that I'm better?"

"It's not that easy. I've seen you fall too many times to count."

"I've never gone this long. I'm not saying I'm cured. I know that this is a disease that I will always have to deal with. But all we're talking about right now is an hour where you go get a tree and I bake cookies with my grandson. I'm not going to set anything on fire."

She had to let her mom off the hook on that particular concern. "I know that, Mom." After one last minute of silent debate, she said, "Okay. It would be helpful if you could watch Brett while I run out to the tree lot."

"Take your time. I don't have anything else going on today."

"All right." They walked back into the kitchen. Brett had stopped stirring the dough and was playing with the unused cookie cutters on the floor. "Brett," she said. "I'm going to run out and do an errand. Grandma will watch you. You're going to be very good, right?"

Brett nodded. "I will."

"I'll be back soon." She looked back at her mom. "Call me or text me for any reason—promise?"

"Yes."

She really hoped she wasn't making a mistake, but her mom could hopefully handle this, and she was only a phone call away.

With that reassurance in mind, she headed for the door. She only had a few days to turn her house into a Christmas wonderland for Brett, and she was going to take whatever time she could get to do that. She might not be able to bring Kelly home, but she could make sure one little boy had a happy Christmas.

# CHAPTER FOURTEEN

As Hannah wandered around the Christmas tree lot, she realized two things: one, most of the good trees were gone, and, two, she would not be able to fit the tree in the back of her small car. She did know someone who had a truck, but was she really going to bring Jake back into her life, when she was trying to get rid of him?

As if on cue, her phone rang, and Jake's number flashed across the screen. A hot tingle immediately ran through her body, but she tried not to think about that. "Hello?"

"Hey, where are you?" Jake asked. "I need to talk to you, but I'm in front of your house, and I don't see your car. I do, however, see your mom's car, which is why I haven't rung the bell."

"Sorry about earlier. She was a little harsh."

"She was protecting you. I respect that."

"Why do you need to talk to me?"

"I got some information from Trevor."

"What is it?"

"I'd rather tell you in person."

"Is it bad?"

"Where are you, Hannah?"

"I'm at Donny's Christmas Tree Lot," she said.

"I'll be there in five minutes. And it's not bad. I just want us to talk about it in person."

"Okay. I'll see you soon." While she was waiting for Jake to arrive, she made another pass through the selection of trees. She was curious as to what he'd learned, but it didn't sound that earth-shaking, so she focused on the trees.

She hadn't bought a Christmas tree in a long time, probably not since Tyler had hit his twenties. Before that, she'd tried to make Christmas special for him. But after that, they'd both been content to order a pizza and exchange one present, which was usually some kind of a joke.

Now things were different. Although, in some ways, the situation with Brett felt remarkably familiar. She was trying to make a happy Christmas for someone whose parent should have been the one to do it. But that wasn't Brett's fault, and she had a feeling he would like a big tree, something that would make his eyes light up. That's what she wanted to see—that spark of joy.

"Well, if it isn't one of the Starks. How are you, Hannah?" an older, gray-haired man asked.

"I'm doing well." She smiled at Donald Ralston, the owner of Donny's Christmas Trees. His family had a Christmas tree farm just outside of town, and she'd gone to school with his son, Andrew.

The Ralstons had been selling trees for decades, and there was a time when their lot had been right next door to her dad's hardware store. Donny and her father had been the best of friends during that period. Donny and his wife, Rose, had tried to support her mom after her dad's passing. Her mom hadn't made that easy, though, and after some embarrassing incident at one of Rose's birthday parties, their families had stopped getting together.

"I didn't think anyone in your family bought Christmas trees anymore," Donny said. "Or maybe you've been getting 'em from Ace's lot or chopping down your own at one of the farms outside of town."

"We just haven't been getting trees, but this year is different."

"Why is that?"

"My sister's son is staying with me. He's four, and he needs a tree that will light up his eyes with wonder and amazement."

"This one should do the trick. It's a seven-footer, good symmetry, and thick branches."

"It looks perfect," she agreed.

"I didn't realize your sister was back in town. When did that happen?" Donny asked.

"Actually, it's just her son right now."

His sharp eyes didn't miss a beat. "Well, that's good. Always nice to have little ones around at Christmas. How is your mother?"

"She's doing well."

"Happy to hear that."

"How's your family?"

"Rose is in charge of remodeling our kitchen, so she's keeping busy. Andrew is selling cars during the week and racing 'em on the weekends."

"He always liked fast cars."

"He did. Of course, Rose would like him to spend more time finding a wife and maybe producing some grandchildren, but he pays her no mind."

"I'm sure he'll find the right person when he's ready."

"What about you? You got someone special?"

"Right now, the only male I'm obsessed with is my four-year-old nephew."

"I wish your dad was alive to meet him."

"Me, too. Brett looks a lot like my father and also like Tyler. No red hair for him."

"That red is beautiful, and it's your fire," Donny said with a smile. "It gives you strength, and Lord knows you've needed it. I'm sorry we fell out of touch, Hannah. I let you and your siblings down. Rose and your mom got so angry with each other, and I was caught in the middle."

"You don't have to apologize, Donny. The only person at fault was my mother. She pushed everyone away. But she's sober now. It feels like she finally came out of the tunnel she went into after my dad died."

"I'm very happy to hear that. Now, what about this tree? Do you have some way to get it to your house? Otherwise, I can have Randy drop it off. However, he might not get it there until later tonight. He had to run a tree over to the west shore, to some fancy celebrity's house."

They'd been getting more and more celebrities staying at the large estates that had recently been built on the west shore, but they didn't seem to wander into town too often. "I should be able to get the tree home. Someone is coming to help me." She handed him her credit card. "Could you ring it up and then we'll figure it out?"

"Sounds good." As Donny ambled back to the cash register, she saw Jake drive into the parking lot, and she quickly moved in his direction.

He'd barely gotten out of the truck when she said, "What did you find out?"

He closed the door and gave her a reassuring smile. "It's not huge news, but it's something."

"Tell me."

"Kelly went to Trevor's cabin to ask if she could borrow his car. She said that hers had broken down. Trevor was drunk at the time, so he said yes, but on one condition—she had to drive him to the motel where he's staying now. Apparently, the cabin had too many memories of his ex-girlfriend, so he needed to move. Kelly agreed. She drove him to the motel Friday night, and he hasn't seen her or his car since then. He did say that on the drive, she kept murmuring to herself that her kid was going to be all right, that he was with her sister, and everything would be okay, like she was trying to give herself a pep talk."

"Did she look like she'd been hurt?"

"No, but he did confirm that she was pregnant. She also kept talking to the baby, saying everything would be all right, and she'd protect her."

She thought about Trevor's story. "It sounds like she was very stressed out. But where was her car? If it was broken down, why wasn't it in front of the cabin?"

"Because she hid it in the trees."

"How do you know that?"

"I called Adam to tell him what Trevor had said, and he told me that they'd just located Kelly's rental car about a mile from the cabin. It was in perfect working condition."

"Then she just needed to switch cars."

"That would be my guess and Adam's as well." He paused, his lips tightening. "They did find some drops of blood inside the vehicle."

Her stomach turned over at that piece of information.

"It might not have been her blood," he continued. "The police are running the DNA."

"If it turns out that the blood belonged to her boyfriend, that won't be good for Kelly," she said heavily.

*Had her sister really been able to stab a man to death?*

It didn't seem possible. On the other hand, if she was fighting for her life, for the lives of her son and her unborn baby, maybe there was no limit to what Kelly had been willing to do.

"Let's take it one step at a time," Jake said. "Now that we know Kelly drove to the motel in Trevor's car, the police will try to track her movement from there via traffic and security cameras."

"What if she switches cars again?"

"Then she'll have to leave Trevor's car somewhere and that will be another clue. But for now, we focus on what we know so far. She's not injured. She's not with anyone. And she has made sure her son is safe."

His determined optimism inspired her to think positively. "You're right. I need to concentrate on all that." She let out a breath. "Now I need a favor. I know—there's no end to the favors I need."

He smiled. "Considering where we're standing, I'm guessing you need help getting a tree back to your house."

"Good guess."

"What were you going to do?"

"Donny said he would deliver the tree, but maybe not until late tonight. I'd rather get it now."

"I assume your mother is watching Brett."

"Yes. And they're baking the cookies I need to take to the hospital party tomorrow."

"How did that all happen?" he asked curiously. "I thought she didn't even want to see Brett.

"She had second thoughts. Once she met Brett, he stole her heart with one smile. I was a little reluctant to leave them alone, but my mom has been sober for almost four years, and there's no alcohol in my house at the moment, so she should be okay, right?"

"I would think so."

"How is Trevor doing?" she asked.

"He's almost to the forty-eight-hour mark without a drink, so he's hanging in there. He thinks the worst is over."

"He's lying to himself."

"Maybe. But he seems determined to get clean."

"By himself? That rarely works."

"I said the same thing, but he tried rehab once and it didn't stick, so he thinks he needs to be able to stop in the real world."

"He has a point, but it can still be physically debilitating."

"I agree. But he has to do it his way. I got him some groceries. I'll check in on him again tonight."

"That's generous and very kind."

He shrugged. "He's not a bad kid. He's just emotional and having a rough time. It doesn't help that it's Christmas."

"What do you do for Christmas, Jake?" she asked as they headed toward the tent where hopefully Donny would have her tree waiting. "Do you spend the day with your family?"

"I'm leading a cross-country skiing group in the morning. I'll drop by for a drink before dinner. My parents usually have about twenty people over for dinner, so it's not just a family thing, which is fine by me. What about you?"

"The last couple of years, Tyler and I would make enormous

bowls of cereal in the morning. We mix three or four different kinds like we used to do when we were kids. We catch a movie in the afternoon and later in the evening we get pizza for dinner."

"You don't see your mother?"

"Not usually on Christmas. But this year is going to be different. It has to be more like a traditional Christmas—cookies for Santa, presents, stockings, a big breakfast, playing in the snow, and maybe a prime rib for dinner. I want Brett to have the kind of holiday I had when I was young, when my dad was alive."

"And your mom will be included?"

"I think so. We'll see how things go between now and then." She paused as they got to the tent.

Donny handed her back her credit card and then he and Jake took the tree out to Jake's truck.

When the tree was safely loaded, Jake said, "I'll meet you at your house."

"Thank you so much for this. I can pay you in cookies."

"That your mother made? I'm sure she would not want you to do that."

"Probably not, but she won't have a choice."

As Jake got into his truck, she walked back to her car and slid behind the wheel. On the way home, she called her mom.

"Everything is fine," her mother said. "We just took the last tray of cookies out of the oven, and Brett is decorating them. I also made spaghetti. It should be ready when you get back."

"That's great."

"Did you get the tree?"

"I did. But I needed help to get it back to the house. Don't freak out, Mom, but Jake is bringing the tree over. He's going to come inside. I'm probably going to give him some of your cookies."

Her mother's sigh was long and heavy. "Fine."

"I need you to be polite. He's doing me a favor."

"I just don't understand how you can give him another chance, but it's up to you."

"It is, and I'm not giving him another chance. I'm just..." Her voice trailed away as she realized she didn't know what she was doing with Jake. She just knew that she wanted to keep seeing him and talking to him. She wanted to kiss him again. She felt more like herself with him than she did with anyone else. "I'll see you soon," she said, ending the call before her mother could ask her any more questions she didn't know how to answer.

# CHAPTER FIFTEEN

JAKE PULLED the tree out of his truck, and with Hannah's help, they carried it into her house. While he was happy to assist Hannah, he wasn't looking forward to seeing her mother again. But he reminded himself that he wasn't a teenager anymore, and Katherine Stark was nowhere close to perfect, either. They'd both hurt Hannah. Maybe they could both find a way to make it up to her.

As they entered the house, he was overwhelmed with delicious smells of vanilla, chocolate, and cinnamon. "It smells like Christmas," he murmured as they set the tree in the corner of her living room.

"Now, we have to make it look like Christmas." She stepped back, her gaze sweeping the tree. "I think the size is right."

"You couldn't have gone any bigger, not if you have an angel to put on top."

Her gaze moved back to him. "We used to have an angel. I think it's still in one of the boxes in my garage."

Brett came running into the room, his eyes lighting up when he saw the tree.

"That's what I wanted, right there," Hannah muttered. "That look on that little face."

"You got it."

"It's so big," Brett said in amazement. "I never had a tree this big. Are we going to decorate it?"

"We are," Hannah assured him. "As soon as I pull out the decorations."

Jake stepped to the side as Hannah's mother entered the living room. She didn't glance in his direction, her gaze going straight to the tree.

"What do you think, Mom?" Hannah asked.

"It's very nice. Do you still have any of our decorations?"

"They're in the garage."

At Hannah's words, he saw guilt move through Katherine Stark's eyes. No doubt she'd missed more than a few Christmases and probably had no idea where many of her things had ended up.

"Well, good," Katherine said. "I've made spaghetti and salad for dinner. It's ready now. Perhaps we can decorate the tree after we eat."

"Thanks for making dinner, Mom."

"It was nothing." Katherine's gaze finally moved in his direction. "If you'd like to stay for dinner, Jake, there's plenty."

Her invitation almost knocked him off his feet. It was certainly a turnaround from the way she'd spoken to him earlier.

"Are you going to stay?" Brett asked eagerly.

He hesitated, his gaze seeking Hannah's.

"You're welcome to stay for dinner," Hannah said. "You did help me get the tree here. And as I recall, spaghetti is one of your favorite meals."

"It is," he admitted.

"Well, I'll just put the garlic bread in the oven," Katherine said. "Brett, why don't you come with me? We'll get your hands washed so you're ready to eat."

As they left the room, his gaze swung to her. "Are you sure this is all right?"

"I wouldn't have suggested you stay if it wasn't."

"I thought you'd be ready to see the back of me by now."

She met his gaze. "I would have thought the same thing. But you're kind of growing on me."

"Not like fungus, I hope," he joked.

She grinned. "You said it, not me."

He smiled back at her. "What did you say to your mom to get her to invite me to dinner?"

"Nothing."

She was lying. He could see that. "Well, whatever it was, I appreciate it."

"We'll see if you feel the same way after dinner," she said dryly.

---

The food was good. The conversation and atmosphere were tense, but dinner with Hannah and her mother wasn't as bad as Jake thought it might be, mostly because Brett talked constantly, asking questions about everything under the sun. Katherine was surprisingly patient with her grandson, which was not a trait he usually associated with Hannah's mother. *But then how well did he really know her?*

When they were in high school, Hannah had never wanted to hang out at her house. He only went there when she was stuck watching her little brother, and on those occasions her mom had not been home. Once or twice, he'd witnessed Katherine come stumbling into the house, but Hannah had always pushed him out the door when that was happening. He'd known there were problems, but he certainly hadn't realized how bad things were or how much Hannah had kept from him. Even now, he didn't think he knew most of it. Or that anyone really knew what had gone on in the house.

But tonight things were different, and maybe that was because of Brett, or perhaps it was because Katherine was now sober. Whatever the reason, he hoped it was a sign of better times to come.

As they finished their meal, Hannah got up to clear the plates and Brett ran off to play, leaving him and Katherine alone at the table. She looked directly at him for the very first time.

"How are your parents?" she asked politely.

"They're well."

"And your brother? Is he still free from cancer?"

"Yes. He's been in remission for eight years now."

"That's wonderful. I heard he's studying to be a doctor like your father."

"He is. He's almost done with medical school."

"And you—you're running a shop now?"

"It's more than a shop," Hannah cut in, as she came back to the table to grab the rest of the silverware. "Jake also runs guided adventure tours, and he volunteers with the search-and-rescue team."

"That sounds exciting," Katherine commented.

"It can be," he said evenly, extending her the same cool politeness she'd shown him. "What are you doing these days, Mrs. Stark?"

She bristled a bit at his question. "I work at Sonia's Flower Shop."

"My mom is very good with plants," Hannah interjected, as she loaded the dishwasher.

Apparently, she'd decided to mediate between them.

"It sounds like the perfect job then," he said.

"I enjoy doing it." She gave her daughter a pointed look. "And I can speak for myself." She turned back to him. "I don't know why Hannah is willing to give you a second chance, but don't blow it. Don't hurt her again."

"I won't," he promised.

"Mom, it's not on you to get Jake to make promises," Hannah said, coming back to the table. "Our relationship has nothing to do with you."

"So, there is a relationship?" Katherine queried.

Hannah sighed. "We're just friends, okay?"

Katherine gave Hannah a disbelieving look. "I didn't believe that the first time you told me that, and I don't believe it now. Jake always had a way of getting under your skin. I hate to see you going down that same road again."

"I know what I'm doing."

"All right." Katherine waved her hand in surrender and then got to her feet. "I should go. I promised I'd stop by Marty's on my way home, and I have to go to work early tomorrow. It's the last day we're open before the holiday, and there are a lot of plants and fresh flower arrangements on order for pickup."

"You don't want to help decorate the tree?" Hannah asked.

"You and Brett can handle that. And, frankly, I'm not sure I'm up to seeing the old ornaments. There are so many memories attached to them."

"I don't know what I still have."

"I think you have the important ones. You were always very worried about them getting broken or lost. You boxed them up and took them with you to Denver when you went to college, when you had Tyler with you." Katherine bit down on her lip, emotion filling her eyes. "Your dad used to make an ornament for you, Tyler and Kelly every year in his woodshop. I'm sure Brett will love them."

Jake watched their conversation with fascination. There was so much emotional subtext under every word.

"Thanks for making all the cookies and entertaining Brett so I could get a tree," Hannah said.

"No problem. I'll check in with you tomorrow." Katherine paused. "You'll let me know if you hear from Kelly?"

"Absolutely."

"Thank you." She turned to him. "Good night, Jake."

He stood up. "I'll see you to your car."

Both Katherine and Hannah looked surprised by his words, but neither one argued, so he followed Katherine down the hall and out of the house. He walked her all the way to her vehicle.

She opened the door and then looked at him. "Why?" she asked.

"Why did I walk you to the car?"

"Why did you hurt Hannah? I thought you were in love with her."

His gut twisted at the question. "It wasn't intentional. I was going through a bad time, and I made a lot of mistakes in one night."

"I know about mistakes, and I'm sure you find it ironic that I would have the nerve to judge you when I've probably done worse things."

"I understand that you want to protect your daughter. I actually respect that."

"I didn't always protect her. I didn't take care of her the way I should have. But I'm trying to be a better person now." She took a breath. "I guess it annoys me that she's willing to give you a second chance but not me."

"Isn't she giving you a second chance?" he countered. "We just had dinner together. It seems like you and Hannah are getting along."

"Because of Brett."

"Whatever the reason, it's a start."

"I hope so. You don't just want to be Hannah's friend, do you?"

"No, I want to be more," he admitted.

"You're going to have to earn it. My daughter doesn't forgive easily."

"I know that. I'm willing to do whatever it takes."

"I used to think you were good for Hannah—until you weren't."

"I used to think the same thing about you," he returned.

Katherine drew in a quick breath as his comment hit home, and he kicked himself for probably going too far, but then she surprised him.

"Fair point," she said. "Let's both try to do better where Hannah is concerned."

"Sounds good to me."

"Good night, Jake." Katherine slid into her car and closed the door.

He stepped back as she drove away, relieved to have the conversation end on a positive note. He didn't want to be another obstacle between mother and daughter. Hopefully, Katherine wouldn't put him in that position.

When he returned to the house, he went into the kitchen and saw the door leading to the garage open. As he entered the garage, he saw Hannah wrestling to get a big box off a shelf while Brett was already looking through another box on the ground.

He was almost to Hannah when he saw the box about to tumble down on top of her head. He grabbed it in the split second before it took her down.

"Thanks," she said with a breathless smile. "I thought I could manage it myself."

"You always think that," he said with a grin. "You hate asking for help."

"I do. But you keep showing up in the nick of time."

They were so close, he could feel her breath on his face, and he wanted to do nothing more than to steal a kiss from her sweet lips, but there was a little boy now edging between them, eager to see what was in the box they'd just taken down.

Hannah shrugged, amusement in her eyes. "I have a little chaperone."

"He has to go to bed sometime."

She flushed at that comment. "Let's just concentrate on decorating the tree. And since you want me to ask for help, why don't you bring this box into the living room, and I'll bring the smaller one?"

"Done."

When they got back to the living room, Hannah put on Christmas music while he untangled the lights and Brett started pulling things out of the boxes, exclaiming with giddy delight at every new ornament that he unwrapped. And there were a lot of them. Hannah's father had been a very talented craftsman and the ornaments were beautifully carved. Hannah got emotional as she went through the ornaments, too, but she managed to keep it together. He knew she was doing that for Brett. She didn't want to mar his happiness with sadness from the past.

Once he had the lights organized, he wound them around the tree, thinking that he couldn't remember when he'd last decorated a Christmas tree. He didn't think he'd done it since he was in high school, and that was a very long time ago. "Is that enough?" he asked Hannah.

"I think so."

"Well, you can decide after I turn them on."

"Actually," she said, putting up a hand as he reached for the switch. "We can't turn on the lights until we decorate the tree."

"Is that a rule?"

"Yes."

"Okay, you're in charge. What's next?"

"Brett can start putting ornaments on the tree. We might need you for the upper part of the tree. Unless you'd like to be done?"

"No, I want to see this thing through to the end."

He stepped to the side as Brett started putting up decorations. "Those are very cool ornaments. Your dad made most of them, didn't he?"

"Yes. He loved his woodshop. He was extremely talented." She took a carved train out of a box. "This one was for me. I loved trains when I was little. When I was nine, my dad took me on a train trip from Colorado to Pennsylvania to visit my grandparents. I was in heaven. We even got to sleep on the train. I thought it was the most exciting trip I'd ever taken. The next Christmas, he made me this ornament."

She ran her fingers around the edge and then she looked up at him. "He's been gone forever," she continued. "But there are days when I still miss him so much. It feels like it was yesterday that he was here, that he was decorating the tree with us. My mom never did it. She was always baking something while we were decorating. When it was done, we'd turn on the lights and eat whatever delicious cookies she'd made." Her voice trailed away as she let out a breath. "I wasn't really expecting to take this trip down memory lane tonight."

"Why didn't your siblings go with you to Pennsylvania?" he asked, wanting to distract her from the sad part of her memories.

"Tyler was only four. He wouldn't have been able to sit still that long. Kelly was fourteen and into her teenage years. She didn't want to leave her friends to visit the old people, as she used to call my grandparents. But I wanted to go, so my dad took me while my mom stayed home with Kelly and Tyler. It was a great trip."

"It sounds like it. I wish I'd gotten to know your dad better."

"He was a wonderful man and a fantastic father. He always made sure to spend time with each of us. With me, it was ice-skating. He was the one who first taught me how to skate and then drove me to practices and competitions. With Kelly, it was all about horseback riding. That was their thing to do together, and with Tyler it was baseball." She smiled. "Sometimes, I wonder how he had time to work."

"He made time for his family," he said shortly, wishing his father had been half the man Hannah's father had been.

"He did," Hannah agreed. "And he'd always tell me that as the middle child, I was the most special, which was a complete lie, but I appreciated the effort. It wasn't always easy to stand out in a line-up of three kids. Kelly had a big personality and Tyler was the cute baby."

He sat down on the couch, propping his legs up on the coffee table. "I think you always stood out, Hannah."

"Probably not in a good way," she said with a self-deprecating smile.

"Well, that's what made you interesting. You were never entirely predictable. And you always had a lot of ideas, especially when it came to revenge."

She grimaced. "I don't think I want to be reminded."

"Remember your old neighbor, Mr. Fordham? You got mad at him because your ball went over the fence, and he wouldn't give it back. He said he'd told you a dozen times not to kick your ball into his yard."

"He was a grumpy, old man, and I think you were the one to kick the ball over the fence," she retorted.

"I was responsible for the ball, but you were the one who painted happy faces all over his stone patio."

"It washed right off, and I thought he should think about smiling more." she said defensively. "But I got grounded for a week."

"Because you didn't realize he had a security camera in his backyard."

"That was a mistake," she conceded. "However, I'm fairly sure I told you my idea beforehand and you loved it."

"I loved you," he said, the words spilling out of his mouth before he could stop them.

She jerked, surprise and wariness filling her pretty brown gaze. "Don't—don't say things like that."

"It's the truth. I didn't actually mean to say it, but it's not a lie. You were the first girl I loved."

"But not the last," she said sharply.

He actually wanted her to be the last, but she was already rattled by what he'd just said. "Who knows who'll be the last?" he murmured.

She stared back at him. "You don't have to hang out. Brett and I can finish the tree together."

"No way. I want to see the end results. My lights are on there. I'm part of it."

"Fine. You can stay, but no more talk of the past."

"Deal. How do you feel about tinsel?"

"What?"

"Tinsel or garlands? It's usually one or the other, but I don't see either in your boxes."

"We never used tinsel or garlands. We had a dog when I was little—Tiger. He would either eat the tinsel or pull the garlands down, so we just stopped putting them on. It was all about the ornaments."

"Is Tiger in heaven?" Brett asked.

"He is," Hannah admitted.

"Stormy is in heaven, too." Brett said. "He's with my dad. Mommy says they can still see us. Daddy knows when I'm being good. He's proud of me."

Hannah gave her nephew a sweet, tender smile. "I'm sure he's always proud of you, honey."

"He liked me a lot," Brett added. His expression shifted. "Russ liked me a lot, too."

Hannah stiffened, shooting him a quick look.

He was as surprised by Brett's comment as she was. From what they'd learned about Kelly's boyfriend, Russ, it didn't seem like he was a good guy or a man who would like children.

"He said he'd always protect me and Mommy," Brett continued. "We didn't have to be afraid. He would take care of us."

"Do you know where Russ is?" Hannah asked carefully.

"He's camping. He's going to catch a big fish. Mommy said he had to stay and wait for the fish to come. I wanted to wait with him, but she said we couldn't." He paused. "Can we turn the lights on now?"

"We're just about there," Hannah said. "We need to put some ornaments on the top of the tree first."

Jake jumped to his feet. "That's my cue." For the next few minutes, he filled out the tip-top of the tree while Hannah worked on the middle, and Brett gave them suggestions on where to put the ornaments. They ended their decorating when he placed a beautiful angel on top of the highest branch. "Now we're done," he said. "Hannah, do you want to do the honors?"

"They're your lights. Go for it. But wait—let me turn off the lights in the room."

As Hannah darkened the room, he hit the switch and the tree lit up. Brett's expression of amazement made Jake's heart flip over in his chest. They'd created a magical moment for this little boy, and in light of everything going on in his life, that was a very good thing.

"Is Santa coming tonight?" Brett asked.

Hannah shook her head. "He won't be here for two more days."

"I hope Santa brings me my present."

"Do you want to tell me what you asked him for?" Hannah asked.

Brett shook his head. "It's a secret."

"Sometimes Santa needs a little help with shopping, so maybe you could whisper it to me," she said.

He thought about that suggestion. And then he motioned for her to lean over.

His whisper was so loud that Jake could hear it across the room.

"I want my mommy to come back," Brett said.

Hannah put her arms around Brett. "So do I."

"Will Santa bring her back?"

"I think he'll do everything he can to make that happen," Hannah said. "But right now, it's time for you to go to bed."

"Can Jake tell me a story?" Brett asked, looking in his direction.

"Sure, I can do that," he said.

Brett clapped his hands with delight.

"Let's get you in your PJs," Hannah said.

He followed them up the stairs, thinking this was how it would feel if he and Hannah were married, if they had a kid, if this was their Christmas as a family. The thought shook him to the core. This wasn't the kind of life he led. He was an adventurer, an explorer, a guy who liked to live on the edge and push himself to the limit. But he had to admit that he'd had more fun tonight than he'd had in a long time. And it wasn't over yet.

# CHAPTER SIXTEEN

HANNAH LISTENED to Jake's story of ships and pirates from the hallway, impressed with the animated impressions he put into his tale. He really brought the story to life. And Brett was loving every word of it.

As Jake finished, Brett said, "Tell me another one."

"Sorry, kid, you have to go to sleep now."

"What are we going to do tomorrow?"

"I'm sure Hannah has a lot of fun things planned for you."

"I like Hannah, but I want my mommy."

"I know you do."

"Do you have a mommy?"

"I do."

"And a daddy, too?"

"Yes," Jake said, tension immediately entering his voice.

"You're lucky," Brett said. "I think Russ might want to be my daddy."

"Would that be good?" Jake asked.

"He can throw a baseball really far."

"Well, that's a good skill to have."

She felt incredibly emotional as she listened to their conversation. And once again, she was confused by Brett's affection for

Russ. She was also worried about what would happen, how hurt he would be, when he found out Russ was not going to be part of the family.

She headed downstairs, letting Jake finish up with Brett. He was really good with the little boy. She could trust him not to say anything that would hurt him. When she got back to the living room, she thought about turning on the lights in the room, but the tree was so pretty, she couldn't bring herself to do it. She needed a little Christmas magic, too.

She sat down on the couch and stretched her legs out on the coffee table. It had been a crazy busy day. In fact, she felt like she'd been on a dead run since Friday, since Kelly had disappeared.

She looked up as Jake made his way into the room. He flopped down on the couch next to her.

"Kids are exhausting," he said.

She gave him a smile. "It is amazing how much energy one little boy has and how much he needs the same energy from everyone around him. But it's not just Brett who has exhausted me. I can't stop thinking about Kelly and what Brett said about Russ."

"He told me that he wants Russ to be his dad. He definitely liked the guy."

"And he said Russ would protect them. But from who? Himself? That doesn't make sense."

"Who knows what Brett really understands? He could have been confused or he's not remembering it right. He's a friendly little kid who likes everyone and believes everyone likes him. Look how quickly he's settled in with us and made friends with our friends. And he and your mother hit it off right away. They're best buddies now."

"You have a point. I can't put much weight in anything Brett tells us. It's just frustrating not to know what's really going on. A man is dead, and my sister is out there somewhere, but I don't know where or what condition she is in."

"I wish I could make it better, Hannah."

She saw the sincerity in his eyes. "I wish you could, too. But we just have to wait—my least favorite thing to do." She let out a sigh, her gaze moving to the Christmas tree. "I have to admit that this beautifully lit tree is making me feel better."

"The magic is working."

"I wanted to do it for Brett, but it turns out I'm getting just as much out of it. Do you have a tree?"

"No," he said with a little laugh. "I have no holiday decorations. But we have some in the store. Does that count?"

"Maybe a little. I heard you live above your store. What's that like?"

"It's a one-bedroom apartment with a great view of the mountains. It's perfect for me. I'm close to my business, which takes up a lot of my life."

"It's great that you found a way to make money doing what you love. And you got to see the world, too. I don't remember you having so much wanderlust in your soul when we were in high school. Back then, it was all about sports, getting a college scholarship, and going pro."

"Like a lot of high school athletes, my dreams were bigger than my talent."

"You were pretty talented."

"Is that a compliment?"

She made a face at him. "They retired your number at the school, Jake. We both know you were a star athlete."

"Well, it's not like Whisper Lake is a hotbed of athletic talent but thank you."

"When did you start wanting to travel?"

"College. I didn't know what I wanted to do for a major, so I started out in archaeology."

She was surprised by his answer. She turned sideways on the couch, pulling her legs up under her so she could see him better. "Seriously? I would not have guessed that."

"I liked the idea of digging for treasure. And that's on you."

"How so?"

"You gave me that book to read—*The Lost City of Valmoor*. The hero was an archaeologist, and he stumbled onto an underground city that had been buried after a tsunami."

A smile spread across her face. "I loved that story."

"Yes. You talked about it nonstop, and you made me read the book. It was actually the first piece of fiction I had read since I was about eight years old that wasn't assigned by a teacher. And then I had to read the second book by that author, and the third and the fourth."

"You kept reading after we stopped talking about books?" She was a little surprised by that. She'd thought Jake was just humoring her by agreeing to read some of her favorites.

"Yes. I found I enjoyed the escape. What I didn't enjoy were the actual classes in archaeology that one had to take in order to have those adventures."

"Real life is not always like the books."

"Definitely not. I switched to business my junior year, but those archaeology classes left me with a desire to see more of the world. I studied abroad the summer between junior and senior year, and after I graduated, I hit the road. I stayed in hostels, in campgrounds, and on couches. I met a lot of incredible people."

She felt a wistful sense of yearning that she hadn't been a part of those adventures. "It sounds amazing, Jake. You were lucky to have that freedom."

"It wasn't just luck, Hannah. I worked a lot of jobs during college to save enough money to travel. While my parents were generous and paid for my education, I knew that anything beyond that was on me. Whatever I was going to do, I had to do my way."

"You had your own vision," she murmured, thinking Jake had always been an independent thinker and someone who wanted to do more than anyone else, be better than average. He hadn't cared about school, about grades, the way she had; his dreams had always been bigger than that.

"You had a clear vision, too. You always wanted to be in medicine. Is nursing what you thought it would be? Do you ever wish you'd become a doctor like you originally planned?"

"Not anymore. Medical school was going to be too big of an ask for me. I didn't have the money. Plus, I had Tyler and my mom to worry about. Nursing was going to be faster and get me working more quickly. In the beginning, I felt some resentment, mostly toward my mom, but what else is new? I also didn't like it when the doctors ordered me around. But toward the end of my first year of nursing, I found a mentor, and she really showed me that I was focusing on the wrong things. She helped me see that what I was doing was really important. I'm with the patient far more than the doctor is. I'm holding their hand. I'm talking to them and to their families. I am a big part of their healing journey, and I'm the bridge between them and everything else in the healthcare system. Because I'm in the room, I can see small changes that might be missed. I can make a difference in whether someone recovers, or they don't. And it changed my whole way of thinking."

He gave her a smile. "I can hear the passion in your voice."

"I love what I do. And I have to admit that I love doing it in Whisper Lake. I wasn't sure I would when I came back, but it was a good decision. Because it's a small town, I get to be more involved in the diagnostics than I was before."

"No regrets then?"

She shook her head. "Nope. What about you? Are you sure Whisper Lake won't be too quiet for such a world traveler?"

"I'll still travel but I don't need to wander the way I used to."

"Why not?"

"Because I don't feel the need to run anymore."

"That's a curious statement. Why did you feel the need to run?"

His gaze met hers. "A lot of reasons."

"That answer is way too vague, Jake."

He shrugged. "I'm not the best at self-analysis."

"Give it a shot."

He thought for a moment. "I hated what I did to you. It haunted me. And it was easier not to think about it when I was far away. I also liked having space from my father. Roaming the world, I could pretend he didn't exist."

"That's kind of sad."

"It wasn't sad; it was the right thing to do. I had to find myself, and I needed to do that completely on my own."

There was an honesty in his answer that resonated deep within her. She felt like this was the Jake she'd fallen in love with, the one she could talk to for hours on end about anything. They'd had an emotional bond that had been just as powerful as the physical attraction. And it was all coming back to her now. That probably wasn't a good thing, but it felt good—at least for the moment.

"It sounds like you did that," she said. "You figured out who you were and what you wanted."

"Yes, but I'm still a work in progress."

"Aren't we all?"

As they shared a smile, she felt butterflies in her stomach, and a deep desire to reconnect with this man who had taken her heart so many years ago. She'd never really gotten it back, not all of it anyway. But as the air between them charged with tension, with expectation, she also felt uncertainty.

"I can't remember who has the ball," she whispered.

His gaze darkened. "Whoever wants it. Do you want it, Hannah?"

That was a trick question. "I don't want to want it," she confessed. "I'd rather not feel anything. I'd rather there be icicles between us."

"Too much heat for that. You've always gone after what you want."

"So have you, Jake. Why aren't you doing that now?"

"I don't want to risk pushing you too hard too fast."

"Risk what?"

"Us."

She drew in a breath at the one simple and yet so complicated word. "There's no us."

"There wasn't for a long time, but that could change. I want it to change."

She ran a hand through her hair, conflict running through her mind. "I don't know what to do. Three days ago, I couldn't stand you. Now I want to make out with you."

A grin curved his sexy mouth. "Then let's stop talking and do that."

"It's not smart."

"Blame it on the mistletoe." He put his hand behind her neck and gently pulled her forward.

"There's no mistletoe."

"In my mind, it's right over our heads. There's nothing to do but kiss…" He leaned in, and her stomach clenched with desire.

It seemed to take forever for his mouth to find hers, but then it was an instant explosion of heat. Jake had always been a good kisser. Even when they were young and fumbling through their first sexual experience, the way he kissed had set her body on fire. It was no different now. Actually, it was different; it was better.

Jake's kiss went from exploring and sensual to hard and demanding, and she liked feeling his impatient need for her. She opened her mouth, taking him in, their tongues tangling in a desperate need to get closer.

She ran her hands up under his sweater, loving the feel of those hard muscles against her fingers. She wanted to see him. She wanted to touch and taste him in every possible way. She wanted to go back to where they'd once been. She wanted to feel that impossibly close connection.

But all those needs made her feel like she was on a runaway train, with an inevitable crash coming up around the next bend.

A voice inside her head screamed caution. This was Jake, a man who could turn her on like no other. But this was also Jake, the man who had shattered her heart.

*How could she trust him not to do it again?*

She finally found the strength to push him away, to slide down the couch and put space between them, to catch her breath and try to think. But it wasn't easy with the blood rushing through her veins and an aching desire in her body.

Jake gazed back at her with glittering lights of gold in his brown eyes, his breath coming hard and fast. But he didn't say anything, and she couldn't find any words.

The silence stretched out between them like a taut wire. She had to break it. "You should go home, Jake."

"I pushed too hard."

"No, you didn't." She couldn't put it on him. He had a lot of blame to carry in their story, but this time was on her. "I wanted you to kiss me. I still do."

"Then why did we stop?"

"Because it's too fast. I still want you, but I don't know what comes after the wanting, and that scares me."

"Then we'll slow it down."

"I don't know what *it* is, Jake. I don't know what you want from me, and more importantly, I don't know what I want from you."

"I can answer the first question. I want you back," he said bluntly.

Her heart skipped a beat. "We had our chance. You could have had me before, and you walked away."

"I was seventeen. I wish you could trust me again."

"I wish I could, too, but I don't know how to get there. It would probably take a miracle."

"Well, it is the season for miracles." He got to his feet. "I'll go, Hannah, but I'm not giving up."

"You should. I'm not big on second chances. My mother could tell you that."

"She already did. But some people, some relationships, are worth fighting for."

She stood up. "I'm not convinced of that. I think some relationships have their season, and that's it. They expire. They're done. You can't recreate them."

"Well, I disagree, and I like challenges."

"Is that what this is about? A challenge to get me back just to prove you can?"

"No. It's about you and me, how good we once were, and how good we could be again. I don't just want to have sex with you, Hannah, although I do want that."

Her cheeks filled with heat at his direct statement.

"But I want a lot more," he said. "I want the girl who laughed with me, who challenged me to read books and look at the world in a different way. I want the girl I could talk to all night long, the one I could say anything to, and she could say anything to me. I want the connection we had. The one where everything felt exactly right. I've never felt that with anyone else."

Her body sang at words that were both beautiful and terrifying. She'd never felt that with anyone else, either.

"I want your heart," he said.

"You already broke it," she whispered.

"Give me a chance to put it back together. Just a chance, Hannah. Let's start with that."

She honestly didn't know what to say.

"Just think about it," he said, and then he left.

As she heard the front door close, she let out a breath, feeling a wild range of emotions.

*Was he worth a second chance? Did she have enough courage to give him one?*

# CHAPTER SEVENTEEN

HANNAH WOKE up Monday morning feeling like she'd been through a mental and emotional war. She'd slept very little, reliving every moment with Jake, every word that they'd spoken. It had pissed her off that she was losing sleep to him for the second time in her life. But as much as she wanted to hang on to that anger, she couldn't do it anymore. She'd gotten to know Jake again, and she liked him even more than she had the first time. She still didn't know if she could give him another chance, but she would have to see how things played out. While she wasn't ready to say yes, she also wasn't ready to say no.

After getting Brett breakfast, she took him out to play in the snow, which they both enjoyed. Then he helped her wrap presents for the hospital party. She tried talking to him a little about Kelly, but he was all over the place in his answers. One thing held true— he adored his mother. According to Brett, Kelly made the best pancakes, she told the best jokes, she gave the best hugs, and she told the best stories. There was no denying that whatever else Kelly might be, she was a good mother.

Her own mother showed up around three, while Brett was napping.

"You look tired," her mom said, as she came through the door. "Has something happened?"

"Aside from entertaining a four-year-old all day? No."

Her mother smiled. "Just think—I had three kids to entertain. How about some coffee? I think we could both use a cup."

"All right," she said, as they moved into the kitchen. "How was your day?"

"Busy. I got in at seven this morning to help get all the Christmas centerpieces out on time. But now I'm off until next weekend. What about your work schedule?"

"Luckily, I have the week off, barring any unforeseen major disasters. I'm supposed to go back to work Friday. Hopefully, Kelly will be back by then," she added, as she started the coffee maker.

"Hopefully," her mom echoed. "Is there any news?"

She sat down at the table across from her mom. "Kelly borrowed a car and the police are now looking for that vehicle."

"Borrowed?" her mom queried. "Is that a polite word for stole?"

"Maybe. I don't know exactly what's going on."

"But you know more than you've told me."

"Yes."

Her mother's sharp gaze met hers. "Are you afraid to tell me?"

"I am. I don't want to trigger you."

Her mom didn't say anything right away, as if she was debating how much she wanted to know. "I can handle it, Hannah. I've had some time to get used to the idea that Kelly is probably in trouble. But I need to know how much."

She had to start trusting in her mom's ability to handle herself. "Okay. Here's what I know about Kelly. She was married to Brett's father, who was in the military, but he died in action when Brett was a baby. Kelly lived in various cities after that, most recently Colorado Springs. She was dating someone named Russ Miller there. They disappeared from their jobs and from the city about three weeks ago. They checked into a campground outside of Denver last week. Two days later..." She drew in a breath.

Her mother's jaw tightened. "Just say it."

"Russ Miller was found dead. He'd been stabbed."

"Oh, my God!" Her mother put a hand to her heart. "I wasn't expecting you to say that. What about Kelly?"

"All I know is that her boyfriend was killed on Wednesday and Kelly showed up at the cabin on Friday. Now, she's missing. Oh, and she's also pregnant."

Her mother let out a breath. "Well, that's a lot of information to get in a couple of sentences."

"I wish I could put context around the facts, but I don't have any, Mom. There's some thought that Kelly was in an abusive situation with her boyfriend. She told a friend she was having trouble with a guy. Now a man is dead."

"Are you saying that Kelly...killed him?" she asked in confusion.

"I don't know—maybe."

"This is worse than I imagined."

"And maybe not even true. Like I said, it's all speculation. Brett told me last night that this Russ Miller was a good guy. He liked him."

"Brett has a big imagination. I'm not sure you can trust what he says."

"I agree. We need to find Kelly. She's the only one with answers. But as the days pass, I worry she's not coming back, and that will destroy Brett. He told me he asked Santa to bring his mom back."

"She'll come back; she has to. That little boy needs her."

"He does. And it's clear that he loves Kelly. He talked about her all day long."

"He talked about her to me, too, when we were baking yesterday. It was a little hard to hear."

"It was," she agreed. "I stopped wondering what Kelly was doing a long time ago. Now, I feel guilty that I didn't know she was married or that she was widowed or that she was raising a kid on her own."

"That was her choice."

"Yes, but as we both know, people can make bad choices. She

was young when she left, and she was in pain from Dad's death, from the blame she was getting."

"And you blame me for that."

"I blame both of you. I know that it was just an accident. And like you, I was angry that Kelly was the reason Dad went out that night. But that wasn't fair to her. And Dad would have hated that we blamed Kelly. He adored her."

"He did. Your father would be so angry and disappointed in how I fell apart after his death. I just couldn't handle my pain. Every time I heard his voice in my head, I would drink, because I couldn't stand to think how I'd let him down, how I let all of you down."

There was a clarity and a self-awareness in her mother's voice that she hadn't heard in a very long time. "I know you're sorry, Mom. I'm glad you're better now. I hope you continue working hard to stay that way."

"I will, Hannah. I don't ever want to be that person again. And when Kelly comes back, I'm going to apologize to her. I'm going to tell her that it wasn't her fault. I want us to be a family again. Having Brett around, reliving our traditions, has brought everything back. We were a good family once. I think we could be again."

She felt a sense of déjà vu. Her mother wanted a second chance. Jake wanted a second chance. *What did she want?*

"In the meantime, what else can I do for you?" her mother asked, changing the subject.

"Want to help me pack up the cookies for the hospital party?"

"Of course. I'd like to go with you to the party, if you're okay with that? Or will you be going with Jake?"

"No," she said quickly. "I'll be going with Brett."

"But Jake will be there."

"I doubt it. He's not close to his father, and it's his dad's party."

Her mother smiled. "But you'll be there, and he wants you back."

"I just don't know if I can let him back into my life."

"Oh, Hannah, he's already there," her mom said with a

knowing smile. "I saw it last night. I didn't want to see it, but I did. There's still something between you, and maybe you need to find out what it is."

"Why would you encourage that? You don't like him."

"I liked him before he hurt you. Maybe he's changed. But one thing is certain, I've never seen you look at anyone else the way you look at Jake."

"You haven't really been around to see me look at anyone else," she said.

"Am I wrong, Hannah? Is there some great love of your life who I don't know about?"

She really wished she could say there was. "I've had other men in my life who I cared about," she hedged.

"But no one who stuck."

"That's part of the problem, Mom. How do I know Jake would stick when he didn't before? And his life—is it really here in Whisper Lake? He's an adventurer. He's traveled the world. He's back now, but for how long? Could he really be content here?"

"I can't answer any of those questions. But I can say that there's never a guarantee you won't get hurt. You have to decide if love is worth the risk."

"But wouldn't it be smarter to love someone who hasn't already hurt me once?"

"Probably. But since when does love make us smarter?"

# CHAPTER EIGHTEEN

JAKE HADN'T BEEN in the new medical center since he'd come back to Whisper Lake, and he had to admit that it was impressive. With his father as chief of staff and his mother in charge of hospital fundraising, the facility had been remodeled and modernized with the latest technology. While he had many reasons to dislike his dad, he couldn't deny that the man was a brilliant doctor and good at his job. He'd just been a terrible father. Maybe not to his brother, Paul, but definitely to him.

His mother and brother had encouraged them to talk to each other, but they'd both managed to avoid that. He didn't want to hear what his father had to say, and he suspected his father felt exactly the same way. Which made him wonder again why he'd decided to come to a party where his father was the host, the center of attention, the leader of all men in the room.

There was only one answer—Hannah.

She'd be here. And since he hadn't been able to stop thinking about her all day, he had to be here, too.

He made his way up to the fourth-floor cafeteria, which had been beautifully decorated with holiday wreaths, a large Christmas tree, and buffet tables filled with food. An older man was playing holiday carols on the piano and there were at least thirty to forty people milling about. Some were in hospital uniforms, but most were in holiday clothes. There were also some kids in wheelchairs being entertained by a puppet show, with their parents and siblings sharing in the experience.

His gaze swept the room, settling on his mother and father. He shared similar features with his dad, Davis McKenna. They were both over six feet tall with brown hair and eyes, while his mother was a short, curvy blonde with light-blue eyes. His parents were laughing with their friends, Dr. Richard Peters and his wife, Cynthia. The Peters were also neighbors and would be attending his parents' Christmas dinner.

"Has hell frozen over?" a voice asked.

He turned around to see a look of amazement in his brother's eyes. "It might have," he admitted.

"I did not expect to see you here, Jake."

"It's been a while since I attended one of these." The hospital Christmas party had been part of his childhood. The tradition had actually been started by his grandfather, who had also been a doctor in Whisper Lake, before he and his grandmother had moved to a warmer climate. "Looks like you'll one day be carrying on this family tradition, Paul."

"One day," Paul murmured.

"Are you sure you don't want to work somewhere else for a few years? Get some big-city experience?"

"I'm considering all my options."

"I'll bet Dad is pressuring you to come here."

"More Mom than Dad," Paul replied. "Now that you're back, she'd like to have the whole family together again."

"You should make the right decision for yourself, not for Mom or for Dad."

Paul smiled. "I will. I'm not a kid anymore, Jake. I can see the benefit of getting broader experience before I come back here, but eventually I would like to settle in Whisper Lake. I got great care from this hospital, and I want to make sure that level of care continues for everyone who lives in this community."

He could hear the passion in his brother's voice and knew that

Paul's career path came more out of his personal experience than just a desire to follow in his father's footsteps. Paul knew firsthand the healing power of medicine. And with his sharp mind as well as his kind, unselfish nature, Paul was going to make a great physician. "That makes sense," he said. "I would love to have you back here, but I just want what's best for you."

"I want the same for you, big brother. So, why are you really here? Does it have anything to do with one very pretty but stubborn redheaded nurse?"

"You think you know me so well."

"I do know you that well," Paul said with a laugh. "And Hannah just arrived with her mom and a little kid. We walked in at the same time."

His body tightened at that information, and he couldn't stop himself from looking around the room. When he saw her putting cookies on the buffet table, excitement rushed through his veins. She looked beautiful and holiday appropriate in tight black jeans and a bright-red sweater.

"You have it bad," Paul commented, his gaze not missing a thing. "So, what's the latest with you two?"

He forced himself to look back at his brother. "I don't know. It feels like two steps forward and one step back with Hannah."

"At least there's some forward progress."

"Some. I just want more, and I want it faster."

"That doesn't surprise me. You always want more, and you usually get it. I guess the question is—what does Hannah want?"

"She's fighting what she wants. But I'm working on her."

"Which is why you're here. Do you want to come with me to say hello to Mom and Dad?"

"I'll catch up to them later."

"All right. Good luck."

As his brother left, Jake looked back at Hannah. They'd gotten close last night, and he wanted to get closer. For that, he might need an ally, someone who could watch Brett, someone who could give him a little more alone time with Hannah.

As his gaze moved to Hannah's mom, he wondered if he might

find one in Katherine. He was probably crazy to think that, but there was only one way to find out.

---

Hannah wished she could stop being so aware of Jake. She'd seen him the second she'd walked into the party, and even though she'd been mingling for the past thirty minutes with her friends and coworkers, she couldn't stop her gaze from moving back to him.

He'd also been mingling, but now he was talking to her mother, and they seemed to be getting along quite well. Her mom was actually smiling at him. *What was that all about?*

Maybe they were just talking about Brett. But Brett had reconnected with Hailey, and they had joined the kids watching the puppet show. Her mom and Jake were on their own. She couldn't believe they had that much to talk about.

"Hannah, there you are."

At Davis's voice, she turned her head, giving him a happy smile. Dr. McKenna was dressed in a dark suit with a bold-red tie, his brown hair starting to pepper with gray at the sideburns. While Jake couldn't stand his father, she liked Davis a great deal. He'd been a mentor to her before and after she'd become a nurse and watching him at work every day had made her respect him even more. He certainly wasn't perfect. He occasionally had an arrogance that was off-putting, but he did care deeply about his patients and the hospital and what more could you ask for from the chief of staff?

"Merry Christmas, " she said. "I like the tie."

He tipped his head. "I bring it out every Christmas. I've been thinking about you, Hannah. I've been hearing some rumors about your sister. She disappeared after dropping her son off with you?"

"Yes. I think she's in some kind of trouble. The police are looking for her." She didn't even bother to ask how he'd heard. Gossip spread fast in Whisper Lake.

"I hope she's all right. How is her son?"

"Brett is great. He's a wonderful little boy, and I'm trying to make it a good Christmas for him."

"I'm sure you will succeed. I remember Kelly as a teenager. She was headstrong but also had such a beautiful laugh. She volunteered at the hospital one summer, and she was good with the patients. I thought she might go into medicine."

"I forgot she volunteered here. I don't really know why she did. But then, I'm starting to realize there was probably a lot I didn't know about her then. And there's certainly a ton I don't know about her now. I guess it's true what they say—everyone has secrets."

His smile dimmed at her words. "That is true. We never really know who anyone is. We only see what they want to show us."

"That's very philosophical."

"And way too heavy for a Christmas party."

She had to admit there was a stress in his eyes that seemed unusual for a holiday party. "Is everything all right?"

"Yes, everything is fine."

"You seem a bit off."

"I'm a little tired. But I actually got some good news a few minutes ago. We just snagged a very big donation that will go into next year's budget. It looks like we'll be getting a new MRI machine."

"That would be wonderful." She was impressed with how hard Davis worked to keep the hospital as technologically up to date as possible. "You're always working so hard for the hospital. I hope you know how much we all appreciate it."

"Thank you for saying that, but it's a group effort."

"You're the leader of the team."

He gave her a somewhat weak smile as his gaze drifted across the room. She realized he was looking at Jake.

"You should talk to Jake," she said quietly.

He straightened, annoyance moving into his eyes as he realized he'd been caught in perhaps a more vulnerable state than he would like anyone to see. "Why?" he asked.

"Because he's your son."

"He doesn't want to be my son. He hasn't in a very long time."

"I don't know what's between you, but I wish you could talk it out. It feels like you both have something to say, but neither one of you wants to be the first to say it."

"Don't worry about it, Hannah."

"I can't help it. I care about both of you."

"You care about Jake? I thought he broke your heart."

"He did, but that was a long time ago, and he's not that kid anymore."

His gaze sharpened as it swept across her face. "Are you and Jake getting back together?"

"Oh, I don't know about that," she said hastily. "But we have called a truce."

"How did that happen?"

"I'm not entirely sure, but it happened. Maybe you and Jake need to do the same thing. You're living in the same town."

"I don't see him any more now than I did when he was traveling the world. I think his mother sees him, but he usually manages to avoid me."

"Why does he do that?" It wasn't her business, but she couldn't stop the question from sliding through her lips.

"He never told you?" Davis asked.

"No."

His jaw tightened. "Well, it's between Jake and me. Excuse me, Hannah, I need to speak to Alan."

She had a feeling he had less of a need to speak to the head of orthopedics than to get away from the conversation they were having, but she simply nodded.

As Davis headed across the room, her gaze reconnected with Jake's. He'd left her mother and was walking straight toward her, and the look in his eyes made her heart jump into her throat. The instantaneous reaction reminded her of high school, of how fast her pulse had raced when Jake gave her his trademark smile—boyish charm mixed with smoking-hot sexuality.

She drew in a breath, wishing she could make a run for it, but he was already too close.

"Hi," he said, exchanging a look with her that was filled with intimate memories from the night before. "You look beautiful."

"Thank you," she said, swiping her lips with her tongue as her mouth went dry. "I didn't think you'd be here. It's your father's turf."

"It's yours, too. And I wanted to see you."

"I should find my mom and Brett," she said, eager to get away from all the unsettled feelings running through her.

"They're getting ready to hear the Christmas story," he said, tipping his head toward the far end of the room. The kids were settling into a circle, getting ready to hear Dr. McKenna's traditional reading of *A Christmas Story*.

"Maybe I'll join them."

"Or," he said, moving in front of her. "We could have some fun."

"I don't think so. I have Brett."

"Your mom offered to babysit."

Her gaze narrowed. "Is that what you were speaking to her about?"

"Among other things."

"Well, the two of you don't get to decide who is going to watch Brett. That's my decision."

"Hannah," he said. "We weren't planning anything nefarious. I told her that I'd like to take you ice-skating after this. She said you haven't been skating in years."

"I don't know how she would know that."

"Is she wrong?"

She frowned. "It doesn't matter."

"Well, your mom said she'd be happy to take Brett home and watch him for the rest of the evening so that you could go skating."

"You should have asked me first."

"I ran into her before I ran into you."

She frowned. "I don't think that's exactly the way it happened."

"Well, I might have wanted to check with her first," he conceded. "She wants to babysit."

"Why would she want to babysit so you and I can go out? She doesn't like you."

"I think she's warming up to the new and improved me. I thought you were, too. Last night was good, Hannah, and I'm just asking for an hour of your time. You used to love to skate. Why don't you do it anymore?"

She had loved to skate, but she hadn't done it since high school. Sometimes, she got a wave of nostalgia when she saw the skaters, because there had been a time when she was a kid when she'd dreamed of being an Olympic skater. "I just got busy."

"You never take time for yourself, Hannah."

"Sure I do."

"Well, not much time," he said. "You've been with Brett all day, and you spend half your life in this hospital. Are you sure you can't sneak out for a little fun?"

"You always make everything sound so tempting."

"Is that a yes?" he asked with a sexy smile that made it really hard to say no.

She was torn. She needed to stop spending time with him. On the other hand, she wouldn't mind cutting out on the party and doing something fun. It had been a stressful few days, and she wouldn't mind a little break. "I need to speak to my mother first," she said, knowing she had to make sure that her mom was up to babysitting.

"Of course."

She made her way across the cafeteria. Her mother looked up as she approached.

"Do you really want to watch Brett tonight?" she asked her.

"Yes, I do. We'll have a great time. If you give me your keys, I'll drive him home in your car, since you have the car seat, and you can go with Jake."

"Are you sure?" She hated the doubt that crept into her voice. Her mom heard it, too, and annoyance entered her gaze.

"I am completely capable of doing this, Hannah. Why don't you stop worrying about everyone else for a change and have some fun? You always say I never help you, so accept my help."

"All right. Call me if you need me."

"I won't need you. Stay out as long as you want. I can always sleep over, too."

"I will not be out that late," she said pointedly.

"Whatever you want," her mom said with an airy wave.

As she left her mom, Jake came over, a questioning gleam in his gaze.

"Are we going skating?" he asked.

"Yes," she said, telling herself it was just ice-skating.

Nothing else had to happen.

# CHAPTER NINETEEN

THE ICE RINK was next to Jake's store, and they stopped in there to get skates rather than wait in line at the rental counter. She hadn't been in his store before. Everything connected to Jake had been off-limits for the past two years, but now she was impressed. He didn't have a lot of retail space, but it was well laid out, and there was a clear focus on the adventure experiences, which seemed to take up one side of the space. There were lots of posters on the walls, showing off the various adventures and their happy participants. There were also monitors hung around a large circular counter.

"What are the TV monitors for?" she asked.

"I have videos showing our tour offerings. I find that when people can actually see what we're offering, they're more eager to sign up."

"How do you get video of the more extreme adventures?"

"I've hired photographers, and I've also used drones."

She shook her head. "If you need to use a drone to capture the moment, you must be on the highest peaks."

"We go as high as we can," he admitted.

"Is there any place you haven't been able to get to?"

"There are a couple of spots on Victory Peak and Shelter

Mountain, but it will happen someday. I just need the right set of conditions in order to make that happen. Now, let's find you some skates."

He led her over to the skate section and pulled out a pair of white boots with a shiny, sharp blade, and her heart skipped a beat.

"What do you think?" he asked.

"They're beautiful." She felt strangely reluctant to take them.

He gave her a quizzical look. "Want to try them on?"

"They'll fit," she said, knowing he'd grabbed the right size. "I just realized I haven't skated since high school, since you and I went out to Baker's Pond."

"Seriously? Not since then?"

"No. But it wasn't because of you," she added quickly.

"Thank goodness. I don't think I could handle being responsible for ending something you loved as much as skating." He paused. "You used to tell me that skating reminded you of your dad. It was bittersweet. But you still seemed to have fun when we did it."

"You made everything fun," she admitted. "After high school, I just stopped thinking about skating, and when I moved to Denver, it got further from my mind. It felt like something from another lifetime."

"But you've been back here for three years. You've never been tempted?"

"A little, but no one pushed me to get back on the ice."

"Good thing I came along."

"Is it a good thing?" she asked with a helpless shrug.

He smiled. "I think so, and hopefully you'll think so, too, at some point."

"Well, I don't need these new skates. I can rent a pair at the rink."

"Think of these as an early Christmas present."

She hesitated.

"Don't say no," he added quickly. "It's just a pair of skates, Hannah. They don't come with strings."

"I'm sure I have my old skates somewhere, and it's not like I'll be needing new skates in the future."

"You never know. You might hit the ice and want to come skate as often as you used to."

"I don't think I have time for that."

He dangled the skates in front of her. "Please take 'em."

"Fine," she said, not wanting to argue about it. "Thank you."

"You're welcome. I'll just grab my skates from upstairs. Want to come with me?"

Since she was somewhat curious to see his apartment, she gave a nod and followed him up the stairs.

As she entered his apartment, her first impression was that it was very masculine, from the hardwood floors and wood paneling to the brown leather couch and matching armchair. What surprised her most was the absence of a large TV, which in her mind was a staple in a single guy's apartment, but there was no television in the living room. There were, however, two floor-to-ceiling book-shelves that were filled with books.

She wandered over to those shelves, noting a mix of fiction and nonfiction on a wide range of subjects. "I like that you still read."

"I didn't see very many books at your house," he commented. "Why is that?"

"I've gone digital. I still have some print, but most everything is on my tablet. It's much easier to take to work and read on my break."

"So you're still reading?"

"Every chance I get." As she looked away from the books, she noticed a comfortable clutter in the room: a couple of coffee mugs scattered between the coffee table and the kitchen island, as well as a sweatshirt tossed over the back of a chair. There were also golf clubs in a corner of the room and a set of skis leaning against the wall. "This apartment feels like you." She gave him a smile.

"Messy and disorganized?" he joked.

"More like comfortable and unpretentious."

"I'll take that."

One of the framed pictures on the wall caught her eye. "That is an amazing photo," she said. The photographer had captured a ski jumper in mid-air on one of the steepest, most spectacular mountains she'd ever seen. "Where was this taken?"

"Norway. My form wasn't bad, so I decided to hang it."

"Wait a second, this is you?" she asked in surprise. "I thought it was just something you bought."

"Nope, it's me from years ago."

She looked back at the photo. The athleticism and fearlessness of the skier was unbelievable. "I can't believe you did this. You're literally flying. Weren't you terrified?"

"I was focused. I'd been training for that jump for several months."

"Several months? Seems like it would take years to really prepare. What drives you to do this kind of stuff, Jake?"

"It's an adrenaline rush, for one thing."

"It has to be deeper than that." She wished she could read his gaze a bit better. "What's behind the wanderlust, the thirst for death-defying adventures?"

"Why does it have to be deeper than just loving the thrill of danger?" he challenged.

"Because it does." She thought about what his motivation might be. "Does it have something to do with your estranged relationship with your father?"

"No." He let out a sigh. "I just like to test myself against the biggest odds. It makes me feel alive. It makes me feel like I'm not missing a moment that is meant to be lived."

His words took her in another direction. "It's about Paul. Your brother is so healthy now I sometimes forget how sick he was and how you used to dedicate your games to him. Did that continue when you started jumping off mountains?"

"Yes, it did. When Paul was first diagnosed with leukemia, he could barely get out of bed. When I'd come home from school, he was always eager to hear what I'd been doing. And it was my job to tell him a story that would take his mind off his pain. I needed adventures and experiences to share, so I went after them. When I left to go to college, I'd share my stories on the phone or in text. We always had something to talk about."

"And the adventures just got bigger and scarier. You kept pushing the boundaries."

"And somewhere along the line, it stopped being about Paul," he said. "I was on my own. I was accountable to no one, and there was nothing to hold me back. When I was challenging myself, I felt alive."

She gave him a thoughtful look. "What changed two years ago? Was there something specific that happened that made you decide you wanted to come home? That you wanted to be done with extreme adventures?"

"I'm not done, Hannah. I'm just taking my life in a different direction. I'm creating and sharing adventures with people who wouldn't get to have those experiences without me. I'm opening up their worlds, and I like that. I like being a part of a moment in their lives where they conquer their fear, try something new and step outside their comfort zone. It's fun and rewarding."

"I can see how it would be."

"But I can still travel. Just because I've reestablished some roots here in Whisper Lake doesn't mean I can't still take a vacation. I'm not trapped here. I choose to be here. And it feels different because it's my choice, because I was ready to come home."

"But you could choose to leave at any time."

"Just as you could," he said pointedly. "Are you trying to find another reason to push me away, Hannah?"

"I don't need another reason. I'm just saying…you could leave."

"I could, but I don't have any plans to do that. What about you?"

She shrugged. "To be honest, I've thought about leaving on occasion, wondering if I need to see more of the world."

"Is something stopping you?"

"Probably things that aren't completely true anymore, but I haven't let go of them."

"Like your mom and your brother needing you to be here?"

"Yes. I know Tyler doesn't need me to be here, but I have been looking out for my mom."

"If you really want to see the world, you should go see it. You know what I think, Hannah?"

"I'm not sure I want to know."

"You've been taking care of everyone else for so long that you don't know how to let them take care of themselves, but they can."

"Deep down, I know that. But it's a recent development."

"Not that recent. Your mom has been sober for almost four years, right? And your brother has been gone a while, too."

She drew in a breath and let it out. "All true. But it's not like I'm dying to go. I love this community. I love my job. There's just been something missing."

"Or someone?" he challenged.

She wasn't going to touch that comment. "I think we should go skating."

He smiled. "We'll get there. It's always easier to look at someone else's life than your own, isn't it?"

"Absolutely. But I think we've talked enough. You said we're going to skate; I want to skate."

"Great. Why don't you leave your bag here, so you don't have to worry about carrying it around while you skate?"

"Are you trying to make sure I come back here after skating?"

"Now that you mention it…"

She couldn't help but grin at his absolutely see-through suggestion. "I'm going to leave my bag because I don't want to carry it around, but that's the only reason."

"Whatever you say."

She headed toward the door, then paused, giving him a pointed look. "And by the way, the ball is back in my court."

His only answer was a really sexy smile.

---

The skating rink was packed with families and kids. Holiday music and spinning lights added to the fun holiday atmosphere. They put on their skates and left their boots in a cubby, then stepped onto the rink.

The first slide of her blade on the ice brought back a torrent of memories, and she braced herself for whatever pain might follow, but it was the joy that came back, the feeling of familiarity, the sense that everything in her world that had been out of kilter suddenly fell back into place.

Yes, there were images in her head that reminded her of her dad, the way he'd watched her from the side as she took a lesson and the happy times afterward when they'd talked about her routine over hot chocolates or hot apple ciders. There were the two-hour drives they'd taken to rinks outside of Whisper Lake so she could compete. She'd loved those drives because they were together and because she got to do something she loved.

Her dad had been very passionate about dreams. He'd always told her to follow her heart and not be afraid to really live her life, even if it was messy, even if she made mistakes.

His advice rang through her head now, and she couldn't help feeling like she hadn't really gone after her life. She did love her job and her friends. *What about everything else? Was she pushing herself enough? Was she taking enough risks?*

She looked over at Jake, knowing he was probably the biggest risk she could take.

He smiled. "This isn't enough, is it?"

"What do you mean?" she asked warily, not sure if he was talking about their relationship or the slow speed at which they were moving.

"Skating around in a circle with me. You need to go faster. You need to spin."

"It's too crowded."

"Not anymore," he said, as the rink changed over to adults only for the next ten minutes, and the kids and families cleared the ice. "You have the room you need. It's up to you to take it."

He gave her a little push, as if he didn't trust her to do it on her own. And maybe she wouldn't have.

"Fly, Hannah, the way you used to," he urged. "Feel the ice. Take this moment wherever you want it to go."

She pushed off, gathering speed as she moved forward. Her hair flew out behind her. She didn't know where Jake was anymore, somewhere behind her. But it didn't matter because she was flying. Her talent and her skill came back in seconds. It was as if she had never taken a break from skating. She was going forward, backward, and then spinning around. When the music stopped, the rink filled with applause, and it took a moment for her to realize they were clapping for her.

She felt a little embarrassed at the show she'd just put on, but as Jake joined her in the middle of the rink, she saw nothing but approval and respect in his eyes.

"That was fantastic," he said. "You never showed me that before."

"I don't know why I did now."

"You let the skater in you come out."

"I thought she was gone."

"She wasn't. How do you feel?"

"Amazing."

"Good. So, want to go slow with me again?" He extended his hand, and she took it.

They skated with the crowd now, and it was as perfect as her unexpected solo. Because she was with Jake. She looked over at him. "Thank you. Not just for bringing me here, for giving me that little push."

"I'm glad you seized the opportunity, and everyone loved the show. You're still good, Hannah. You must have been spectacular when you were a kid. I know you must have told me how skilled you were, but you didn't show off those skills in high school."

"When we went to the rink back then, I was more interested in holding your hand than skating," she admitted. "And maybe it was still too close to the loss of my dad. He was the one who shared my love of skating, who got me on the rink, who drove me to practices. I lost a lot of interest in skating after he died. Tonight, I felt like he was with me. I haven't felt his presence in a very long time.

It felt good." She paused, looking at his handsome face. "You feel good, too. So good, I think I want to stop skating now."

His eyes sparkled. "Are you sure? We haven't been here very long."

"I know, but I'm ready to go whenever you are."

"Whatever you want."

They stepped off the ice, put on their boots, and walked in silence back to Jake's apartment. As they went up the stairs, her nerves tightened, and by the time they got into the living room, she was a nervous ball of tension and anticipation.

"Should I take you home?" Jake asked.

The uncertainty in his eyes surprised her. Jake always seemed to know exactly what he was doing and where he wanted to go. While she was often unsure, especially when it came to him. But tonight felt different. She felt different. "Not yet," she said, licking her lips. "I have the ball, and...I want to kiss you good night."

Surprise and desire flared in his gaze. "Okay."

"Actually, that's not true," she said hastily. " I don't want to kiss you and say good night—I want to kiss you and stay a while."

He sucked in a breath. "I was not expecting you to say that."

She took off her coat and tossed it on a nearby chair. "I was not expecting myself to say that, either, but it's the truth. I want us to be honest with each other. It's the only possible way this could ever work."

"I agree," he said, taking off his jacket.

"I told you what I want. What do you want, Jake?"

"You," he said simply. His warm gaze swept across her face. "Not the way we were, Hannah. The way we are. I like this version of you. I like the confident, independent, strong-willed nurse who knows her mind and acts on what she wants and is also the most beautiful woman I've ever laid eyes on."

Her heart sang at his words, at the need in his gaze. "I like this version of you, too, Jake. I like how you've made your passion your job, how you care about your employees, how you put your-self out there to people even when they don't deserve it. When we were younger, it always felt like you were trying to outrun a speeding train. You had so many thoughts, so many dreams, but you didn't know where to start. You figured all that out. You took your restlessness all over the world, and it changed you. Now, there's a humbleness to your cockiness that makes me want to throw myself at you."

"I have no idea what that means, but I'll take it," he said with a smile, opening his arms.

She moved forward, putting her arms around his neck, as he pulled her up against his chest.

"I'm nervous," she said.

"Me, too."

"No way. You're fearless."

"Not when it comes to you, Hannah."

His words touched her heart. "Can we really go back, Jake? Everyone says you can't. It's never the same."

"I don't care what *everyone* says. And I don't want it to be the same. Because we're not the same. We're better." He lowered his head and kissed her.

The touch of his mouth made her gut ache with longing and hunger. All of her remaining doubts fled from her mind. It might be a mistake, but she wasn't going to regret this choice. She wanted to be with Jake again. She wanted a second chance with him, too, even though she didn't want to admit it.

Their kisses went from tender and tentative to deep and compelling. Even though she was nervous as hell to be with him again, she was much more confident than she'd been the first time they'd gotten together. But every touch, every taste, brought back memories. She knew how she wanted him to touch her. And she knew how she wanted to touch him.

"Too many clothes," she murmured as they came up for air. Pulling back from his kiss, she pulled her sweater up over her head, shaking out her hair.

He smiled as his gaze moved to her breasts. She'd filled out since she was a teenager, and she was secretly a little thrilled to show him that.

"Sweet," he said with eager male appreciation, his hands

moving to cup her breasts, the lace providing a delicious friction from the sensuous movement of his fingers.

Anticipation shot down her spine as she wanted his hands all over her. She grabbed his shirt and helped him off with it, running her hands across his solid male chest. He'd always had an incredibly hot body but now he was even more muscularly built, the result of all those adventurous sports.

"Wow," she said. "I feel a little intimidated."

"No way." He reached around her back and flicked the clasp of her bra open in one quick move. "You're beautiful, Hannah."

"That was faster than the last time," she said breathlessly as they shared a smile.

"I've gotten a little better in some areas," he said with a grin.

"I can't wait to see."

"I can't wait to show you." He pulled her bra off her shoulders as he pushed her up against the wall and ran his mouth down the side of her neck while his fingers played with her nipples.

Each stroke sent ripples of heat through her, and while Jake seemed content to draw this out, she felt an overwhelming impatience. She reached for his jeans, unbuckling the snap and then lowering the zipper.

He groaned and stepped back. "You gotta slow down."

"Who says?" she challenged.

"I want to make this good for you."

"Then don't make me wait. I want you now."

His eyes lit up. He grabbed her hand and pulled her into the bedroom.

As they headed toward the bed, they stripped off the rest of their clothes and tumbled onto the mattress together. She finally had him exactly where she wanted him. And he had her.

Despite his desire to go slow, the fire was burning too hot, and with only a quick break to grab a condom out of the bedside drawer, they were sliding into each other.

It felt familiar and different and wonderful all at the same time. There was a sense of belonging, of being in exactly the right place at the right moment. This was Jake. This was the boy of her dreams. This was the man she'd loved for as long as she could remember—the one who'd always made her feel whole in a world that was constantly shattering around her.

And Jake knew how to touch her, how to drive her crazy. She tried to reciprocate, but he made it clear this time was all about her. *How could she argue with that?* Her entire body was tingling. Her heart was pounding out of her chest, and every move took her pleasure to new heights until she couldn't take it anymore, until they found the perfect release in each other's arms.

Long minutes passed before she could take a full breath, before her brain could refocus. And that was just fine. Stretched out on Jake's ruggedly masculine body was not a bad place to be. In fact, she didn't think she wanted to move ever again. But as he shifted slightly, she raised her head. "Am I too heavy?"

"Not a chance." He gave her a satisfied smile as he wrapped his arms around her back. "I like this."

"Me, too." She paused. "So…"

"I'm not going to compare." He answered her unspoken question with a shake of his head. "I loved being with you the first time, and I loved this time, too.

"I feel the same way."

"No regrets?"

"No," she said, even though she knew there would be a lot of second thoughts coming, as well as questions. *Where did they go next? Did this mean she trusted him? That she'd forgiven him?*

As the questions raced through her head, she frowned.

"Don't do that," Jake said. "Don't start thinking."

"I don't know how to stop thinking. My brain always works overtime."

"I have an idea," he said, rolling her onto her back.

She looked at him in surprise. "Seriously? Already?"

"It's been a long time for us. And I want you again—before you start coming up with a lot of reasons why we shouldn't."

"There are a lot of reasons." But as she ran her hands down his back and felt him growing hard against her soft core, she didn't want to think about any of those reasons. "I don't think we should talk about them now."

"Thank God," he said with such an immense relief she grinned.

That was the other thing about Jake—he'd always had the ability to make her smile, to make her laugh, to make her feel like they were alone together in a perfect cocoon of love. When he was with her, the outside world completely faded away.

"On one condition," she said.

He gave her a wary look. "What's that?"

"This time we make it about you."

"Could you be any more perfect?"

She gave him a wicked look. "Let's find out."

---

He'd known sex would be good with Hannah, because it had been good before, but the word *good* didn't seem big enough to encompass what had just happened between them.

He rolled onto his side as he looked at Hannah. Her hair was a tangled mess from his impatient fingers and there was a rosy hue to her cheeks. She pulled a sheet up over her breasts, while he was happy to let the air cool him down.

She gave him a happy look, her eyes bright, her lips swollen from the pressure of his mouth. And God help him, he already wanted her again.

"No way," she said, clearly reading his mind. "I'm exhausted."

"I didn't say I wouldn't let you rest."

"I also have to go home, Jake."

"Your mom can't stay the night?"

"I don't want to push it too much."

He was disappointed, but he understood. "I get it." He reached out and brushed a piece of hair off her forehead. "Beautiful Hannah. I never thought we'd get back here."

"Me, either. A part of me feels like we wasted so much time."

"I've thought that, too. But it wasn't wasted. We had to grow up. We had to become who we are now."

"If you'd asked me a week ago if we'd even talk again, much less have a night like this, I would have said you were crazy. I had my walls up."

"They were incredibly high. At times, they felt insurmountable," he said. "When you'd see me and run away, it hurt me, Hannah, every single time."

"Seeing you hurt me, too. When you came back, I wasn't ready to deal with you again. I had locked you away, and I didn't want to let you out. I was afraid to see you as you are, because I didn't want to want you again." She let out a sigh. "I was right to be afraid. It's been four days, and here we are."

"But it took more than four days to get back here," he said quietly.

"I know." Her expression shifted from pure bliss to one of uncertainty, and he hated to see the change. "I'm not sure where we go from here, Jake."

"Do we have to decide now?"

"Maybe not. But you know me, I like to plan things out. I like to have structure." She paused. "We're different that way. You're good at winging it, taking a leap into the unknown. I like to know exactly where I'm headed and how I'm going to get there."

"It's good that we're not the same. We complement each other."

"I suppose. You do push me in a way no one else ever has. What do I do for you?"

He thought for a moment. "You make me want to be the best version of myself."

She gave him a doubtful look. "I do? That has to be a recent thing, because it wasn't true before."

"Not that recent. The desire started about five minutes after I realized how badly I'd hurt you."

"I don't want to talk about that."

"Neither do I," he said quickly, sorry he'd brought it up.

"But you know what makes me crazy about that night, Jake?"

"I thought you didn't want to talk about it. Let's stay in this happy place that we're in. It's nice, don't you think?"

"It is nice," she said with a sigh. "But it was nice before, and then it ended, and I still don't know why. You had so many different excuses for doing what you did. I wish I could understand what really happened that day."

"Does it matter anymore?"

"I think it does, Jake. You want me to trust you again, and to do that, we need to have everything in the open. No secrets. No misunderstandings. No confusion. Complete and total honesty. That's how we move forward."

"I think it's how we move backward," he argued. "There's nothing I can say that will make you feel better about what happened. There's no way I can give you any kind of guarantee that you won't get hurt again. I can make the promise, but you have to find a way to have faith in me, in us."

She thought about that. "Maybe the promise would make more sense if I had context about what happened."

He sighed. "You are so stubborn."

"You're being just as stubborn," she retorted. "Why won't you tell me?"

He could lie and say he didn't know, but he'd done that before, and she hadn't believed him. He could make up a reason, but he'd done that before, too, and she hadn't believed him. She might believe the truth. It might change her feelings about his actions, but his hands were tied.

"I made a mistake, Hannah. I got drunk. I hooked up with Vicki. And I hurt you. Those are the facts, and I'm incredibly sorry about each and every one of them."

She stared back at him. "But there's something you're not telling me. I can hear it in your voice. I can see it in your eyes. It's between us. It's been between us for twelve years. And it's always going to be there until you share."

"Does it have to be between us? Can't we build from here? Can't we make new memories, Hannah? Do we have to keep rehashing things?"

"I don't know, Jake. It bothers me that I feel like you're hiding something from me. I have a problem with secrets. My mom's drinking was a huge secret for a long time. I had to lie about a lot of things so no one would take me and Tyler away from her. And when we did get taken away, I had to tell more lies to get her back. I don't want to live with secrets anymore. I don't want to be with someone who can't tell me everything. Maybe that's unfair, but it's the way I feel. I shouldn't have to settle for less than complete honesty."

He realized her need for the truth went way beyond him. "You're right. You shouldn't have to settle. And you shouldn't have to lie."

"Where does that leave us?" she asked.

He wished he could give her a different answer. "For now, I guess I should take you home."

Disappointment filled her eyes. "Really?"

"I can't tell you what you want to hear, at least not right now."

"Then when?" she asked in confusion. "What's holding you back?"

"Nothing I can talk about."

She let out a weary sigh. "Okay. Then I guess you should take me home." She slid out of bed, taking the sheet with her.

As she moved into the living room to find her clothes, he rolled onto his back and cursed. But swearing wasn't enough. If he wanted anything to change, he had to do something, and it was long past time to do it.

He got out of bed, threw on some clothes and went into the living room where she'd finished getting dressed.

"I can call for a car," she told him in a tense voice.

"No. I'll take you home."

"It's going to be awkward."

"Probably. But no more awkward than it's been before," he returned.

He grabbed his keys and put on his jacket as they left his apartment. When they got downstairs and stepped outside, there was a light snow coming down.

Hannah shivered as they got into the truck, and he quickly turned on the heat. "It should warm up fast."

"From hot to freezing in ten seconds," she muttered.

"In more ways than one," he said, thinking how fast things had changed between them.

A buzzing sound drew her gaze to her bag. "Oh, my God it's Adam," she said, shooting him a scared look. "He wouldn't call this late unless he had news."

"Can you put it on speaker?"

She did so, then said, "Hello? Adam? Have you found Kelly?"

"No, but we tracked the car she was driving to a gas station on the road leading into Black Falls. Your sister bought gas and snacks there. She was alone and appeared to be in good condition. The image we received from their security camera was blurry, but we were still able to make a positive identification."

"Black Falls is only fifteen miles from here," Hannah said with surprise in her voice. "I thought she'd be farther away by now."

"Well, that's where she was yesterday morning. Do you know of any place in that area where she'd be going?"

"We used to camp there with my dad, but that was in the summer, not in the winter. I have no idea where she'd go."

"If you think of anything let me know. I'll be in touch as soon as I have any additional updates."

"Thanks for working so hard on this, Adam."

"I'm determined to bring your sister home, Hannah."

Jake pulled into her driveway as she ended the call. "That's good news," he said.

"Is it?" she mused, dark shadows in her eyes. "I want this to be over, Jake. I want Kelly home. And I have no idea why she'd go to Black Falls or where she'd stay if she did. There's a big storm coming in tomorrow. If she's outside, if she's hurt in any way…"

"Adam said she appeared in good condition."

"On a security video. Who knows what kind of detail that picked up? And she's pregnant, Jake. If she's not eating or drinking enough…"

He could hear the frustration and fear in her voice, and despite the wall they'd just rebuilt between them, he couldn't just sit there and do nothing. He pulled her into his arms and held on tight.

"You have to keep the faith," he murmured, happy that she was actually letting him comfort her. "Focus on what you do know. She's alive. She bought gas and food. She didn't ask anyone for help."

Hannah pulled back and lifted her gaze to his. "She wouldn't ask for help if she's running from the cops."

"True. But the important thing is she's all right."

"Yesterday morning she was all right, but I don't know about now. I wish I could do something to help."

"You are doing something. You're taking care of Brett."

"Not tonight I wasn't. I was just having fun."

"Hannah, stop," he said forcefully, refusing to let her wallow in guilt. "You took a short break. That's not a crime. Brett was bonding with his grandmother, which was good for both of them. And whether you'd sat at home all night or gone skating, whatever is happening with Kelly would still be happening."

"I know, but I feel helpless. I hate this feeling of being out of control."

"I get it. But Kelly is alive and well, even if we don't know where she is. One thing we do know is that your sister is a survivor. She's very resourceful. She's been on her own since she was nineteen. She has a son and a daughter on the way. She'll fight for them. She'll do whatever she needs to do."

"Except maybe turn herself in."

"There could be a reason she's buying herself time. She could be trying to build a case for self-defense. Or maybe it's something else entirely. She could have asked you for help, but she didn't. All she wants you to do is take care of Brett, and that's what you're doing."

"Maybe." She didn't sound convinced, but the bleak look was fading from her eyes. He suspected that had more to do with her fighting spirit than his words, but he was still happy to see her bouncing back. "I should go in." She put her hand on the door, then looked back at him. "I know this night has gone a lot of different ways, Jake."

"That's an understatement. Look, we don't have to decide anything tonight, Hannah."

"I think it's already decided," she said with a heaviness in her voice that disturbed him.

"I don't agree. We need to have another conversation. We'll talk tomorrow," he said firmly.

She hesitated, then shrugged. "All right. Good night, Jake."

"Good night," he said, happy she hadn't said good-bye. It gave him hope that he could turn things around. Because he intended to do just that.

He would tell her everything, but first he had to tell someone else.

# CHAPTER TWENTY

HANNAH WOKE up Tuesday morning to the ringing of her doorbell, a small boy jumping on her bed, and a splitting headache. She'd gotten stress headaches ever since her dad had died, but she hadn't had one this bad in a while. Apparently, having sex with Jake had not been the stress release it should have been.

Actually, it was the after-sex part that had created all the tension, as well as the sleepless night she'd spent trying to figure out if she was willing to push Jake away because of something he didn't want to talk about that had happened twelve years ago.

She still hadn't come to a conclusion on that. Thankfully, she had way too many distractions to worry about it at the moment. She heard voices downstairs and realized that her mom was talking to someone. Her mother had been on the pull-out couch in her living room when she'd gotten home last night and said she would just spend the night there, so she didn't have to go out in the cold. She'd offered her mom her bed, but that invitation had been declined, and she'd been too tired to argue.

"Is Santa here?" Brett asked, drawing her attention back to him.

"No, that's not Santa. He won't come until tonight, long after you go to sleep." She slid out of bed and threw on a robe. Her tension eased when she recognized the familiar voice downstairs. "That's your Uncle Tyler. Want to meet your mom's brother?"

Brett nodded and followed her down to the living room. When she saw her brother's smile, happiness flooded through her. He'd made it home. At least, one thing had gone right.

"Tyler," she said, giving him a big hug. Her little brother was five years younger than her but six inches taller, with brown hair and her mother's green eyes. "You look good."

"You don't," he said dryly. "Bad night?"

"You could say that."

Tyler turned to Brett. "Hi, Brett. I'm Tyler."

"Mommy said you like baseball."

Silence followed Brett's unexpected words.

All three of them were shocked that Kelly had spoken of Tyler at all. He'd been nine when she'd left home.

"I do like baseball," Tyler said, a thick note of emotion in his voice.

"So do I," Brett said. "Mommy throws me the ball sometimes. She says I have a good arm."

Another painful reminder that Kelly might not have been present in their lives, but she had certainly been present in her son's life, and Brett needed his mother.

"We'll have to play catch sometime," Tyler said.

"But not today, not in the snow," her mom said in a decidedly cheerful voice. "I'm going to make chocolate chip pancakes in honor of Tyler, because they're his favorite. Brett, do you want to help me?"

Brett gave an enthusiastic smile and took her mom's hand.

As they left the room, she turned to her brother. "I thought you were going to call when you got a flight."

"I figured I'd surprise you just in case the flight got canceled or delayed again, but I was able to beat the storm." He paused, giving her a speculative look. "I have to admit I didn't expect to find Mom sleeping on your couch. Is there a reason she couldn't drive home?"

She gave him a reassuring smile. "It's nothing bad. She was watching Brett for me last night, and she just decided to stay over.

She's actually doing really well, Tyler. Since she decided to meet her grandson, she has really changed for the better. It's like she remembered how to be a mother once she realized she was a grandmother."

"That's great news," he said with relief.

"It really is. I've had trouble trusting that she's okay and not about to go off the wagon again."

"What else is new?"

She made a face at him. "I know. I'm very good at worrying about things that might not happen. Anyway, I think she's trying her best to be our mom again, although she's still clueless. You don't like chocolate chip pancakes."

"Nope. Blueberry waffles are my thing. And you made 'em the best."

"I had a lot of practice perfecting those waffles for you." She paused. "I think it was Kelly who liked the chocolate chip pancakes."

"I'm sure they'll be good enough to eat and no reason to mention her mistake," he said easily. Tyler had always been the peacemaker, probably because she'd protected him from a lot of the really bad stuff, so he didn't have the same memories that she had.

"No reason to do that," she agreed. "Not with everything else going on."

"Is there any news about Kelly beyond the texts you've sent me?"

"Only that she was spotted at a convenience store on the road to Black Falls. Adam wanted to know if I had any idea where she was headed. I told him we camped there a few summers, but that was in Butterfly Canyon, and there aren't any cabins there. Anyway, the police are doing everything they can to find her."

"Good." He grabbed his bag. "I brought a few presents this year. I know we don't usually exchange, but once I heard about Brett and that you'd gotten a tree, I thought we'd need something to put under it." He paused, as his gaze moved to the tree. "Looks like you beat me to it. There are already presents there."

She was actually surprised to see those presents. "Mom must

have wrapped some of mine. Or she bought some of her own." A warm memory ran through her head. "Remember how she used to hold off on wrapping our presents until the night before Christmas? She wanted us to wake up Christmas morning and think the presents were from Santa."

"I remember that. I'd go to bed with just one present under the tree, and the next morning there would be five or six."

They exchanged a smile at the shared memory.

"This is going to be a good Christmas, Hannah," Tyler said with an optimistic note in his voice. "Kelly will make it home."

She wanted to believe that. "If Kelly comes home, it would be the first time in fifteen years that we're all together."

"I can't believe it's been that long. This has to be the year."

"I hope so." She sent up a silent prayer that they would get the miracle they needed. But at the moment, that felt like an impossible dream.

---

Four hours later, Hannah felt like one part of her impossible dream was coming true. They didn't have Kelly back, but the rest of the family was becoming closer. Brett, her mom, Tyler and she had had an incredible day. After breakfast, they'd taken a walk into town to pick up groceries for Christmas dinner, and to drop off presents at charity organizations. They finished their errands with lunch at Chloe's café, and when they'd gotten back to the house, they'd decided to build a snowman. She couldn't remember having this much fun as a family since her dad had died.

Brett's childhood joy and innocence awakened something in all of them, but especially her mother, who seemed like a completely different person. It was quite amazing. Maybe her mom would be able to remain sober and present in all their lives.

Tyler, too, had turned into the fun-loving kid she remembered. He seemed to enjoy letting go of the stress of law school to build a snowman with Brett. When they were finished, she ran inside the house, grabbed a red scarf, and came back to drape it around the snowman's neck. Then they all stood back to admire their work. It wasn't a snowman that would win any awards, but it was still pretty good.

"Can we build another one?" Brett asked.

She smiled at his never-ending energy. "It's time for you to take a nap."

"I'm not tired."

"Well, you'll have to try to get a little sleep."

"Is Santa coming tonight?"

"Yes, he is," she said, as she grabbed his hand and took him into the house.

Her mom and Tyler followed, and they all tossed their coats and gloves onto a big pile on the chair by the stairs.

"I'll put Brett down for his nap," her mother said.

"Are you sure? You've been doing a lot of the heavy lifting," she said.

"It's past time for me to do that." Her mother turned to the little boy. "Come on, Brett, I'll read you a story before you go to sleep."

As her mom and Brett went upstairs, she and Tyler made their way into the living room, flopping down on opposite chairs.

"That was fun," Tyler said. "Even though at times it felt like we'd entered some alternate universe with Mom. But I'm not complaining."

"I know what you mean. Brett has awoken something in Mom, and it's beautiful to see. But now he needs his Christmas wish to come true, and that's for Kelly to come back. I've been trying to think of where she might go to hide, and I just can't come up with anything."

"I wish I could say I knew her well enough to guess, but, honestly, I don't remember her that well. That sounds terrible, but it's the truth. I have images of her in my head, but they're fleeting moments in time. Sometimes I'm not even sure I remember the scene or if someone just told me about it. Like, I have this vision of her pitching a softball game. Was I there or did you just tell me what a great pitcher she was?"

"You were there. You were usually playing in the dirt when she was pitching."

"Then I guess I do remember something." He cocked his head to one side, giving her a thoughtful look. "What do you remember about her?"

"She used to do my hair and nails when she was stuck babysitting us. I remember her talking on the phone a lot. She had a laugh that sounded like a musical melody. It started out slow and just kept going, like a song that starts to wrap around your heart."

"I kind of remember that."

"She was fun, reckless, and impulsive. In some ways, she was a lot like Mom. Maybe that's why they couldn't get along. But in the end, she was Daddy's girl. She was definitely his favorite."

"Did that make you feel bad?"

"Middle children are always out in the cold," she said lightly. "Not the desperately wanted first child, or the adorable third child, just the one in the middle."

"I don't even think of us as being three. It was really just you and me."

"We were a good team; we still are."

His expression turned serious. "Sometimes, I feel like I let you carry too much of the load, Hannah. I didn't help enough. You were going to be a doctor, but you didn't go that route, because you were raising me."

"Well, I love being a nurse, so don't go thinking I'm not happy with my career choice. I ended up exactly where I was meant to be."

"That's good." He paused. "Are you seeing anyone?"

She hesitated. "Not really."

"What does that mean?"

"Well, I've actually reconnected with Jake. I don't know if you remember—"

"Of course I remember Jake. He was a great guy until he broke your heart and made you cry for about a year straight. You're getting back together with him?"

"I don't know. He's the same but he's different; he's better. He's been really supportive through this whole situation, and I still really like him. I'm just afraid we'll end up in the same place. I told him last night that I think we should be done."

"You're letting fear stop you from doing what you want?" Tyler asked.

"I wouldn't put it that way."

"There's no other way to put it. You just said you were afraid, so you ended it."

"He hurt me, Tyler. While he has apologized, he has never really said why he did it. And I can't deal with secrets. I need to be in a relationship where all the cards are face up on the table."

"Where's the fun in that? There's nothing wrong with a little mystery."

"There's plenty wrong."

"Well, I think *you're* wrong," he said pointedly. "You're also not acting like yourself. You are the girl who goes against all odds to achieve her goals. But you're letting something from a long time ago stop you from being happy now? That doesn't seem smart."

"I didn't say it was smart. It's just that Jake has so much power over me. He sweeps me off my feet so easily. I could lose myself in him. And it took a tremendous amount of effort and a lot of years for me to get over him the first time. Why would I put myself through that again?"

"Love."

She stiffened at his simple answer. "What do you know of love?"

"I might have met someone," he admitted.

"Really? Is it serious?"

"It could be. We're going to spend New Year's together in Aspen."

"That sounds romantic." She felt an unexpected wave of jealousy. She had a feeling her New Year's Eve was going to be another night alone or watching her friends fawn all over their boyfriends and husbands. Aside from Keira, the single circle was getting quite small.

"I plan on pulling out all the stops," Tyler said, an excited sparkle in his eyes.

"Good for you. When do I get to meet her?"

"We'll see how New Year's goes. What are you doing that night?"

"I have no idea. I can't think past Christmas or Kelly." She let out a sigh. "I feel so frustrated, Tyler. I want to go out and find her."

"Black Falls is a huge area. Where would you even start looking?"

"I don't know, but I feel like I have to do something. This inaction is driving me crazy."

Tyler gave a big yawn, then gave her an apologetic smile, "Sorry. You're not boring, I just need some coffee. I had to get up at three thirty this morning to catch my flight."

"Why don't you take a nap? You can use my room. Mom is planning to spend the day and evening here. She can watch Brett if I run out for a bit."

"Where are you going to go?"

"Maybe nowhere. I'm still thinking about it."

"Well, let me know what you decide," Tyler said, as he got to his feet. "In the meantime, I'm going to make some coffee."

As Tyler left, she felt a restless urge to do something; she just didn't know what.

Part of that restlessness had to do with Jake. She hadn't talked to him all day, and she found herself missing him. That was crazy, since she was the one who had told him they needed to be done. Now, less than twenty-four hours later, all she wanted to do was talk to him, kiss him, wrap her arms around him. Her body still tingled with memories from last night. It would have been a lot smarter to break up with him before she had sex with him, but then they wouldn't have had sex, and it was very difficult to regret those hours together, which had been some of the best hours of her life.

Forcing her mind off Jake, her thoughts returned to her sister. It was almost two, ten hours until Christmas, and only another eight hours after that before Brett would wake up and expect to get his Christmas gift from Santa.

*Where could Kelly be? Had there been some other clue that they'd missed?*

She'd gone through the suitcase and Brett's backpack a dozen times.

*Was there anything at the cabin she'd overlooked?* Adam had gone through the house and said they'd found nothing of interest. *Could there have been something there only she would recognize, like the unicorn necklace?*

Jumping to her feet, she knew where she needed to go. It was a thirty-minute drive to the cabin. But she had nothing else to do this afternoon, and she'd be back before the storm hit.

As she went to grab her coat, her mom came down the stairs.

"Brett fell asleep before I finished the story," her mom said.

"That's good. Are you going to stick around for a while?"

"I'd like to." Her mom gave her a quizzical look. "Unless, you'd rather have Tyler to yourself?"

"No. Actually, I was going to run out for an hour, and I'm not sure Tyler will be able to stay awake to keep an eye out for Brett. He got up early this morning."

"I'll be here. Where are you going?"

"I just have a last-minute Christmas errand to run," she said vaguely.

"Well, don't be too long. The weather is supposed to turn."

"I'll be back before that." She grabbed her coat and gave her mom a smile. "Thanks for helping out so much."

Her mother smiled back. "Thanks for letting me." She paused. "It's almost Christmas, and I have a good feeling about this year. I think Kelly will come home and for the first time in a very long time, we'll be a family again."

"I hope so."

# CHAPTER TWENTY-ONE

HANNAH TRIED to hang on to her hopeful feeling, but as she neared the cabin, her stomach churned, and anxious thoughts ran through her head. The temperature had dropped another ten degrees, and the snow was coming down at a steady rate, blanketing the trees and road in powdery white. She didn't know if it was the incoming storm or the fact that it was Christmas Eve, but the highway around the lake was nearly empty, and when she turned off onto the narrow road leading down to the lake and the four cabins at Wicker Bay, there wasn't a car in sight.

When she arrived at the cabins, there were no vehicles parked in front of any of the buildings. She pulled into the short driveway and turned off the engine. Then she made her way up to the porch. She unlocked the door and walked inside. It was very cold in the living room, which wasn't unusual since the property manager turned off the heat in between rentals.

Everything looked the same as when she'd left it. She saw a few drawers pulled out in the kitchen and some pillows knocked off the couch, but that was probably from when the police had gone through the place.

She walked over to the sofa and picked up two pillows and put them back. That's when she heard a noise.

Her heart began to pound. She walked down the hall. The bedroom door was closed, but there was light coming from beneath the door.

*Someone was in the bedroom.*

Her breath came short and fast.

*Should she leave? Go back and get her purse and then call 911 from the car?*

She was still debating when a scream rang through the air filled with pain and fear and a tone of familiarity.

She opened the bedroom door. A woman was sprawled on her side across the bed, her blonde hair falling over her face as she writhed in pain, her hand pressing against her abdomen. She'd taken off her jeans and panties, a long black sweater falling to her hips. And that's when Hannah saw the blood on her thighs. The woman turned her head.

*Kelly!*

Shock ran through her, even though she'd known it was Kelly from the second she'd opened the door. But meeting her sister's gaze…it was familiar and different at the same time.

Kelly was older now, but it wasn't her age that bothered Hannah the most; it was the bruises on her face and the muscles in her face contorted with pain.

"Hannah," Kelly gasped. "Thank God! The baby is coming. I'm bleeding. I don't know what to do. It's too early."

She put every question out of her head and immediately went into nurse mode. "It's going to be okay," she said, moving to the bed.

"I'm scared."

"I'm sure you are."

"You must hate me."

"Right now, I just want to help you. I'm a nurse, Kelly."

"I know. I've been following you online."

That comment shocked her, but she needed to focus on the immediate crisis. "Let's see what's going on with the baby. Can you roll onto your back?"

Kelly gasped and groaned as she shifted onto her back.

Hannah did a quick check, her anxiety tripling when she realized the baby was breech. This wasn't going to be an easy birth, but there was no way she could get Kelly to the hospital now, which meant she had to deliver the baby. She hadn't done that in several years, and only once had she dealt with a breech birth. But she could do it. She would have to do it unless she could get the ambulance out here before the baby came, but that appeared doubtful. Kelly was already fully dilated.

"What's wrong? Something's wrong," Kelly said, fear in her eyes.

She met her sister's panicked gaze. "The baby is turned the wrong way. It's coming feet first, Kelly." She put as much calm into her voice as she could. "I'd like to try to turn her and see if we can get her into the right position."

"Okay," Kelly said.

"But first I'm going to grab my phone and call 911."

Kelly grabbed her arm. "You can't call 911, Hannah. The police will know where I am."

"I know you're in trouble, Kelly. I also know that Russ Miller is dead. But the police are already looking for you. I have friends in the department here. You can trust them. If you killed Russ in self-defense, they'll help you."

"I didn't kill Russ," she said, shock in her gaze. "You think I killed Russ?"

"The police thought he was hurting you, and you killed him trying to protect yourself."

"No, Hannah. It was Tom Washburn. He's a cop. He got obsessed with me after I had drinks with him one night. But I was never dating him. I never slept with him. I was in love with Russ. When I told Tom I was pregnant, he got crazy. He kept stalking me and harassing Russ. He even started thinking the baby was his. He's freaking insane. He's monitoring the police radios now. If we call for help, he'll know."

"That doesn't really make sense," she began.

"Trust me. He will find us, and that can't happen."

She didn't know what to make of Kelly's story, but she couldn't discount what her sister was saying. "I still think we can talk to the Whisper Lake Police. Tom doesn't work for them, right?"

"He has friends everywhere. I tried to get help from a cop in Colorado Springs, but he told Tom I was trying to make trouble for him. So, Russ and I had no choice but to run. Somehow, Tom found us, and he killed Russ. Now he's trying to get to me. He caught up to me earlier today. I rammed his car with mine, and I managed to get away. I didn't know where to go so I came back here."

"I didn't see your car."

"I hid it in the woods. By the time I got to the house, I was bleeding. I guess when I rammed his car, the impact triggered labor." Kelly let out another scream of pain. "Oh, God! The baby wants to come. How am I going to do this?"

"You're going to be fine, and so is your daughter." She pushed up the sleeves of her sweater. "I refuse to allow for any other outcome. You used to boss me around. Now it's my turn. You're going to do exactly what I say."

"I will. I'm sorry, Hannah. I'm sorry for everything. But I had to leave Brett with you. I had to make sure he was safe. I waited for you to come. I made sure you were there for him before I left."

"You should have stayed and talked to me."

"I was afraid."

"There will be time for apologies and explanations later. Right now, we need to get your daughter into the world. And first, we need to get her turned around." She looked at her sister. "This is going to hurt, Kelly. But we have to do it."

"Okay." Kelly breathed in and out. "If I don't make it, you'll take care of Brett and this baby, right?"

"You're going to make it. I'm going to take care of them and you. We are going to be a family again."

"I want that. I want to start over," Kelly said, a desperate plea in her eyes.

"We'll start now," she promised.

Jake had been avoiding his father for too long, but that ended today.

He arrived at the medical center just after three o'clock. He'd been debating this trip ever since he'd gotten up in the morning. He'd thought about it while taking a dozen tourists on an early-morning cross-country ski trip. And it had consumed his mind during a holiday lunch with his employees. Now, he had the afternoon free and the opportunity to do something to change Hannah's mind about having a relationship with him.

The past few days together, especially last night, had shown him how much he needed and wanted Hannah in his life. He'd lost her before, but he wasn't going to lose her again. She needed to trust him, and he could think of only one way to make that happen. He had to deal with his family issues.

He headed into the building and took the elevator to the fifth floor, to the offices of the chief of staff, Davis McKenna. His dad's assistant was sitting at a desk outside his father's office. She gave him a surprised look. He'd known Judy for most of his life, and certainly she was aware of the tension between him and his father.

"Hello, Judy."

"Jake," she said, a speculative gleam in her eyes. "How are you?"

"I'm doing well. Is my father available?"

"I'm sure he is for you. Go on in. He's just doing some paperwork."

He walked past Judy, then paused, needing one last double check. "He's alone, right?"

She nodded. "Yes, why?"

"Doesn't matter." He put his hand on the doorknob, flashing back to another door twelve years earlier. He should have stopped when he heard the sound of laughter. Or, at the very least, he should have knocked. But he hadn't. And his life had turned upside down.

Today, he would turn it right side up.

He opened the door and entered his dad's office, which was spacious and well-decorated, befitting the head of the hospital. His father sat behind a large desk, a computer to his left, a stack of charts to his right. Behind him was a window with a fantastic view of the mountains. The walls on either side of the room were filled with medical books, and a couch and two chairs in a seating area completed the space.

His father stood up, giving him a wary look.

He closed the door behind him before moving farther into the room.

His father came around the front of his desk, his arms crossed in front of him. His dad seemed to take that hostile but defensive posture every time they crossed paths.

"Why are you here, Jake?"

"We need to talk."

"About what?"

"You know what."

At his pointed words, his dad frowned. "Jake, please, that was a long time ago. Why do we need to discuss anything?"

"Because we do. I need to talk, and you need to listen."

His father stared back at him. "All right. Maybe it is time to get all this out in the open."

"It's past time. Twelve years ago, you made me promise to keep a secret. You made a compelling argument about protecting my mother and my brother," he said bitterly. "But you shouldn't have asked me to do that. You shouldn't have put that burden on me."

His father paled, his dark gaze narrowing in anger and guilt. "You're right, Jake."

He'd been prepared for a counterattack, not for an agreement. "Yes, I am right," he said forcefully.

"What I did was wrong. And it put a wedge between us."

"A wedge? That's an incredible understatement. You destroyed our relationship. You put me in the middle of a situation I never should have been in."

"I didn't know you were going to walk in on Louise and me."

He hated hearing that woman's name on his father's lips. Louise had been one of his father's nurses. She'd left town a few weeks after he'd interrupted their afternoon office affair, and his dad had assured him that it was a one-time thing, that it was a mistake, and it was over. As far as he knew, Louise had never come back, but whether or not his father had made the same mistake with someone else was something he didn't want to know.

"You can't tell your mother now," his father continued. "It would kill her, and what would be the point? I have been faithful to her ever since that day. Seeing the pain in your eyes, hearing the accusation in your voice, I knew I'd made a horrible mistake. And all my excuses for doing what I did were worth nothing. It didn't matter that your mom had been obsessed with Paul's care and couldn't have a conversation with me that didn't require my medical knowledge. It didn't matter that I felt helpless because I couldn't cure my youngest son."

"You can't blame Paul's illness for your infidelity."

"I know. I realized that after I'd crossed a line I never should have crossed. I made a vow then to be a better husband. Your mother and I worked on our marriage. We rebuilt it. We came back together, and we became stronger than we were. You just weren't around to see that part."

"I couldn't be around. I didn't want to look at you. I didn't want to watch you deceive my mother."

"It wasn't like that, Jake," his father said, shaking his head. "I've always loved your mother. I just made some horrible decisions. The cheating was bad enough but bringing you in on it was even worse."

"Making that promise to you drove me to make my own mistake. That night I bailed on Hannah. I abandoned her on the night of the prom. I got drunk and had sex with another girl and everyone knew. I hurt and humiliated Hannah because I was so caught up in a world of pain and I couldn't tell anyone."

"She told me that you'd cheated on her," his father said slowly. "But I didn't know it was that same night."

"I was out of my mind, and I wanted to escape. That decision ended Hannah and me."

"Maybe she would have forgiven you if you'd stuck around."

"If I'd stayed, I would have told her your secret, because I told her everything. I couldn't have kept it from her. I had to leave."

"But now you want to tell her," his father said heavily. "You want to get back together, isn't that right?"

"Yes," he admitted. "Hannah knows I've been holding something back all this time. And she can't trust me if I don't open up to her. I'm not going to tell Mom; I'm just going to tell Hannah. But I won't ask her to keep it a secret. I don't know if she'll tell Mom or if she'll want to protect you. I suspect she'll probably choose the latter, because you're her mentor, and she has tremendous respect and loyalty for you."

"I doubt that will continue after she hears what you have to say."

"Maybe not, but I've kept your secret long enough. If you've truly rebuilt your marriage with Mom, then you should tell her. And you should tell Paul."

"It would destroy them."

"I guess it's always been easier just to destroy me."

His father sucked in a quick breath as the knife went deep. "It has never been easy. You probably don't believe that, but it's true. I am sorry, Jake."

"Are you? I've never seen any evidence of that."

"I didn't know how to fix it. You were gone before I could figure that out, and you stayed away for a long time. I kept thinking one day we'd talk it out, but the days and the years kept passing."

"Wasn't it easier for you that I was gone? The only person who knew your dirty little secret wasn't around to blow your life up."

"It wasn't easy. I missed my son. And your mother missed you even more. She'd cry when you didn't come home for the holidays. That's when we started opening up our Christmas dinners to extended family and friends. It helped her get through the day without you. When you came back, she was unbelievably happy, but she still hates that you and I don't get along."

"And does she ask you why?"

"She's asked me many times, and I always tell her the same

thing—that I let you down, I wasn't there for you, and you can't forgive me."

"You've never thought about telling her the truth?"

"I've thought about it a thousand times, but I'm afraid I'll lose her if I do. I love her, Jake. I always have. What we went through with Paul tested us in ways you don't understand, because you weren't a parent. You saw it through the eyes of a sibling. It was different for you than for us. And I'm sad to say that I failed the test. But I did try to do better after that. I've tried to make your mom and Paul as happy as I can. And I'd like the opportunity to make things up to you."

It hurt to know that his dad was willing to put everyone else in the family over him, but at least he was being honest for the first time in a long time. And he could be honest, too.

"I've never wanted to tell Mom or Paul," he admitted. "I hated that you asked me to keep the secret, but the real reason I kept it was because they were fragile, especially right when it happened. I thought about coming clean later, but everyone had moved on, and you and Mom seemed happy enough. I thought Hannah was gone forever, but that's changed. I have a second chance with her, and I have to take it. I have to, Dad. She's the one. She's always been the one."

"And she can forgive you for cheating on her?"

"I'm very aware of the irony," he admitted.

"What if I asked you for a second chance?"

"It's not the same."

"It's not, but it is. It's about forgiveness. It's about accepting that people can be weak. They can make mistakes, but that's not their entire story."

His dad made a good point. "You're right. A mistake is not the whole story. But I've never thought you wanted my forgiveness, only my silence."

"I've wanted both."

"Well, I'm glad you can admit that." Jake paused as his phone began to buzz. He pulled it out of his pocket, his body tensing as he saw a stream of texts coming in from Hannah. "Damn," he muttered. Her texts were all short and panicked.

*With Kelly at cabin. She's in labor with complications. Call Adam and get an ambulance up here. Tell him Kelly is being stalked by a cop—Tom Washburn. She didn't kill Russ; Tom did. I'm trying to deliver her baby, so I can't talk, and she doesn't want me to call 911 to dispatch ambulance to this address. She thinks Washburn will use it to get to her first. He can't know where we are.*

His mind raced with questions, but he quickly texted her back: *Done. On my way.*

"What's wrong?" his father asked.

"I have to go. Hannah is with her sister at their cabin in Wicker Bay. She's in trouble. I don't know what's going on. But she needs an ambulance at her cabin, and she can't call 911."

"Why not?"

"I don't know, but she can't."

"All right, Jake, take it easy. I know where the cabin is. I'll arrange for the ambulance."

"You can't mention Kelly's name or Hannah's, for that matter. And, again, I don't know why. It just seems to be very important."

"I'll take care of it, Jake."

"Thank you." While his dad was doing that, he punched in Adam's number, as he headed toward the office door. Thankfully, Adam answered.

"Kelly is back at Hannah's cabin," he told Adam, as he jogged toward the elevator. "She's in labor and in trouble. Hannah is with her. She said that Kelly is being stalked by a cop."

Adam swore. "Who is it?"

"His name is Tom Washburn. Kelly seems to think this cop can track anything broadcast through the police or 911. My father is sending an ambulance from the hospital. I'm on my way. What about you? Can you meet us?"

"Yes, but I'm in Black Falls, Jake. I'm probably an hour away. I'll call Brodie and get him up there as soon as possible."

"Great. I'll be there in thirty minutes, twenty if I can," he promised.

"Be careful, Jake."

"I'm not worried about myself." As he ended his call, he was shocked to see his dad keeping pace with him. "I thought you were getting the ambulance."

"Both our ambulances are out on calls. Judy is contacting the fire department. She will make no mention of Kelly or Hannah's names. I don't know what's going on, but it sounds bad."

"Kelly has a stalker who's a cop. He killed her boyfriend. Now she's in labor, and Hannah said there are complications." He flipped open the locks on his truck. "I'll talk to you later."

"I'm coming with you," his dad said forcefully. "And I'm bringing my medical bag. Hannah and Kelly might need my help, especially if we can't get an ambulance out there fast."

He didn't argue. As much as he hated to admit he needed his dad for anything, he might need his medical expertise. He jumped in behind the wheel, as his dad got into the passenger seat, and he tore out of the parking lot.

His father didn't have much to say as he sped down the slick highway, occasionally bracing himself with one hand on the side of the door.

When he skidded a few feet around one curve, his father finally said, "Jake, we need to get there. Slow down."

"I know you're right, but I'm worried." He slowed the truck down as gusty winds sprayed blinding snow across the windshield. His wipers were working fast, but they couldn't keep up. The storm had arrived.

"Tell me what's going on," his father said.

"Hannah is trying to deliver Kelly's baby and there's a killer stalking Kelly, which means Hannah is now in the line of fire." He picked up his phone and punched in Hannah's number. He had to know what was going on, but he had no reception now. "Dammit," he swore. "Phone isn't working."

"We'll be there soon," his father said.

"I hope it's soon enough." A bad feeling was churning his gut.

*Hannah had to be all right. She had to be. He could finally tell her the truth. He could finally be completely honest with her.*

"Hannah is a survivor," his father reminded him. "She'll fight to the end."

"That's what she told me about her sister."

"It's true for Kelly, too."

"I just wish..."

"That you'd told her the truth all those years ago?"

He glanced at his dad. "I wish I hadn't cheated on her. God, it took me until just this second to realize that the mistake was mine. I've been blaming it on you for twelve years."

His father stared back at him in surprise. "Well, it was my fault. You were shocked by what you saw and the promise I begged you to make."

"But I had a choice. I could have just gone home. But I didn't. And I hurt the only girl I've ever really loved. But even if she can never forgive me—even if we can never be together—I just want to know she's having the life she deserves, that she's happy."

"I'm sorry, Jake. I should have let you out of that promise years ago. I want you to be happy, too. And if Hannah needs the truth, then you should tell her."

"I will."

As he turned off the highway, the road became much more difficult to navigate. The wind picked up, and his windshield was quickly covered with snow. He only had a mile to go, maybe less. But then he heard an enormous roaring sound. He didn't understand where it was coming from until branches hit the top of the truck, and to his horror, he saw an enormous pine tree coming down just ahead of them. He slammed on the brakes, which caused the car to skid.

He wasn't sure if they were going to slide off the road or get crushed by the tree heading straight for them, but there was nothing he could do except hang on...

# CHAPTER TWENTY-TWO

"I CAN'T DO IT," Kelly screamed.

"Yes, you can," Hannah said firmly. "You're through the worst of it now. Violet has changed positions. She's headfirst now, and she's crowning. On the next contraction, you're going to give me a good push. Here we go."

As Kelly bore down with a scream, Hannah put her hand under Violet's head. "Her head is out. We're almost there, Kelly."

"I'm so tired."

"One more push, Kelly. Take a breath, and let's meet your baby."

Kelly pushed with every last ounce of strength she had, and Hannah brought baby Violet into the world.

Violet blinked and then let out a cry. It was the most wonderful sound Hannah had ever heard, and tears came into her eyes. She'd delivered babies before, but this one was special. This one was her niece.

She wrapped a towel around the baby and placed her on Kelly's chest. "Your little girl is beautiful," she said, her heart breaking at the beautiful sight in front of her.

Kelly was smiling and crying as she held her child. "She's so small. Is she going to be okay?"

"I think so, but we'll want to get her checked out as soon as we can since she's several weeks early."

"I can't believe everything I've put her through this past month —all the stress, the running around, the skipped meals, and then the crash."

"She's a tough cookie, like her mother." She paused, grabbing her phone. "I need to find out where the ambulance is." Unfortunately, she had no signal. But her last text from Jake reassured her. He was sending an ambulance and he was on his way.

However, that text had come in almost thirty minutes earlier, and neither Jake nor the ambulance had arrived. They had to be on their way, she thought desperately. While both Kelly and Violet seemed stable, Kelly had lost a fair amount of blood and Violet was premature.

As she helped clean Kelly up and get her ready to go to the hospital, she finally had a chance to talk to her. "Can you tell me now what happened, how you ended up here?"

"It's a long story."

"Give me the short version."

"Seven months ago, Tom Washburn, a police officer, moved into the apartment across the hall from me. I thought he was nice. We were friendly neighbors. We had drinks one night at the bar across from our building when Brett was on a play date. I didn't think much about it. I was dating Russ, but he was out of town for a few months, so I was at loose ends. I told Tom I had a boyfriend, and he seemed cool with it. We had a few other casual meals, mostly with Brett, or just grabbing a coffee at the bakery. I had no idea that Tom was getting all kinds of crazy ideas until Russ came back," she said, letting out a tired breath.

As much as Hannah wanted to hear the story, she was a little worried about the pallor of her sister's skin. "We don't have to talk about this now. You should rest."

"No, I want to tell you. I need to tell you. When Russ came back, Tom suddenly seemed to show up wherever we were. Then Russ got stopped for speeding twice, not by Tom but by his friends. I knew Tom was behind it. I told Tom that I wasn't interested in him, that I was actually pregnant with Russ's baby. I started spending most of my nights at Russ's house, so I wouldn't have to see Tom. He seemed to back off for a while. And then last month, I ran into Tom at the market. I was really showing by then, and he started acting weird. He made comments like he wondered what our baby would look like. I went to the police, and the man I spoke to said Tom was one of their finest officers, and I must be imagining things. Then Tom really started to threaten me. He said I'd regret trying to make trouble for him."

"Oh, Kelly, I'm so sorry."

"The tipping point was when Tom went to Brett's school in uniform and picked him up, and the school let Brett go with him, because he was a cop, and he said I'd been in an accident. He wanted me to know that he could get to Brett at any time. When he brought him back to me, he said he wanted us to be a family. That night, Russ and I left town. We went to a campground, but Tom tracked us down."

Kelly's voice filled with anger and pain. "He killed Russ, and I ran. I didn't know where to go, so I came here. I couldn't take the chance you or Mom would tell me no, so I used a fake ID. I lured you to the cabin and left my necklace so you might realize Brett was my son."

"Why didn't you just say so in the note?"

"I didn't know if you would call the police and show them the note, and then Tom would find out. But I waited until I was sure you were with Brett. I love my son."

"I know you do. I'm so sorry, Kelly."

Tears slipped from Kelly's eyes. "Russ was a good man. His only mistake was to fall in love with me, and now he's dead. The fathers of both my children are dead." She gave a helpless shake of her head. "And Tom is coming for me."

She zeroed in on that piece of information. "You said you hit his car?"

"Yes. He found me near Black Falls, and he tried to run me off the road, but I turned my car into his, and we crashed. His vehicle went off the highway, and I got away. I didn't see what happened to him. But if he's alive, I'm sure he's still tracking me, and I don't know how he found me yesterday. I had switched cars."

She frowned, wondering the same thing. "Maybe he put some kind of tracking device on you or in your purse or something."

Kelly's eyes met hers, and there was a new fear in her gaze. "If he did, he's coming here. What are we going to do?"

Kelly had no sooner asked the question then the front door of the cabin crashed open and footsteps came down the hall.

Hannah desperately wanted to see Jake come through the doorway, but it was another man, a big bear of a man with blood smeared across a jagged cut on his forehead, and two black eyes.

She jumped in front of her sister as he raised the gun in his hand.

---

Jake blinked his eyes open. The truck had come to a crashing halt, the airbag hitting him in the chest. As he came fully awake, he realized that the vehicle was surrounded by a sea of branches, pinecones, and needles, all coated with a heavy snow. He couldn't see the road. He couldn't see anything but the tree that had engulfed them.

He glanced at his father, who was also coming back to consciousness, and he was relieved to see his eyes opening. "Are you all right, Dad?"

His father gave him a bemused look, putting a hand to his head, where blood was dripping from a cut.

"Are you hurt anywhere besides your head?" he asked. "Do you feel any pain in your legs, arms, chest?"

"No," Davis said finally. "I—I'm okay. What about you?"

"Same." He took his phone out of his pocket. He had no signal. They would not be able to call for help. He looked around as he unfastened his seat belt, trying to assess the situation. One thing was clear. "We've got to get out of here."

His father tried to take off his seat belt, but the door on his side was bent inward and had jammed the mechanism. "I can't get it off."

"It's okay." He reached into the glove compartment and pulled out an emergency box of tools, which included a pocketknife. It took him a few minutes to cut through the belt, and every second that passed added to his tension and frustration. Not only did they need to get out of this truck, they needed to get to Hannah.

Finally, the seat belt released. Then he worked on getting his door open. Once outside, he was able to cut through some branches to make some space. His dad couldn't get out of his side of the truck but was able to maneuver his way out of the driver's side, and he brought his medical bag with him.

When they were both on their feet, he could see that they were at the far end of the tree branches. The heaviest part of the tree had missed them by about ten feet, probably because they'd skidded completely off the road. Most of the tree was behind them, which was better. They couldn't go backward, but they could go forward, and that's where Hannah was.

"The cabin is that way," he told his dad.

"Are you sure we didn't get turned around?"

He wanted to be more certain than he was. But even though it was only afternoon, it was dark, and the snow was thick. It was not easy to see in any direction. "My gut tells me we need to go that way," he said, looking at his dad. "Whether I'm right or wrong, we can't stay here."

His father nodded, giving him a grim look. "No, we can't. You lead, I'll follow."

He was oddly touched by his father's trust in him. He hadn't felt that trust in a long time, maybe not ever. There had been no respect between them since he'd been seventeen years old. But now they would need to work together in order to survive and to get to Hannah and Kelly. God knew what was going on with them. But he couldn't think about them. He couldn't let fear or worry get in the way. He had to focus on one step at a time.

Using the knife at times, he was able to cut their way through some of the brush. They finally came out on the other side and made their way down the road. As they went around the next curve, they stopped abruptly. His heart sank. The bridge over the Whisper River had cracked and broken away, half of it now submerged in the icy water below. It wasn't a long bridge, just twenty feet across, but that twenty feet now seemed almost insurmountable.

"Damn," his father said, giving him a troubled look. "We're trapped."

"Not trapped," he said decisively. "We'll just have to cross over at another spot."

"There's no other spot, Jake. We can't cross the river. The ice isn't solid enough."

"Don't tell me what we can't do. Tell me what we can do," he snapped, angry at the situation more than at his father, but he was the closest target.

"Why don't you tell me?" his father countered.

"I'm thinking," he grumbled. "We're not giving up. We just have to figure it out. There has to be a way." His mind raced with possibilities, but each one seemed impossible. They couldn't cross the river for the reason his father had given. They could follow the river in either direction and possibly find a narrower place in which to climb across, but he didn't know this area that well, and they could waste far too much time, only to end up exactly where they were.

"We need something to get us across the river," his dad said. "Something long and sturdy enough to take our weight."

"Like a huge branch of a huge tree?"

His dad smiled. "Think we know where to find that?"

They were both so excited to have a possible solution that they practically flew down the snowy road. The wind had eased, which was helpful as the snow wasn't so blinding. After searching for the right branch, they found one they thought was long enough. He cut through some extraneous thinner branches to release the one they needed, and then they dragged it toward the river.

It took more than a little effort to get back down that road, but adrenaline was giving them the push they needed.

Then came the most difficult part: getting the branch across the river. It took them several tries, and Jake groaned in frustration more than once. Finally, they were able to span the distance. The branch was still somewhat precarious, but it was probably the best they were going to be able to do.

"I'll go first," he said.

"Be careful," his father said, worry in his eyes. "Even if it doesn't break, if it gets dislodged, you could end up in the river."

"I know. Once I get to the other side, I'll be able to secure it better so you can cross." As he took one step onto the thick branch, he felt like he was about to walk the high wire. He wasn't as worried for himself as he was for everyone else. There was no way an ambulance or the police could get past that tree in the road, not without some heavy-duty equipment to clear the way. There was no help coming, and if they didn't get somewhere warmer, they could freeze to death before they had a chance to help Hannah. There was a lot riding on this high wire. But he was up to the challenge.

Every fearless thing he'd ever done in his life had prepared him for this moment. He had the agility and he had the confidence. He could not be stopped.

He lowered himself close to the branch as he made his way across the makeshift bridge. It creaked and groaned at times, and the wind whipping up the branches didn't help, as it sometimes blinded his gaze with snow. He didn't look back. He put his focus on the hilly incline in front of him. He could hear his dad shouting words of encouragement, which felt more than a little surreal, but he had to admit it was nice to have the support.

He was almost to the end when the branch suddenly shifted and slid three feet down the opposite embankment. He held on, not breathing, until it came to a stop against a rock. How long that rock would hold was anyone's guess. He moved once more as carefully as he could. Finally, he was able to step off the branch, his feet hitting the ground.

He took a few breaths, then looked around for some rocks to bolster the stability of the branch. He set them around the bottom of the branch and positioned himself in a way that would hopefully prevent the branch from sliding again. Once that was done, he motioned for his dad to cross.

He'd never really thought of his father as an athlete, even though he'd heard about some of his athletic accomplishments as a kid. But all the while he'd been growing up, his father's expertise had been in science and medicine. His brilliant brain had been his most impressive quality.

Now, watching his sixty-two-year-old father cross the river on a narrow branch without much more trepidation than Jake had had was quite an eye-opener. Maybe he'd gotten more from his dad than he'd realized. He might not be following him into the world of medicine like his brother, Paul, but they both had a cocky confidence and enough athletic skills to overcome some tough obstacles.

When his dad reached his side of the river, he gave him a hand and helped him to the ground. Then they made their way up the embankment, which wasn't that easy, either, with the thick snow making every step difficult. When they got to the top, they moved through the trees and he felt an enormous sense of relief when he saw the clearing and the circle of cabins.

That relief faded when he saw an unfamiliar vehicle next to Hannah's car. He hoped it was Kelly's car, but it certainly wasn't the one she'd stolen from Trevor.

He paused, looking at his dad. "I don't know who that other car belongs to."

"It looks like it was in an accident," his father commented, nodding his head toward the shattered windshield.

That sight sent another chill through him. Hannah had said Kelly had a stalker, someone who was tracking her. *Was he here? Was he inside?*

"I'm going to get closer," he said. "Stay here, Dad."

"No. We're doing this together."

"Then we need to see what's going on inside, before they see us."

"Agreed."

They slid through the trees toward the house, avoiding the porch. There appeared to be a light on in the bedroom, so they made their way around the structure. They were almost to the back windows when he heard a baby crying.

*Kelly had had the baby.* At least, the child was alive. Hopefully everyone else was, too. But as they moved around the corner, he could see a large shadow in the window. The person was tall, and he had something in his hand.

His heart stopped. It was a gun.

*He had to get inside—now!*

A hand came down on his shoulder, his father's soft voice in his ear. "Careful," he said. "We need a plan. We can't rush in."

"We also can't wait here," he growled, but he knew his dad was right. "We need a distraction."

His dad met his gaze. "I'm on it. We're not going to lose Hannah, son. We're not going to lose Hannah or her sister or that little baby."

"No, we're not," he said, praying that they weren't already too late, because at this moment, he had no idea who was in that house or what condition they were in.

# CHAPTER TWENTY-THREE

HANNAH STARED at Tom Washburn as he paced back and forth, his footsteps jerky, his anger palpable. But there was something else at play—uncertainty.

Tom had been holding them at gunpoint for almost thirty minutes. At first, he'd wanted to grab Kelly and throw her into his car, but her condition and the arrival of the baby had thrown him. He also didn't seem to know what to do about her.

He'd ordered Hannah to sit on the floor, her back against the wall, which she'd done without complaint, not wanting to upset what appeared to be a fragile mental condition.

"Please, Tom, just go," Kelly pleaded again, her arms around her baby, who was fitfully crying. She'd begged him before to leave, but he seemed unmoved.

"You're mine. I'm not leaving you or our baby," Tom replied.

"She's not *our* baby. She's *my* baby," Kelly said.

Hannah frowned, wishing Kelly would stop talking, because she didn't think reminding him that the baby was not his was the best approach. The man was clearly unhinged. He'd be more likely to hurt a child who didn't belong to him than one who did.

"They both need to go to the hospital," she interjected quietly.

"Shut up," he said, his evil gaze swinging to her.

"Kelly lost a lot of blood. Look at her face," she continued. "Look at how white it is. If you love her, and it seems that you do, you don't want anything to happen to her, do you?"

"She's fine."

"She's not fine. She could be bleeding internally. I'm a nurse. I know these things."

"You're lying."

Kelly started to gasp. "I don't think she is, Tom. I feel like I'm dying."

Hannah didn't know if her sister was playing along or if the pallor of her skin really was a sign that she was bleeding. "Can I check on her?"

"Stay where you are," he ordered. "You're both lying." He moved back and forth in front of the window.

She thought she heard something outside. Maybe the police had finally come. Or else it was just the wind. Perhaps the ambulance hadn't been able to get through the snow. Jake might have been stopped, too. Although, now she hoped he had been stopped, because if he got here first, he could walk right into a volatile situation. There was no doubt in her mind that Tom would shoot anyone who walked through that door.

Her heart pounded against her chest as an image of Jake rushing to help them, only to be gunned down, entered her mind.

*Why had she texted him? Why had she listened to Kelly?* She should have called the police first.

She forced those regretful thoughts out of her head. She couldn't change what she'd done. She had to figure out a way to get that gun away from Tom.

"Oh, God," Kelly gasped, suddenly using her free hand to clutch her stomach. "It hurts. It hurts so much." Her sister started to breathe so hard that Hannah scrambled to her feet.

"I told you to sit," Tom ordered.

"Then shoot me, because I'm going to help my sister." She got up and moved to the bed, putting her hand on Kelly's abdomen.

She was looking for contractions, rigidity, but she felt nothing. Kelly had to be faking it. *Now what?* She needed to get Tom out of the room.

"I need a knife," she said abruptly.

Kelly's eyes widened in shock.

"From the kitchen," she told Tom. "I need to puncture her abdomen. It's filling with air. She's going to die if I don't do that. Can I get it?"

"No way. You're just going to run."

"Then you get it. We're not going anywhere. Unless you want my sister to die. Is that it? I thought you loved her."

"I do love her. She's mine. The baby is mine. We're going to be a family," Tom said, his words becoming more frantic and desperate.

"Then help me save her life. Please." She had no idea what she was going to do with the knife if he actually brought her one, but if she could get him out of the room, she could lock the door and maybe buy them a little more time, although the flimsy lock on the door probably wouldn't hold him back long. Her mind raced as she calculated how long it would take her to shove the dresser in front of the door. He could shoot his way through the wood.

This could be the worst plan she'd ever come up with.

Kelly screamed in agony, even as her hand stroked Violet's back. The baby began to cry, too.

Hannah felt like joining them. She needed to release the tension and the fear, but she had to stay strong. "We're going to lose her," she said. "Help me, Tom."

"You're lying," he said, shaking his head. "You're not going to cut up your sister. She's faking. She's not dying."

Her ruse was not working, and a sense of overwhelming despair came over her.

*What was she going to do now?*

And then she heard a loud bang.

Tom's gaze flew to the door. Another bang came from the front of the house, louder this time.

Her heart sang with relief, as Tom raced out of the room. She ran to the bedroom door just in time to see the front door of the cabin swing open. Tom took several wild shots.

She screamed, terrified that it was Jake that Tom was shooting at.

But then out of the corner of her eye, she saw Jake come out of the kitchen. He launched himself on Tom's back, taking him down to the floor. The gun flew out of Tom's hand. She closed the bedroom door and then raced forward to grab the gun. Once she had it in her hand, she didn't know what to do. The two men were fighting for their lives, knocking over furniture, landing punishing blows, but they were so tangled up together, she couldn't pull the trigger and accidentally shoot Jake.

Tom had at least fifty pounds on Jake, but Jake was punching with a ferocity she'd never seen. Still, she didn't know if he could take Tom down. She wanted to help. She had to do something. She had to save Jake and her sister and her niece and herself.

As Tom shoved Jake off him with almost superhuman strength and lunged to his feet, she had her chance. She fired a single shot, hitting Tom square in the chest.

Tom's eyes widened in shock as he fell to his knees and then onto his back.

Another man came through the door, and she turned her gun in his direction.

Davis McKenna quickly put up a hand. "It's me, Hannah."

She blew out a breath, her hand still shaking. She needed to let go of the gun, but she couldn't get her fingers to move. And then Jake was there.

"Give me the gun, Hannah," he said quietly.

She met his gaze and his eyes reassured her. She let him take the gun, relieved when it was out of her grip. She was reeling. Blood was racing through her veins and her heart was beating way too fast.

As Davis checked on Tom, she said, "Is he dead?"

Davis looked back at her. "Yes. He's dead."

"I killed him." She felt numb with shock. She should feel bad that she'd killed a man. She'd spent her entire career trying to save lives, not take them. But she couldn't get to that expected feeling of remorse. She kept remembering Tom's madness. He'd killed Kelly's boyfriend, and he'd threatened to kill all of them.

"Where's your sister?" Jake asked. He put the gun on the nearby mantel and took her hands in his.

"She's in the bedroom. I should get to her."

"I'll check on her," Davis said. "Take a minute, Hannah. Get your feet back under you."

As Davis left, Jake gave her a searching look. "Are you all right? Did he hurt you?"

"No. But if you hadn't come, he would have killed me, maybe Kelly and Violet, too." She drew in a much-needed breath. "But you came—just in time."

"I'm sorry it took so long for me to get here. We ran into a few problems on the way." He looked back at the man on the ground. "I assume he was alone. Is there anyone else we have to worry about?"

"No. He was alone. He was crazy, Jake."

"I'm so happy he didn't hurt you. I heard a woman scream, and my heart stopped."

"That was Kelly. She was faking pain. We were trying to get him to go into the other room."

"Thank God." He put his arms around her and gave her a tight squeeze. "I was so worried about you, Hannah."

She savored the comfort of his arms for a long minute, wanting to stay there forever, but the sound of Violet's cries brought her head back up. "Want to meet my niece?" she asked.

He smiled. "I do."

They walked into the bedroom where Davis was examining Kelly and the baby.

"You did well, Hannah," Davis said approvingly. "Everyone looks good."

"Hannah was amazing," Kelly said, meeting her gaze.

"Although, for a minute there, I was scared you were going to cut me open."

"I was just trying to get him out of the room."

"I know. I tried to play along."

"You were almost too good. I started thinking you might really be in pain."

"I feel wonderful now. Dr. McKenna said Tom is dead." Her sister's gaze sought hers for confirmation.

"Yes, he is. He can't hurt you again, Kelly. You and Violet and Brett are safe."

Her sister's eyes watered, and tears slid down her cheeks. "Because of all of you. I didn't know what was going on when I heard the shots, but I just had faith that the next person to walk through the door would be someone who wanted to help me." She looked at Davis. "I couldn't believe it was you, Dr. McKenna."

Now that Hannah thought about it, she couldn't quite believe it, either. She looked at Jake. "How did you and your father end up coming here together? You never do anything together."

She saw Jake and his father exchange a look, and then Jake said, "That might change. It turns out we're a better team than I thought."

"Jake has a lot to tell you," Davis added.

She didn't know what that meant, but seeing that the anger was gone between them, she felt very hopeful that they might be finding their way back to the relationship they'd once had.

"I want to hear it all," she said. "But we need to get Kelly to the hospital."

"That won't be happening for a while," Jake said. "A tree fell across the road and the bridge is down."

"Are you serious? How did you get here then?"

"Jake found a way," his dad put in. "He's very resourceful."

"So are you," he told his father. "You drew Tom's attention without managing to get yourself shot."

"You needed a distraction; I gave you one."

"So, what are we going to do?" Kelly asked.

"We'll stay here until help comes," Davis told her. "Don't

worry, Kelly. I will take care of you and your baby until we can get you to the hospital."

"You're being so nice to me, Dr. McKenna—all of you are," Kelly said, her eyes tearing up once more. "I don't deserve it. I abandoned my family years ago. And then I came back and left my son for Hannah to take care of." Kelly's gaze sought hers. "I thought you might hate me, Hannah."

"I could never hate you. You're my sister."

"But I left you behind."

"It hurt," she admitted. "But we were all in survival mode after Dad died."

"I made so many mistakes."

"We've all made mistakes," Davis interjected. "It's what you do after that, that matters."

"He's right," she told her sister. "We all make mistakes, and we hope that we can do better and maybe eventually someone forgives us." She looked at Jake. "Or we forgive them."

His eyes darkened. "You said that might take a miracle."

"Well, I think we got one. And as you told me a few days ago, it is the season for miracles. We even have a newborn." She smiled, suddenly realizing the best part of all. "And this year I also get to help Santa Claus deliver one little boy his only wish—to get his mother back for Christmas."

"Is that what Brett wanted?" Kelly asked, her eyes tearing up once more.

"Yes. He adores you."

"He's my heart. It was hard to leave him, but I had to get him to safety."

"You did what you needed to do," she told her sister. While she still had mixed feelings about Kelly's disappearance so many years ago, she did believe her sister had done the right thing when she'd left Brett in her care.

"I thought about you a lot over the years, Hannah," Kelly said. "I've been following you online. You don't post much, but sometimes your friends do, and you're in the picture."

"Following my life online would never tell you the real story," she said. "There's a lot you missed, Kelly...a lot with Mom."

"What happened with Mom?"

At that question, she realized that Kelly hadn't known how bad their mother's drinking had gotten. "Too much to get into now," she murmured. "But people tried to find you over the years, and they never could. I guess you changed your name after you got married."

"There's a lot you don't know, too," Kelly said with a heavy sigh.

Seeing how exhausted her sister was, Hannah knew this wasn't the time to fill each other in. "We'll talk later. You should rest."

"I'll get my bag," Davis said. "I left it on the porch."

As they left the bedroom, her gaze went to Tom Washburn, who was lying in a pool of his own blood. Jake picked up the heavy afghan on the back of the couch and covered Tom's body. "Thank you," she said, relieved not to have to look at his face.

Davis collected his medical bag, then went back into the bedroom.

Needing some air, she stepped out onto the porch, happy to see that the storm had abated. It was a little past five, but it was no longer snowing, and dusky light was breaking through the thinning clouds. She was less happy to see that the road leading to the cabins was piled high with snow. It could be a while before anyone could get to them. She pulled her phone out of her back pocket. "I still don't have a signal."

"Neither do I," Jake said, taking a look at his phone. "But I spoke to Adam on my way up here. I told him everything you told me. He was in Black Falls at that time, but he said he would send Brodie here and an ambulance."

"That was a long time ago, wasn't it?"

"Yes. They must not be able to get through."

"Can they do what you and your father did?"

"That would be dicey. We used part of the tree that knocked out my truck as a bridge. I'm sure Brodie could get across, but there's no way Kelly and Violet could make it." He paused, and then stepped forward, putting his arms around her.

Her heart sped up once more as she gazed into his warm brown eyes. "I was worried about you, Jake. I was afraid you'd come in and Tom would hurt you before you even knew he was there. I shouldn't have texted you. I shouldn't have involved you."

"Are you serious? Of course you should have texted me. And you gave me enough information to be cautious in my approach."

"I'm so glad you're all right, although your face is kind of bruised."

"I'm pissed he landed even one punch. But you don't have to worry about me. I'm fine." He gave her a searching smile. "Did you mean what you said in there—about forgiveness?"

She smiled back at him, certain in her answer. "Yes. I forgive you, Jake."

"Really? You're not just high on adrenaline and relief?"

"No. I forgave you a couple of days ago."

"You could have let me in on that."

"I did have sex with you. That should have been a clue."

"It gave me hope, but afterward…You gave me your body, but not your heart, and I want both."

"I want both, too. That's why I pulled back. Because I didn't feel like you were a hundred percent in."

"I am in. I've wanted to tell you everything for a long time. And now I can."

"Why?" She wrapped her arms around his waist. "Why can you tell me now?"

"Because I finally confronted my father, and I told him that I was going to be completely honest with you."

Her gut twisted at his words. Deep down, she'd had a bad feeling that whatever Jake was holding back had to do with his dad, and now she wasn't sure she wanted to hear it. "If it has to do with your father, then maybe you shouldn't tell me."

His gaze narrowed. "You wanted this, Hannah. You told me it was a dealbreaker."

"I thought I needed it, but I don't think I do. You've earned my trust a thousand times over the past few days, Jake. I'm ready to move forward. I can let the past go."

"I'm ready to move forward, too, and to let the past go, but I want to tell you, Hannah, at least part of it. Will you listen?"

"Of course."

"The afternoon of the prom, I found out something about my father. It shook me up so much, I got drunk, and you know the rest. I promised him I would never tell anyone what happened, because it would hurt my family, and I couldn't do that. Paul was just starting to get his life back. My mom could finally stop worrying about losing my brother. And you..." He shook his head, his eyes filled with regret. "I really wanted to tell you, Hannah, but I couldn't. I knew that if I saw you that night, I would tell you. And I knew that if I spent any time around you after that, I would tell you. I had to let you hate me. I had to let you think that I just got scared about how serious we were. You said my excuses kept changing, because I couldn't find a way to make it better without hurting you more. It just about killed me. As soon as I could leave town I did, and I stayed away, so I wouldn't be tempted to tell you or anyone else."

There was so much raw honesty in his eyes that she knew he was telling her the truth. She could also read between the lines of his story, and she felt a rushing wave of disappointment toward Davis, not as much for whatever he'd done—although she could guess—but for the promise he'd asked his son to keep. "I'm sorry, Jake."

"You're sorry?" he asked with surprise.

"That your father put that burden on you."

"I hated him for it."

"Now I understand what went down between you."

"I could never look at him the same way again. It wasn't just what he did, it was the promise."

"I understand. That was the worst part. He was willing to sacrifice your relationship for his bad behavior." She paused, tilting her head as she thought about what had transpired over the past hour. "But you came here together. How did that happen?"

"Oh, right. I went to tell him I wasn't going to keep his promise anymore. After last night, I knew I had to do that. I told him I wasn't going to tell my family, but I was going to tell you, because I needed to be completely honest with you."

"I can't believe you decided to do that after all this time."

His arms tightened around her. "I'm in love with you, Hannah. I've been in love with you since I was seventeen years old. But the love I felt for you then doesn't compare to what I feel for you now. If you would be willing to give us a chance, I would be the happiest man alive."

"I'm willing," she said, her heart swelling with love for him. "I love you, too, Jake. I could only hate you as much as I did, because I still loved you. I tried to fight it. I tried to stay angry, because I was afraid. You hurt me in a way no one else ever has."

"I wish I could take it back."

"But you can't, and it's part of our story. But it's not a part I want to think about anymore. I want you to know that you have also made me happy in a way no one else ever has—back when we were teenagers and now. You know me better than I know myself. You know what I need sometimes before I know I need it. You push me, and I like that."

Happiness filled his gaze. "I'm glad I make you happy, and I will never hurt you again," he promised. "I would die for you, Hannah."

"You almost did tonight."

"But you saved me. You picked up that gun, and you took the shot. You were incredibly brave, Hannah."

"You saved me, too. And I'm not just talking about that horrible man inside the house. When you picked me up on the side of the road last week, you forced me to stop hiding from you, stop hiding from myself. I've been closed off for so long. I've felt like I had to only depend on myself. But then you kept showing up, and it scared me because I was starting to depend on you, too."

"You can depend on me. But you're strong on your own, and I love that about you. When I saw your texts today, I was scared, but I knew you would take care of your sister. I knew you would bring that baby into the world. I never had any doubt that you couldn't handle yourself; I just wanted to be there to help."

"You did help. So did your dad. I still don't really know why he came along."

"Because you were in trouble. I told him what I knew, and he shocked me when he grabbed his bag and said he was coming with me, that you might need him."

Even though she was feeling a lot of fury for his father at this moment, she was touched that he'd jumped into action the way he had.

"On the way up here, we talked a little more," Jake continued. "I started to realize that I couldn't ask you to forgive me if I wasn't willing to do the same thing for him. We both made big mistakes."

"We all make mistakes..." She paused and smiled. "Except me, of course. I've been perfect."

He laughed. "That is true, Hannah. You really haven't done anything wrong."

"I'm joking. I'm not perfect. I'm stubborn, bossy and opinion-ated, and I have a great capacity and willingness to carry a grudge. I'm going to try to work on all of that."

"Not too much. I don't want you to change, Hannah. I love you as you are."

"Thank you for telling me your secret, Jake. I won't say anything to anyone."

"You can do whatever you want. I don't want to put the burden on you. And if you want the details, they're yours."

She felt honored by his willingness to trust her, because if the secret could hurt his family, then she could hurt his family. She was also starting to understand that the Jake who had hurt her so badly had done so because he'd been hurt himself. It didn't excuse his behavior, but it made her happy to know that she hadn't completely misjudged his character the first time around.

"I don't need to know anything more," she said. "And I promise not to brag about your dad as much as I have in the past. I partly did it just to annoy you."

"It worked. I hated that you had so much respect for him

when... See, I still want to tell you. I'm never going to stop wanting to tell you."

"You don't have to tell me. I know. He cheated on your mother."

Jake frowned. "Are you guessing, or do you actually know that?"

"I'm guessing from what you just said about protecting your mom and brother."

"He swore it only happened the one time and he has tried to make it up to my mother every day since then. I told him he should tell her, but I don't know that he will. And maybe he shouldn't. They do seem happy. I never wanted to break the family up."

"Keeping his secret didn't stop that from happening, because it broke you. And you broke with your family."

"But they were still okay. That was what kept me going."

"I get it. I have looked up to your father, and I am grateful to him for a lot of things, but I never thought he was perfect. I'm disappointed in what he did. Maybe it will change how I feel about him going forward. On the other hand, he helped save my life tonight and the lives of my sister and my niece. I can't discount that."

"He does have some good qualities, but I don't want to talk about him anymore," Jake added with a smile. "Actually, I don't want to talk at all." He lowered his mouth to hers and his hot kiss made her heart melt and her body shiver all at the same time. They kissed for several long minutes until somewhere in the distance, she heard sirens. Help was coming.

"They're here," she said breathlessly. "Should we go down to the bridge and help?"

"In a few minutes. Trust me, we have plenty of time. That was a hell of a big tree that fell on the road."

He kissed her again and again until they heard shouts and saw lights. And then they went down the road as the police and fire department put together a makeshift bridge to cross the river.

Seeing the branch that Jake and his father had come across made her stomach flip over. They both could have lost their lives.

Thankfully, they hadn't. "I can't believe you crossed over the river using that branch. You really are fearless."

"More like extremely motivated," he said, gazing back at her. "You were worth the risk, Hannah."

She met his gaze. "You're worth the risk, too, Jake. I'm sorry it took me so long to see that."

"I'm just glad we're there now."

"Just in time for Christmas," she said, as she kissed him again.

# CHAPTER TWENTY-FOUR

It took the rescuers over five hours to clear the tree and the road and put together a bridge safe enough to transport everyone out of the area. While Hannah thought it might be a good idea for Kelly to go to the hospital, her sister insisted that she could recover just as well at Hannah's house. She wanted to have both her children with her for Christmas. With Dr. McKenna concurring that Kelly and Violet would be fine to recover at home, Hannah had no choice but to give in, but she was determined to keep an eye on both of them.

Since Jake's truck was completely disabled, Jake and his father took her car back to the medical center, so she could ride in the ambulance with her sister and the baby. Jake told her he'd meet her at her house as soon as he got his dad home.

"What do you think Mom is going to say when she sees me?" Kelly asked, as the ambulance took them home.

Since Hannah knew both paramedics, they'd allowed her to ride in the back with her sister while they sat in the front.

"I have no idea," she said. "But Mom will be very happy that you're safe. She'll also fall in love with Violet in one minute, which is how long it took her to fall in love with Brett."

While Brodie had contacted her mother, letting her know that both of her daughters and her granddaughter were safe, she had yet to get a signal on her phone to allow her to do so. But they would be home soon and then the whole family could celebrate together.

"You said there was a lot I didn't know about Mom," Kelly said. "Want to fill me in?"

"It's a long story."

"Give me the highlights."

"Okay. You know that Mom started drinking after Dad died."

"Yes. She was falling asleep with a bottle of wine every night. It was disgusting."

"That was nothing compared to what happened after you left. She completely fell apart. She moved on to harder alcohol and drugs."

"Oh, my God! I had no idea," Kelly murmured, her gaze shocked. "Who was taking care of you and Tyler?"

"Me," she said simply. "And for a very short time, we went into foster care."

"No." Horror moved through Kelly's eyes now. "I can't believe that."

"The social worker said she tried to find you, but she couldn't. I'm not sure how hard she looked, because after about two weeks, Aunt Joan showed up to take care of us. She stuck around for six months until Mom got her act together. Mom got better after that. She held it together for the last three years I was in high school, but a month before graduation, she fell off the wagon. That started another downward spiral. By then, I knew what to do, and I was old enough to take care of Tyler. Eventually, I took Tyler with me when I moved to Denver for college. I had to get him away from Mom."

Her sister shook her head, regret lining her face. "I am so sorry, Hannah. I can't imagine what you went through. I never would have believed that Mom would fall apart like that. If I'd known, I would have come back."

"You should have known, because you should have checked on us," she said, not willing to give Kelly a pass on everything. "I get that you were angry with Mom. She blamed you for Dad's death, which was unfair and really horrible. But at some point, you should have been there for me and Tyler. We lost our dad, too, and we were a lot younger than you."

"You lost him because of me," Kelly said, her voice laced with pain.

"I never blamed you for that. You didn't know there was going to be an accident. It wasn't your fault. I told Mom that."

"You're wrong, Hannah. It was my fault."

"Just because you stayed out too late doesn't make you responsible."

"What about if I was driving the car—would that make me responsible?"

The question stole the breath out of her chest. She stared at Kelly for a good minute before she said, "But you weren't driving." She stopped, seeing the truth on Kelly's face. "Why wouldn't anyone know that you were driving? Did Mom know you were driving?"

"No." Kelly bit down on her lip, then took a big breath. "Dad asked me to drive. He was having trouble seeing with the rain and the lights."

"Had you been drinking?"

Kelly immediately shook her head. "Absolutely not. I was late because I was arguing with Jim. He wanted to break up. I was trying to talk him out of it, but we were not drinking. I swear to you that's the truth."

"Okay."

"When Dad asked me to drive, I was fine with it. I wasn't worried about driving in the rain, and, frankly, I thought it was better if I drove, because he was mad at me. I never imagined that I couldn't handle it. But the rain started coming down so hard, I couldn't see. I braked, and the car skidded, and I couldn't stop it. We were going down Grammercy Hill, and halfway down we flipped over. Dad was ejected from the car. I managed to crawl out, and I ran to him."

Hannah drew in a shaky breath, her heart racing. She didn't

want to hear this. But now that Kelly was talking, she couldn't be stopped.

"Dad didn't look that bad," Kelly said. "But I couldn't get him to open his eyes. I shook him. I tried to hear his breath, but all I could hear was thunder and rain. The police came minutes later. When they arrived, I was with Dad in the middle of the street. I was in shock. I knew it was bad, but I still thought he was going to wake up. I don't know if anyone asked me if I was driving. I don't think they did." She bit down on her lip. "When we got to the hospital, they put me in an exam room, and they took Dad somewhere else. And then Mom came in with you and Tyler. I remember how scared you both looked."

"I don't need to hear anymore."

Kelly ignored her. "Mom started screaming when she found out he was..." Kelly shook her head as tears dripped down her cheeks. "She said it was all my fault, that he wouldn't have gone out in the storm to pick me up if I'd come home on time. I knew she was right, but I couldn't make her hate me more by telling her the truth, and it just never came out. I killed Dad, Hannah. And when Mom blamed me, it felt right, because I was guilty. I couldn't look at any of you without feeling awful. That's really why I ran away, and that's why I stayed away. I thought you were better off without me."

She shook her head in confusion. "I can't believe you kept this a secret all these years." She thought about her sister's words for another long minute. "Is this the whole story, Kelly? You're not holding anything back? You're not lying about being sober that night?"

"I'm telling you the truth, Hannah, all of it. I wasn't drinking. That wasn't the reason we crashed. I guess I wasn't a very good driver."

Considering the horrific storm that night and the fact that her sister had been a senior in high school who had just broken up with her boyfriend, it was actually easy to see how it had happened. In fact, even if there had been no emotions involved, it could have happened just because of the weather conditions.

"If you weren't drinking, then the accident was still just an accident." It was difficult to say the words. There were waves of anger rushing through her, and she had to fight off a desire to blame and judge. She repeated the words inside her head several times...*it was just an accident...just an accident.*

"I couldn't face you and Tyler and Mom knowing I'd taken away the most important person in your lives. So, I ran as far away as I could," Kelly said. "But I wish now I had known how bad things got. I never imagined Mom would fall apart like that. That you would have to raise Tyler." She took another breath, shaking her head with more regret. "You must hate me, Hannah. Are you sorry you saved my life tonight?"

"No. I'm not sorry about that." She tried to put her thoughts in some kind of order. "I'm trying to process everything. I've looked at that accident from one way all these years. And now you're saying it was different." She paused for another minute, her mind racing through all the data points and settling on the most important ones. "I'm angry that your actions that night contributed to the accident, the fact that Dad went out to find you because you broke curfew. But you were a teenager, and you couldn't have predicted what might happen. I'm also angry that you abandoned Tyler and me. At some point, you should have reached out to us."

"I know. You probably won't believe this, but I've thought about you both a lot. I moved from Florida to Colorado Springs because I felt like I needed to come home, but I couldn't get myself all the way back."

"I wondered why you came back to Colorado. I know that you've gone through some pain yourself. And at some point, I would like to hear about the men in your life, about Brett's father and Violet's father."

"They were both really good men, heroes beyond belief—Travis for his country and Russ for me and Brett."

"Brett told me that Russ would protect him. I didn't understand what was going on. I thought Russ was the bad guy, but that didn't go with how Brett felt about him. Brett clearly recognized Russ for who he was."

"Brett was crazy about him. I don't know how I'm going to tell him that Russ is gone."

"That's a problem for later. Brett will be so happy to see you, that will be enough for now. I am sad for you, Kelly, for all you've gone through." She paused, thinking about all the anger and pain, the misunderstandings and human weaknesses that had ruined their lives for so long. She didn't want to start that circle all over again, especially not now that there were kids involved, children who needed their whole family. "Maybe we can start over."

"Can we do that?" Kelly asked warily.

"I think so. I'm trying to stop judging everyone so harshly and accept that sometimes life brings out the best in us and other times the worst. But we are all works in progress. We're all trying to be our best selves. There has been too much space between us. I want to focus on the positive going forward. Mom has pulled her life together. Tyler is about to finish law school, and he has some woman he's excited about. I haven't met her yet, but they're planning to have some romantic adventure in Aspen on New Year's Eve."

"It's weird to think about Tyler being a man. I've seen photos of him on social media, too, but in my head he's still nine. I wonder what he thinks about me."

"You don't have to worry about Tyler. He has always been much more forgiving than me. He's very chill. He accepts people for who they are. I'm going to work on that, too. Because we both know life is too short to hang on to grudges."

"It certainly can be too short," Kelly said heavily. "But focusing on the positive..." She gave her a curious smile. "I couldn't help but notice how close you were to Jake McKenna. I know you were friends in middle school. Did you get together a long time ago?"

She shook her head. "That is another long story. We were together in high school, had a nasty breakup, and didn't really speak again until just this week. Surprisingly enough, your disappearance brought us back together. He wants a second chance, and so do I."

"Well, he risked his life to save you, and it was clear to me that he's crazy about you."

"He would have risked his life to save anyone; he's that kind of man. But I'm crazy about him, too."

"I'm glad something good might come from all this. Thank you for taking care of Brett and helping me bring Violet into the world. I owe you so much."

"You're welcome. I think you should stay in Whisper Lake, Kelly. I would love to have you and Brett and Violet in town, and I know Mom would, too. We need to be a family again, and maybe we'll convince Tyler at some point to come back as well."

"I would really like that, Hannah."

"Good, because it's time to come home." She smiled as the ambulance came to a stop. "And it looks like we are home."

The paramedics came around and opened the back doors. They helped Kelly into the house, while she carried Violet inside. Her mother, Tyler, and Brett were waiting, and enveloped them with hugs and questions.

"I know it's almost midnight. I didn't get Brett up until a few minutes ago," her mom told her. "When I heard you were all right, and you were coming home. I knew he would want to see Kelly right away."

She smiled reassuringly. "That was a good call, Mom. Thank you."

"Thank you, Hannah, for bringing her back." Her gaze drifted to the baby. "And this little one, too. She's beautiful—like her mother."

Hannah glanced over at Kelly, who was fighting back tears as she settled on the couch. Clearly, she'd heard her mother's words, but now her son was climbing into her arms, and all her attention was focused on him. Mother and child were finally reunited.

"You came early," Brett said. "Santa was supposed to bring you tomorrow."

Kelly's smile was filled with tenderness as she stroked her little boy's head. "I couldn't wait one more minute to see you."

"I missed you. You took a long time to come back. What happened to your face?"

"I bumped it, but I'm fine," Kelly said. "And I'm here now. I'm not leaving again."

"What about Russ? Is he coming back, too?"

Kelly's lips trembled. "We'll talk about that later. Do you want to say hello to your baby sister?"

At Kelly's words, Hannah took Violet over to the couch, sitting down next to Brett and Kelly.

"Did Santa bring her, too?" Brett asked. "I thought she was coming on Valentine's Day."

"She couldn't wait that long to meet you," Kelly said.

Her mom and Tyler sat down in the chairs across from them. Her mother wiped a tear from her eye, and Tyler gave her an emotional smile.

"You did good, Hannah," Tyler said.

"She did more than good," Kelly said. "She brought Violet into the world, and she saved my life. My little sister is quite amazing."

"I've known that for a long time," Tyler said.

"Me, too," her mother said. "And, Kelly, I'm glad you're finally home."

Kelly looked at her mother and Tyler with her heart in her eyes. "I'm sorry, Mom, Tyler. I have so many regrets."

"No time for those now," Tyler said. "We're all together. That's what counts."

"You're so big now, Ty."

He laughed. "We all grew up."

The doorbell rang, and Hannah got to her feet. She took the baby to her mother. "Want to hold your granddaughter?"

"I can't wait," her mom said. "Thank you for trusting me."

She nodded as she deposited Violet safely in her mother's arms and then went to open the door.

Jake stood on the porch, his face showing the bruises from his fight with Tom, but he'd never looked more handsome. She stepped onto the porch and moved into his arms. "I missed you."

He gave her a loving smile. "I missed you, too. It felt like it took forever to get back here."

"About twelve years, but we finally made it." She gazed into his eyes, knowing she was revealing all the love in her heart. She was completely vulnerable to this man. But she wasn't scared anymore. She trusted him.

"I won't let you down," he said quietly.

"I know you won't. Really, Jake, I know that. I don't want to start the next stage of our lives with you feeling like you have to pay off a debt. We're starting fresh. We're equal. We're zero-zero, at the bottom of the mountain, the start of the game…" she finished with a laugh.

His grin warmed her heart. "I get it, and I like it."

"Good. How was the drive back with your dad?"

"It was fine. That relationship may take a little time, but I'm going to work on it, too, not so much for him, but for my mom and my brother. I realize that our fight has been hurting them, which is the opposite of what I wanted to do. I don't know if he'll tell Mom the truth. I don't really care, actually. I want everyone to be happy."

"We're all on a good path."

He gazed deep into her eyes. "I love you so much, Hannah. There's never been anyone else for me. You asked me before if I'd had a serious relationship, and I made up some lame excuse about traveling too much, but that was never the reason. I just couldn't get over you. That's really why I came home. I had to see you again. I had to find out if there was a way to get you back. I couldn't give up on us."

"I'm sorry I made it so difficult for you."

"No, you're not," he teased. "You wanted me to earn it."

"And you did," she said with a laugh. "But I'm a little sorry, because we wasted so much time. I could never get over you, either. Everyone else seemed boring. I love you, Jake. I fell in love with you the first time we kissed. That's all it took—just one kiss. No one else has ever come close to making me feel the way I feel about you, and it's not just the incredible chemistry we have together, it's everything else. You were always my best friend."

"I want to be your best friend and your lover and everything else. I want to spend every minute of my life with you."

"That could work, except when you're jumping off a mountain," she said with a laugh. "You might have to do that minute alone."

"Or maybe I'll convince you to go with me," he said with a sparkle in his eyes.

"God help me, you probably could."

"But I don't want to take over your life, Hannah, I just want to share it."

"I feel the same way. I do have one important question, however."

"What's that?"

She gave him a happy smile. "Who has the ball now?"

He laughed. "I think I do."

"What are you going to do about it?"

"I have a lot of ideas. None of them involve your whole family, though, so my ideas might have to wait. In fact, I should probably go home and let you have this time with everyone."

"No way. You're not leaving, because you're my family, too."

"Good. Because there is no place I'd rather be." He lowered his head and covered her mouth with his, creating a lovely island of heat and love in the middle of a cold, dark night. But that was Jake. He'd always been able to bring the light into her life. She wanted to do the same for him.

He lifted his head as the bells rang from St. Mary's Church. "It's midnight, Hannah."

"Merry Christmas, Jake. I'm going to love you forever."

"I'm counting on that."

# # #

## ABOUT THE AUTHOR

Barbara Freethy is a #1 New York Times Bestselling Author of 70 novels ranging from contemporary romance to romantic suspense and women's fiction. With over 13 million copies sold, twenty-five of Barbara's books have appeared on the New York Times and USA Today Bestseller Lists, including SUMMER SECRETS which hit #1 on the New York Times!

Known for her emotional and compelling stories of love, family, mystery and romance, Barbara enjoys writing about ordinary people caught up in extraordinary adventures. Library Journal says, "Freethy has a gift for creating unforgettable characters."

For additional information, please visit Barbara's website at www.barbarafreethy.com.